ALL UNWARY

ALL UNWARY

CLARE CURZON

St. Martin's Press ♏ New York

A THOMAS DUNNE BOOK.
An imprint of St. Martin's Press.

ISBN 0-312-18037-3

First published in Great Britain by Little, Brown and Company

First U.S. Edition: February 1998

10 9 8 7 6 5 4 3 2 1

1758 3707D 584 719

This one is for
ex-Chief Inspector Laurie Fray
of Thames Valley Police,
with the author's sincere thanks for all past assistance
and warmest good wishes for his retirement.

Three little maids who, all unwary,
Come from a ladies' seminary . . .

The Mikado

One

Saturday, February 7

Between tall brick pillars the iron gates stood open. Two women in graduate gowns paused in their conversation at the doorway of the lodge as Detective-Sergeant Rosemary Zyczynski nosed her car into the driveway. Both turned to watch its progress and were momentarily silent.

The frost-whitened tarmac described a long S-bend, close-walled by dense rhododendrons, before opening on to extensive lawns with a half-profile view of a distant Edwardian mansion. The whole scene was monochrome, flat as an early lithograph, all colour filtered by the floating mist which the low morning sun barely penetrated to raise a brief sparkle from a patina of frost.

On closer approach the house showed pale gold sand-stone. Fronting it the terraced lawn, stiffly white, dropped to a games field with low goalposts at either end.

Hunched in the passenger seat beside Zyczynski, DS Beaumont disregarded the scene's wedding-cake beauty and plumped for the politics of envy. 'Gracious living for the privileged female young,' he grunted acidly. 'What sort of spoilt brat scarpers from this?'

Zyczynski made no reply, disturbed by complex memories. 'Will you wait in the car,' she asked, 'until we know the report's genuine?'

'So that I don't put my chauvinist trotter in it? My pleasure; women *en masse* daunt me.'

1

Zyczynski went up the wide steps, rang at the glass inner doors, showed her ID and was let in. The dim hall was warm and welcoming, with a scent of wax polish. Dark woodwork gleamed richly. The uniformed maid switched on overhead lights as she left, and brass ornaments sprang out like the stroke of a gong. And a gong there actually was in an angle under the mahogany grand staircase, hanging in a frame with a fat leather-knobbed stick alongside.

A pawn on the chequerboard tiles, the policewoman felt the years slide off. In memory an expectant four-year-old, she was holding her mother's hand. Not clinging, because she'd still felt safe at that age: doors opened on to new delights. The only ogres were in fairy tales. And parents were for ever.

Impatient at this momentary surrender to the past, Zyczynski took fresh stock of her surroundings. Solid and traditional, this set-up was intended to reassure. Yet there was no true security in the concept of school. A sudden substitute for family, it implied rupture, a cold replay of the birth cord's cutting.

All those years back she had willingly let go of her mother's hand, tempted by a dappled rocking-horse, then a wooden jigsaw puzzle. And when she looked round later she'd found herself abandoned, among other children deposited like herself, in the care of a stranger with a false-kind face.

She had been too appalled to protest, but could still feel the hollow dread inside. With hindsight she saw it foreshadowing the more maiming desertion of six years later when news was brought of her parents' tragic death.

'Gone to live with God, dear,' people said, meaning to comfort her. But Mum and Dad had left her behind, over-looked. Of the long procession of betrayals to be endured without rebellion, nursery school had been the first. And remembering still had the power to disturb her.

At least she'd been a day-girl throughout her school life. How did these others cope, dismissed from family

2

and home for months at a time? In private how did they account to themselves for such treatment?

Unsettled by the sudden replay of trauma buried under adult reason, she felt rising anger. The eyes she turned on the small woman who had come up quietly behind were hostile.

'Mrs Walling?' she accused her. At the other's silent smile she introduced herself briskly, again displaying her ID. 'I've come about the missing child.'

The Head's sitting room was upstairs, entered through a small office. To reach it they went up side by side on the broad, slightly squeaking treads, her own shoes loud against the noiseless crêpe soles of the other woman. Zyczynski knew she had started badly, projecting cold officialdom. Her terseness could make such a quiet person withdraw further. And complete openness was vital.

They passed under a leaded glass window displaying the school escutcheon between two saint-like supporters, and it briefly stained the colourless woman with its purple, blue and crimson. Today was all symbols, Z thought wryly. This to remind me she didn't get here by being a dud.

'I hope you like coffee?' Dr Walling asked as they entered a room that was bright and comfortably lived-in. 'I asked to have some sent up when you arrived.'

Z thanked her and resolved to be less assertive. Before sitting she went across to the long, angled window which looked out on two directions from this corner room.

'Yes,' said the headmistress, 'I do have a comprehensive view of things outside.' Her tone was humorous, for all the lines of pain at her mouth. She came alongside, gazing down on the frosted lawns and flower beds. As they watched, a straggling line of hearty-looking girls came galumphing up a path from behind a band of shrubbery, bound for some point beyond the women's view. They were in games kit, toting grips and lacrosse sticks. Their hair was tousled, their faces and limbs shone red and their breaths streamed out like school scarves behind them.

3

'I never played lacrosse,' said Z.

'It has some advantages over hockey, a freer pitch, more lusty action. We do a term of each. Then in summer, tennis for all, rounders for the juniors and cricket the seniors.'

'I'm not a prospective parent,' Z reminded her, smiling at last. 'I'm not even married.'

But she pulled herself up: why the need to drag that in, however off-balance she temporarily felt? (Obviously because Max had dropped the subject on her last night. A quite impossible notion for either of them, so caught up in separate, active careers.)

'Well, we're here if ever the need should arise,' the Head said pleasantly. 'Though not myself. I retire at the end of the coming summer term.'

'Then the sooner that we get this little mystery solved, the more carefree your final year will have been.'

'I hope so.' She waved the detective to an easy chair. 'Of course, it's not the first alarm of its sort that we've had. You might be surprised how much goes on under the seemly surface of a girls' boarding school.'

An admission of the very deceits Z had been pondering shortly before. Now she had to admit she was warming to the woman, perhaps to the place itself.

Dr Walling smiled ruefully. 'Real life is full of drama, and we do try to provide a human situation.'

Yes, well, true enough. But to the job in hand. One fifteen-year-old girl absent since last night, not long enough yet to warrant a real Missing Person shout, and there must be dozens of possible hiding places on an acreage like this. But overnight heavy frost and freezing fog wouldn't invite many to surrender a solid roof and reasonable comfort, whatever teenage crisis suddenly overtook them. And the absentee was a minor, which certainly gave official cause for anxiety. Even starting out as a prank, it could yet have a tragic ending.

Zyczynski had been given only the sketchiest briefing on the case. 'Who reported her absence, and when?'

'Apparently her head of dormitory noticed the empty bed just before lights out, that's at 9.40, but she assumed May would be with her housemistress for some reason. Miss Goss occasionally invites one or two girls to take hot chocolate with her in her room last thing. In which case it would normally have been cleared with Matron.'

'So was Matron informed?'

'No. And Stella, the prefect, failed to check it with her when Matron looked in just after lights-out. Then at 2.15 a.m. one of the younger ones shook her awake to report May absent. She has the bunk above May's and had needed to go to the bathroom. As she started to climb back her torch showed the lower bunk hadn't been slept in.'

'And then?'

'Stella knocked on Matron's door, who checked for herself, then informed the housemistress, Miss Goss, that May appeared to be missing.'

'Which was when you were informed?'

'I'm afraid not.'

Zyczynski looked up from her notepad.

'Miss Goss personally conducted a search of the entire building, together with her Head of House, Greta Chilvers. When they were satisfied that May wasn't hiding indoors, Miss Goss phoned through to the groundsman, dressed and went with him to search the outbuildings and spinney. When they failed to find the child Miss Goss decided it was a deliberate attempt to challenge her authority, that May had managed to evade them, warned off by the light from their torches, had found somewhere cosy to hide up and that by breakfast time she would creep back in, repentant.'

The elderly woman's voice was calm, but barely hid a note of censure. 'It became evident when register was taken at 8.50 a.m. that May Matsukawa was officially missing. That is when I was informed.'

'Matsukawa?'

'Mayumi Matsukawa is half-Japanese, with an English

mother. Normally an exemplary pupil in every way; hard-working, serious, perhaps even over-disciplined, as Asian students do often appear to us. Which is why I feel particularly anxious about her disappearance.'

Zyczynski turned a page of her notebook. 'I shall need to question Miss Goss and the two girls you mentioned. Also any from May's dormitory who were close friends.'

'This is a list of their names. I've asked them to keep free of classes and wait until called. In what order would you prefer to see them?'

Clearly this Mrs Walling was a paragon of quiet efficiency. A pity she hadn't been on hand when the girl's absence was first noticed.

'Miss Goss first, I think. Then we'll go back and take it chronologically.'

Unlike the delicate and elegant Mrs Walling, the house-mistress was a heavily built woman in her late thirties, short-haired and chinless, with a small forward-thrust head that made the large nose even more obtrusive. Her high colour might have been normal to her or only the result of present discomfiture. Z recognized she was under considerable strain, but saw no reason to let her off lightly. The woman's firsthand account accorded with the Head's version, and further details emerged with questioning.

Mayumi had worked in study after supper, was ticked on Matron's bath list for 8.30 p.m. and her dormitory prefect, Stella, was pretty certain she'd been present in her dressing gown about ten minutes before lights-out.

'Perhaps we can get confirmation on that from other girls?' Z said hopefully. 'How many are there to that dormitory?'

Twelve, she was told. Only final-year students had twin bedrooms. Cavell House had three dormitories, two junior – each with six little girls from eight years upwards plus two prefects. This senior dormitory had ten teenagers, with two sixth-formers as prefects on a rota basis.

'Cavell House is our smallest,' Dr Walling put in. 'There

6

are three other houses – Hill, Astor and my own here, which is School House.'

'So this isn't the building May escaped from?'

There was the slightest pause in which Z knew she could have chosen a happier way of expressing it.

'May *disappeared* from Cavell House, yes.'

'Then I'd like to go there. With my male colleague who's waiting in the car. Mrs Walling, thank you. I don't think I need to trouble you further for the moment. Miss Goss, shall we go?'

'*Dr* Walling,' the large woman corrected her firmly, then led the way from the building by the rear. They encountered DS Beaumont hovering in a walled walk, contemplating the winter remains of a broad herbaceous border where the cut-down stalks of delphiniums and lupins stuck up in stiff brown spikes from the frosted earth. 'Need me?' he asked, and fell in behind at Z's nod.

Cavell House proved to be less gracious than School House, built post-World War II for the express purpose of providing studies and sleeping accommodation for the pupils. Its double-storeyed walls of red brick were uncompromisingly functional, the tall sash windows uniform. Entrance was by double doors painted dark green which opened directly on to a passage, and opposite a Spartan office furnished with a single table, four upright chairs, a noticeboard and a large built-in cupboard. This Z mentally dubbed the guard room, it being clearly intended for checking pupils in and out.

'Is this the door May would have left by?' she demanded.

But no, it had been locked and bolted at 8 p.m. until when a junior staff member had remained on duty in the office there.

'The downstairs sash windows aren't barred,' Beaumont observed.

'This isn't a prison!' Miss Goss gobbled indignantly. 'We have adequate locks and an intruders' alarm system which

7

has been recently modernized. Unfortunately the circuit had been - er, rendered inactive. During my rounds to find Mayumi in the small hours I discovered one of the common-room windows slightly open at the bottom. That is obviously where she climbed out.'

'Or was removed,' Beaumont murmured, enjoying getting a rise out of her. 'Let's go see.'

'The alarm circuit was tampered with from the inside.'

'So what strangers or visitors have been here recently? Yesterday, for example.'

Miss Goss's face grew more choleric. 'We don't have tradesmen delivering. All meals are prepared and served at School House. But I believe a plumber called, to renew some radiator valves. We've used the same man for years. He's utterly reliable, and was gone by 4.30 p.m.'

'Was the window checked after that time?' Z asked.

'Presumably. When the curtains were drawn. The senior girls do that themselves. We're most particular that no one can see in, once the lights are on. There have been occasions when outsiders have got into the grounds, so we take strict precautions against Peeping Toms.'

'Yes. Doubtless the girls get up to private things in there when they're on their own,' Beaumont suggested.

'Nothing at all questionable, I assure you. But after study there's Indoor Activities time, when they're free to follow their hobbies: drama, needlework, music, drawing and so on. There's also a small television room off the common room; for supervised viewing, of course.'

'Free Association,' Beaumont muttered, mindful of more lenient-seeming adult prisons.

Z was allocated a room for conducting interviews, and the girls were called in one by one, with Miss Goss standing by. Dr Walling had put a star against the last two, as Mayumi's study-mates: Madeleine Coulter and Julia Olney-Pritchard. Z asked to have them in together.

'Perhaps,' she suggested to their housemistress, 'you would wait outside? If these two are May's special friends and she's confided in them, they could be more open with complete strangers.'

The woman was affronted but, as Beaumont ushered the girls in, confined herself to introducing them before stalking out tight-lipped.

'Maddie,' the first corrècted. 'No one calls me Madeleine.' She was small and stood rigidly erect. She tilted her head to survey Beaumont from top to toe before addressing herself to Zyczynski. 'How does a woman get on in the police?' she asked. 'Do they try and put you down?'

'All the time,' Z assured her with a slight smile. 'But they don't often succeed.'

Beaumont's wooden expression masked his discomfiture. 'Look,' he said, grabbing the photograph provided by the Head's secretary, 'I'm taking this back for faxing, with the list of clothes she'd be wearing. Japanese girls aren't all that common round here. The sooner uniform branch get on to it the better. We should have her found in no time.' He marched out, leaving Maddie grinning.

'That's an old photo' Julia burst out. 'We've got better ones taken recently. She looks quite different now.'

The girl grunted as Maddie appeared to stumble against her. 'Ow! Pig! What's the matter?'

DS Zyczynski's eyes narrowed. 'Maddie doesn't seem to think that's such a good idea. Maybe she doesn't want Mayumi found just yet. Is that it? You think she's done a runner and deserves a chance to get right away?'

The two girls stared at her, Maddie defiant, Julia still annoyed, rubbing at her ankle.

'I'd like to see those recent photos, maybe borrow them. But meanwhile tell me about Mayumi. Or do you call her May?'

'Sometimes. But Doll, mostly,' Maddie admitted. 'Because that's how she looks. A perfect china doll. And she isn't really all that Jap. Sometimes you could take her for Welsh.

9

But bags of black Asian hair, and green eyes with long, dark lashes. Smashing skin, sort of peachy.'

'Really pretty then?'

The girl nodded. Pretty Maddie wasn't, but there was an attractive impudence about her small monkey-face, the tip-tilted nose, saucy eyes and a brown mole high on her left cheek that somehow added piquancy. And her voice had a challenging lilt that was personal, owing nothing to local accent, the clipped consonants precisely enunciated, for all her tendency to slang.

The other girl was of bigger build, tall, with long blonde hair severely tied back; long-featured with a narrow forehead. She kept her gaze down, and her thick, pale lashes masked her eyes. She seemed less quick-witted. Her well-muscled limbs suggested she might perform better on the games field than in class.

'Do you all get along well together?' Z asked.

'Like a three-piece suite,' Maddie claimed. 'No; more like a three-piece cruet, because we're all so different, but we are a set, definitely.'

And Julia's, 'Oh yes,' was equally unforced. Z found she believed them.

'So was there anyone here she didn't get on with?'

'Only Goosewoman,' Maddie said. 'But that goes for us all. The woman's a toe-rag. She runs Cavell House as a Fascist operation.'

Maddie had to mean Miss Goss, and she had it right. In caricature a lumbering goose was the woman's animal type; upthrust head with prominent beak and unwinking eyes; heavy bust slung forward, counter-balanced below by the massive rear; short legs and an ungainly waddle on large, flattish feet. It wasn't just the word Goss that had inspired the nickname.

Z's questions continued. Only towards the end was there something that she felt might provide a lead. In the post the previous morning, distributed at break, there had been a letter for Mayumi. The stamp had been British. Doll

10

hadn't discussed it. Just seemed to wilt a bit, then tucked it away after reading. Maddie had assumed it came from her mother, at present living in Wiltshire.

Who must by now have been contacted by Dr Walling and be anxiously waiting for news. So Z's next move would be back to the Head at School House, for fuller details on the Matsukawa family.

Two

'The firm manufactures electronic toys,' Dr Walling explained. 'Animated puppets, talking dolls, the sort of thing which the Japanese are so clever with. Mr Matsukawa must be a multimillionaire in whatever currency you choose to name. Which is something we had to take into account before accepting responsibility for a child from such a family. There are intrinsic dangers, as I'm sure you understand.'

Z felt a sudden chill. 'Do you mean we could be dealing with a kidnapping?'

'I was given no specific warning, but there's always that possibility with such a background. I take some comfort from the fact that May's departure was organized from inside, and that despite her previous good conduct it looks on the surface as if she could have meant to run away. Perhaps when we manage to contact her mother she will be able to throw some light on what was in the girl's mind. So far I've only been able to leave a message on her answerphone. That was some two hours ago, and she hasn't rung back yet.'

Z asked for the address and made a note of it. 'We'll get the Wiltshire police to check on her. If Mayumi has headed there, found the house shut up and her mother away, she could be feeling quite lost. Her friend Maddie mentioned a letter she received yesterday morning which appeared to upset her. She thought it might be from Mrs Matsukawa, but Mayumi kept its contents to herself.'

'May is a very private person. If she had confided in any-one, that would certainly have been Maddie. Did you get the impression that she was keeping something back?'

'I think it's possible. She was against Julia offering us more up-to-date photographs. However, when I insisted that it was necessary, she dropped her protest.'

'How odd. May I see these photos?'

'Julia will be bringing them here when she's collected them from their study. She'd said the one from May's school file was an old one and unlike her.'

'I'm afraid it could be by now. It was her application photograph when she was thirteen. Girls change fast at puberty. And May had her long hair cut off during the Christmas holidays. It was her own decision, and her parents haven't yet seen her like that. I'm expecting some disapproval from them over it.'

'I see. Do you mean that Mayumi didn't spend her holidays with her parents?'

Dr Walling sighed. 'Mr Matsukawa has been sharing his time between Japan and the United Kingdom for the past two years, supervising his factories in both countries, but he's now planning to settle at home for a longer period. His wife was required to accompany him to Kyoto at the beginning of December and make arrangements for Mayumi to join them permanently at the end of this school year.'

'And how did Mayumi take this proposal?'

Dr Walling hesitated, then replied cautiously. 'With apparent equanimity. She isn't given to any display of strong emotions. But doubtless Maddie would be aware of her true feelings. Mayumi is more dutiful than we would expect of a modern Western girl. And it was not so much a proposal as a paternal edict. Female emancipation has barely brushed Japan as yet, and even there Mr Matsukawa, I believe, is considered to be of the old persuasion.'

'But the English wife . . . ?'

'Confided her misgivings to me. I was not entirely

13

surprised to learn that she has now returned to her child-hood home in Wiltshire. But for how long and with what arrangement in mind I can't foresee.'

'This letter Mayumi received yesterday. Would it be possible to check on whether this was from her mother?'

'My secretary has already confirmed it. The envelope was handwritten and posted in Salisbury. We do watch incoming post, for security reasons, and in this case there was no reason to have Mayumi open the letter in front of her housemistress.'

'And the letter itself?'

'Must be with Mayumi. The study she shares with Maddie and Julia has been searched thoroughly this morning to see what she took with her. It wasn't there.'

'What had she taken?'

'A shoulder bag with her current pocket money of five pounds, and whatever cash she had left over from last month. A few items of make-up which she is allowed to use in the evenings and at weekends, her bath bag with toiletries, and a change of underclothes. She would have been wearing her Sunday uniform, a pale grey flannel suit with either a scarlet or aquamarine sweater, nylon tights and flat-heeled, black pull-on shoes. They are all on the list Miss Goss was to provide you with.'

'Thank you. Detective-Sergeant Beaumont is already having that circulated, together with her general description.'

There was a knock on the door and Dr Walling's secretary came in. 'I'm sorry, Headmistress: Julia hasn't been able to come up with any other photos.'

'Thank you. I was afraid of that. They should have surfaced in the search. Mayumi must have taken them with her, possibly to show to her mother. More and more I'm convinced she must be on her way to her now.'

'Unless Julia was mistaken,' the secretary suggested, 'and there actually weren't any other photos.'

'Oh come, she'd hardly be wrong about that. Even Julia.' Dr Walling smiled at Z. 'If there's a wrong way round to get things, Julia will often find it, I'm afraid. But if Maddie didn't deny there were photos, then photos there certainly were. It's possible that her brother took them during the Christmas holidays. He's quite a well-known fashion photographer.'

'I still feel Maddie is deliberately holding something back,' Z said shortly.

Dr Walling nodded. 'If May has confided in her she could feel that loyalty demands total discretion. I'll have a quiet word with her and let you know the outcome, shall I?'

'Would you? I'd be grateful.' There was something about this quiet woman that convinced Z she would handle the girl well. 'You said just now that the photos could have been taken in the Christmas holidays. So did Mayumi spend them in England with her brother?'

Dr Walling frowned. 'She has no brother. Oh, I'm so sorry. I misled you. It's *Maddie*'s brother who is the photographer. Mayumi was invited by the Coulter family to spend a fortnight with them at Petworth.'

Coulter, at Petworth. It rang a bell. Now Z made the connection. 'So Maddie's some relation to Gilbert Coulter, the royal portrait painter?'

'He's her father. The son, Gregory, was eleven when Maddie was born and their mother died later that same year. There have been two stepmothers since then and countless unofficial aunties. But Maddie's resilient, a strong character, which is why I had such confidence in her taking care of Mayumi.'

'And you feel Mayumi needs special care? Because a family break-up is on the cards?'

'Originally I put the two girls together because she is the only part-Japanese girl we have here. Young people can be hurtful to any comtemporaries they consider different from the common run. But no one is going to display

15

racial prejudice when Maddie's around. And now her matter-of-factness about divorce could help May see her own situation in perspective.

'Sad to say, a broken home is not an uncommon problem for my girls. It's often the reason that they're sent here in the first place. Dysfunctional families, as they're called now. I'm old-fashioned enough to believe – well, never mind.'

'So how likely is it that the Matsukawas are seriously considering divorce? Do you really believe May could have rushed off to have some say in the matter?'

'That is something she could have confided to Maddie.' The Head was silent a moment. Then she rose and went across to lean on the windowsill. When she turned back she was frowning.

'As I said, Mrs Matsukawa is English, and I suspect she has delicate health. For whatever reason, she panicked at the thought of returning to Japan. She'd been back in this country for nearly three years, while her husband travelled to and fro. They had a family house built near Wrexham when he set up his British factory in North Wales. Since the New Year she has returned from Kyoto to her family home in Wiltshire, which I find significant.

'In general it seems that Japanese businessmen see little of their families at the best of times. But now that he intends to concentrate on the factory recently rebuilt in Kobe he requires to have his wife with him. Mayumi is to be allowed to remain until she is sixteen then resume her studies in Tokyo. With this in mind, the Matsukawa parents spent a month together in Japan, despite Mrs Matsukawa's reluctance. Now she is back here alone. When she rang to ask after Mayumi last week she sounded – quite distressed.'

'The case got further complicated,' Z complained to Superintendent Yeadings later, 'the more I dug into things. It started with a straightforward runaway school-girl, possibly holed up somewhere in the grounds. Then there was a suggestion of possible abduction, someone holding her for a slice of the Matsukawa billions. Then an undercurrent of domestic fracas, the English wife resisting an autocratic husband with feudal standards. Which made me wonder: had Dad sent some heavies to collect Mayumi as a bargaining counter against rebellious Mum? Or even staged a pre-emptive tug-of-love custody move? Finally there's May's connection with this arty-crafty Coulter family in Sussex.'

Yeadings grunted. 'That's certainly something to follow up. Gilbert Coulter has quite a reputation as an ageing Bohemian. Mayumi could have fallen for the free and easy life-style she sampled in his home and rebelled against the idea of perpetual kowtowing to her own father's commands. Which brings us back to the likelihood of her running away in a bid for freedom.

'Z, this is too iffy for you and Beaumont to handle alone. And there are international implications. It could blow up into something quite serious. Until we know otherwise I'm classifying it as Serious Crime. The Missing Person shout is to be nationwide, using a touched-up version of the existing school photograph. I'll get DI Mott to take the case over, Beaumont to liaise with the Met.'

'London, sir? You think she'd have gone there?'

'Statistically it's possible. That's where youngsters go to get lost. And we know that the wrong people are more likely to pick them up there than the do-gooders. Our vice squad can check on girlie spots in Thames Valley, but unless we hear soon from the Wiltshire force that she's tried to contact her mother, I think she's more likely to have taken the adolescent path to the bright lights of London. Always assuming, of course, that she's free to make a choice!'

'Sir,' Z requested, 'I'd like to have another word with the girl she stayed with over Christmas. If Mayumi was

17

planning a breakout as early as that, Maddie would have known – might even have been encouraging her. And I'm sure she's holding something back. She hadn't wanted us to know about the photos her brother took.'

'Right. Do that while I'm getting Mott relieved from his Slough GBH case. And you'll need to check up on this Coulter brother. His interest in Mayumi could have gone significantly farther than camera work.'

In their shared study Maddie was facing Julia with slitted eyes. 'You need your mouth stitched up; you know that? What were they going to think once they saw those photos?'

Julia stuck out her chin, hands defiantly on hips but trembling just the same, finding it hard to blink back tears. 'It did no harm. Anyway, May must've taken them with her.'

Well she didn't, Maddie rejoiced silently. But I'm damned if I'll let you know where they are. 'You're a double-dyed mental defective. D'you know that? Why the hell don't you engage brain before opening trap? If that policewoman comes back, or the ventriloquist's doll she brought along, *say nothing!* You hear me? Or by God I promise you'll regret it.'

She watched Julia gather up her books to return to class. Only ten minutes to lunch break, so it wasn't really worth the bother of following her. The taller girl, downcast, left without another word.

Leaning on the hot ribs of the radiator, Maddie pressed her forehead against the windowpane, gazing down past her nose, just making out the little white marker half hidden by a winter-flowering heather. The surface of the soil remained even and undisturbed. Even the frost had avoided it, protected by the sill's overhang.

It was last term, in October, three days before her fifteenth birthday, that Maddie had found the casket during a gardening session. It seemed a lifetime ago now. It

18

belonged to an age of innocence. Because of the circumstances of its finding she would always think of it as a tiny coffin.

Her dismissal to the nettle patch was meant as punishment. She might have qualified for isolation through any of three small misdemeanours, but it had been a quite mild sin of omission – a mislaid library book – which proved the last straw and brought the familiar flush to the housemistress's face.

So Maddie seethed at sensed injustice as she attacked the black earthiness with a passion little short of necrophiliac arousal. With heavy duty gloves she had cleared the surface of nettles and torn at yellow roots as tough as electric cables, marvelling at their invasiveness while revelling in the act of destruction. In malicious imagination, confining her efforts to a space six feet by four, she dug deep. Burning with bile against the housemistress, she indulged in the fantasy of burying her *bête noire*. Stimulated by the moist ground's black scents, she transformed the physical effort into a near-religious rite. She was working in the two-foot pit when her spade struck something more substantial.

When cleaned off, the box proved to be of dark-stained wood, rectangular, in size about fourteen inches by eight, and six inches deep, its sides carved with vine leaves and grapes. Digging into the hardened soil on the lid, she found the entwined letters TDT.

And the box was empty. This, above all, seemed the most fascinating thing about it. Buried, yet empty.

Why was she so sure that when it was laid in earth it had contained something of enormous importance, which had shrivelled away, made to disappear as if by magic?

She checked that she wasn't watched. The others' voices reaching her were distant, carrying only the emotion behind the lost words. Julia, on the strength of her father owning a string of garden centres, had been let loose on the roses. She was up a step-ladder fixing stays on the Albertine rambler, loud with self-satisfaction; Petra, below,

19

whining with boredom at holding the base steady. From beyond them came the prattling rise and fall of girlish enthusiasm or disgust at digging up beetroot, encountering half-worms, coping with a reluctant bonfire of rank weeds.

All coming under the official heading of *Hobbies, Weekend,* sub-section *Horticulture,* but frank exploitation in Maddie's opinion. She loudly scorned the school's prospectus with its blah about 'Awareness of the Greater World Around Us'. Despite a grudging fondness for the Head, she'd dubbed Dr Constance Walling the Great Con. The fact that, like most of the girls, she enjoyed the earthy exercise and relief from bookwork still didn't excuse it in Maddie's eyes.

'What,' she had once demanded of her housemistress, 'about the jobbing gardeners we deprive of employment?' And was required to write 300 words on the Value of Voluntary Service.

Goosewoman's gobble was coming closer now. Maddie shovelled a pile of nettles and loose earth over her treasure and continued with the grave.

Three days later, unwrapping birthday presents after lunch, the box had drawn interested eyes, glistening now with linseed oil she had filched from the cricket cupboard in the sports pavilion. Maddie kept to herself the blank note meant to cover it. There hadn't been time to decide what to write. She acted secretive about the gift's mysterious sender, revelling in the status boost it gave.

Invited to examine the box, Mayumi had run a gentle finger round the initials on its lid. 'TDT. What does that stand for, I wonder?'

'Poison,' Julia confidently informed Mayumi. With her garden-centre background, she was a self-appointed authority on all things green.

'Ages back someone wrote a book about it called *The Silent Spring,* because this awful TDT had killed off all the

20

micro-orgasms, all the bees and bugs and that, so the world went barren.'

Maddie hooted. 'Orga*ni*sms, you wally! And that was *D*DT. These initials mean something quite different.'

'Such as what?'

'Ah, that would be telling!'

She was glad they accepted that the letters stood for some*thing*, instead of another person's initials. Because the box was specially her own. TDT could have related to what was put inside it, which was buried and had magically disappeared. The Dreadful Thing perhaps: some grisly object that had to be disposed of. Like a shrunken Goosewoman's head.

Julia, unabashed, had wandered off, but Maddie appreciated that Mayumi was clearly intrigued. Being Japanese she must believe in magic myths and the supernatural. Or, half-Japanese, half-believe in them. She would think a magical box no more weird than that oriental crap of fortune-telling with sticks, a carp that could talk, or a goddess who gave birth to a string of divine islands. Yes, she might well tell Mayumi what the letters stood for, and about the box's powers. In exchange for help with her algebra.

Four weeks later Maddie had put her box to the test, burying it under the window of the ground-floor study she shared with the other two. Of course, it was really nonsense. The thing in it would still be there inside when she came to dig it up again, but at least down in the earth it was safe; no one was going to find it.

On the last day of term she had to make sure, telling herself it was because she wanted to take the box home. Which was true, but not the whole truth. With a serving spoon taken from the dining hall hatch she delved for it. The loose soil fell easily away and the box cleaned up as well as ever.

She dared to open it. It was empty. So no need to burn The Dreadful Thing. The magic really worked. And she was safe.

That afternoon her stepmother arrived in the new Merc to drive her down to Sussex, and was peeved because Maddie's cabin trunk wouldn't fit in its boot. An inch too long, so she expected Maddie to leave it behind! But the Great Con was watching from a window, came out herself and ordered the groundsman to set it in obliquely across the rear seats, despite Stephanie's fears of scratching the fabric.

And that meant the holidays started badly, totally souring relations with Stephanie, which had never been sweet to begin with. But at least, Maddie thought, my school report has to be better news this time. Pure B for maths in the final test; Dad should be really chuffed. Perhaps this Christmas wouldn't be too shambolical.

In the event she had to point out the improved test grade, then he read the report through a second time, grunted and waved it impatiently. 'Has Stephanie told you about Wengen?'

'Dad! You're taking us *skiing*? Brilliant!'

'Not you, I'm afraid.' He had the grace to look shame-faced. 'I left it rather late for booking. Only managed to get these two cancellations. Sorry, Maddie, old girl. Next year perhaps. But we'll have Christmas Day together, then fly out on the twenty-sixth. And Greg will be staying over. He'll be here to drive you wherever you want to go. I was wondering, if there's a friend you'd like to invite . . .'

He was disinclined to meet her baleful stare, and she seethed. Wasn't it enough to dump her at boarding school all term, but he had to do this too? What was wrong with her that he couldn't stand having her around? No, that was wrong. Not him; Stephanie, damn her. The sugar plum stepmother.

It was then that she remembered Mayumi isolated at school, her father recalled to Japan, and this time her English mother had gone too. Things hadn't been working out well between the two of them just lately, and this could be a desperate last chance to get their marriage together.

22

So Mayumi, like herself, was seen as an unneeded marital complication.

'As a matter of fact, there is,' she claimed.

'Is what?'

'There is a friend I want to invite.'

It wrong-footed him, satisfied with merely offering. He looked doubtful. 'There is? Well, do you think that at such short notice . . . ?'

'I'll ring the school,' she offered. 'You can ask Dr Walling yourself. She'll be glad to have one less juvenile bod to look after. Dad, you must remember Mayumi from Open Day in July.'

'That little Japanese?'

'Only half-Jap. Her mother's English. So she understands about Christmas. And she's the sort who'd fit in anywhere. She'll be absolutely no trouble at all, I promise.'

That was all in the past now. Just six weeks ago, but since then the whole world had stood on its head. And she had to admit it was nobody's fault but her own.

Three

Past the wooded dip in the long gravel driveway, at the point where the manor house again came into sight, Elizabeth Matsukawa recognized a police car parked up by the front door. All the rest of the way, driving between rough pasture railed off on either side to contain the home-farm cattle, she worried over what the police visit must mean. A break-in, an accident, something even worse?

She didn't need more stress in her present state of uncertainty. For a moment she suspected – then discarded as ridiculous – the idea that Yasuhiko might have invoked some feudal oriental right and demanded her extradition. But she'd done nothing that a British court would accept as beyond the law. Only wanted her freedom, and to recover the lost years.

In Japanese eyes her original and unforgivable failure was to be foreign, and therefore inferior; a *gaijin*, an outsider freak. In a way, they couldn't escape this prejudice. It was due to their insularity and the implanted national assumption of divine origin. Even Yasuhiko, for all his wealth and influence, was regarded by racial purists as tainted, through long exposure to life abroad.

Perhaps she should be proud that he was willing to withstand sniping critics in upholding their marriage, except that she was sure it was no longer done from love for her as a person, but as part of his ongoing obsession to measure himself against others' opposition and come out supreme. What he had once decided he stood by for ever. Nothing would break or bend him. He reminded her of the oak tree and the bamboo in the allegorical *haiku*. He had to be tougher, more enduring than either of those.

If she failed to return he would lose face. It would be public knowledge that he had wedded not only a freak but a rebellious, therefore dishonourable, woman. Such a breach would be intolerable. Any recollection of their earlier pleasure in each other – could she still say love? – would be overshadowed by what he'd see as her treachery. She would be dismissed, as formally as any disloyal employee.

Not that divorce was at all uncommon now in Japan, but among people of his conservative kind it was demeaning. And if, braving ridicule, he did eventually have recourse to it, there was little chance that a Kyoto court would grant custody of their daughter to a distant English mother.

If only, she told herself again, he could have delayed his return home until Mayumi was of an age to choose for herself. If she went back to him this summer nothing could prevent her being drawn into that other way of life. She was too young, too pliable to withstand the pressures: a woman within herself, but as yet having no adult rights. Yasuhiko would have his way and May would be sacrificed to a dynastic marriage. For status and money, ever more money and power for the commercial moguls. And her opening young life would be crushed under heel.

She drew up behind the patrol car and rolled down her window as the uniformed man got out, bulky in his luminous Traffic jacket. 'Mrs Matsukawa?'

'Yes. Is something wrong here?'

Now a policewoman had joined him, settling her check-banded hat on firmly. 'Could we speak with you indoors?'

Instead of answering, Elizabeth got out and ran her gaze over the face of the old stone house. Nothing looked out of place.

She thought a woman constable was normally sent when

there was bad news to break, and her insides seemed to shrivel. 'Is it my husband?' The hesitant way they looked at each other meant it wasn't.

Surely not Mayumi. She was safe at school. Unless there'd been a fire there, or the team minibus had—

On the steps she turned to face them. 'Tell me now. I have to know. Is it my daughter?'

The policewoman had nodded. Elizabeth went cold, became an automaton, fitting her key to the lock and leading them inside. The house was warm and familiar, with a slightly musty perfume like old pot-pourri. She had to halt at the foot of the stairs, collect herself, then show them into the morning room, switch on lights against the oncoming dusk.

'What has happened?'

'She appears to have left school. We were hoping she might have turned up here. Could she have got in while you were out?'

All colour had drained from her face. She looked haggard, the rather faded prettiness quite gone. 'But why? I mean – when was this?'

'Can I make you some tea?' the man asked, hovering over her so that she couldn't avoid moving back against one of the wing chairs.

It was suddenly unbearable. 'Stuff the tea!' she said in anger. 'No. No, I'm sorry. Thank you for offering. But just tell me, *please*. Everything.'

'The headmistress has been trying to contact you all day,' the policewoman said. 'A Dr Walling. But you've been out, so she left a phone message on your machine. It will probably tell you more than we know; which is that your daughter disappeared sometime last night. If she left a message it hasn't been found yet. But if you ring the school I'm sure they can give you fuller details.'

Slumped in the chair, Elizabeth covered her eyes with one shaking hand. Yasuhiko, she thought. He's one step ahead of me. He's taken her. Paid someone to snatch her.

He hasn't even waited for my answer, or for her to finish this year at school. I may never see her again unless I give in and go back.

'Mrs Matsukawa,' the policeman said, 'are you all right?'

She was anything but all right: appalled, angry, desperate. But there must be something she could do.

'Can you have the airports alerted?' she demanded. 'And any ships due out for Japan?'

'Do you think she's run away home?'

'No, you don't understand! Her home's here. She wouldn't go willingly. My husband . . .'

The man stiffened, nodded to the policewoman and went outside to use his radio handset.

The girl – she didn't look that much older than May: PC Jarrow, Elizabeth suddenly remembered she'd called herself when she showed her card – the girl knelt beside her. 'There's still a chance she left of her own free will.'

'If so, she'd have come here. To me.'

'There was something about a letter you'd written her. It was delivered the morning before. Is that right?'

'I wrote, yes.' But so discreetly. Could May have read more between the lines than she'd intended? Was she more aware of the true situation than her mother supposed?

'I told her I had come back to England for a while. I explained there was no need for me to stay on while my husband was so busy with the recovery programme. In Kobe. There was that awful earthquake, you remember? Everyone is quite obsessed with rebuilding, getting it all working efficiently again. There was nothing for me to do. I could be of more use here.'

'Then isn't it most likely that she's on her way to you? Maybe she was short of money and couldn't afford the train journey. She could be coming in stages.'

'Dear God, not hitch-hiking!' Elizabeth whispered. Every new alternative seemed increasingly dangerous. Little Mayumi in company with some rough-handed heavy goods

27

driver? Oh, he might have young daughters of his own, treat her with respect, but a lone girl travelling that way, he could take her for something she wasn't. One heard of such terrible things.

'You said she disappeared *last night!*' Elizabeth suddenly recalled. 'If she was coming here, she'd have arrived by now. Someone would have seen her in the village. Did you ask there? Otherwise . . . No?'

So it *was* Yasuhiko. An abduction. Either he'd suddenly returned himself or sent his British chauffeur, caretaker at the Wrexham house.

'All the same,' Elizabeth said, desperate again, 'you've got to take precautions. It may not be too late. You must prevent her being taken out of the country.'

'Is your husband in Britain at present, Mrs Matsukawa?'

'He doesn't need to be. Anyone he employs could be paid to carry out his orders. She could be shipped out with some regular consignment for Japan.'

If so, pray God they'd deal gently with her and the police would catch up in time. The memory came back of the young accountant from Kyoto they'd accused of making false entries. He'd disappeared from the North Wales factory and then suddenly he was answering some fraud charge in a Japanese court. She'd heard the whisper that he'd been drugged and crated for loading on a freight jet. At the time she'd refused to believe it, but now . . .

'What can I do?' she whispered. 'There must be something.'

'Contact the school,' the policewoman said again. 'Shall I get you the number?'

Elizabeth pushed herself out of the chair. 'I'll see to it.'

The number was on a pad by the hall telephone. She listened first to Dr Walling's recorded message, which told her nothing new. Then she dialled, got the Head's secretary, then Dr Walling's calm voice took over.

There'd been no positive development, only more details being uncovered of how Mayumi was assumed to have left

28

the school. The Head made no mention of a dark saloon car seen parked fifty yards from the main gates at 9.30 p.m. because the police hadn't yet traced it. It could have had no connection with the girl's disappearance, and either way it would only give the distressed mother something extra to worry over.

'I'm coming to you,' Elizabeth said impulsively. 'I can be there in a little over an hour and a half.'

'Really, Mrs Matsukawa, I wouldn't advise it. Mayumi could be heading towards you even as we speak. She will need you there when she arrives.'

'But she hasn't turned up yet, and it's getting dark. If she left school yesterday evening, this will be the second night . . .'

'Put all the lights on, so that she can see you're at home. And wait until she makes contact.'

Of course, Elizabeth thought, if she's lurking out there she'll have seen the police car. The house front was exposed on its hill. You could see it from the main road. Any sign of a police presence would put her off. She must get rid of them quickly.

She mumbled something as she rang off.

The policewoman was fussing again.

'No. No,' Elizabeth insisted, 'I don't need anyone to wait with me. I'm all right. I shall do as Dr Walling said, and put on all the lights. If Mayumi does come I need to be here for her. Just leave a phone number and I'll ring you at once if anything happens.'

In the front seats of the car they had shared a bottle of Coke and a bagful of goodies from a pastrycook's in Salisbury. 'Hardly a gourmet meal, but better than school grub, I bet,' the man said.

Mayumi licked her finger ends – delicately, as she did everything. He watched amused, glad he'd overlooked paper napkins. For the moment, fascinated by her difference from the women he was accustomed to, he forgot the trouble they were in, and the other trouble that had brought her to him.

'Feeling better now?'

'Thank you. You've been very kind. I think I should walk from here to the station.'

She shivered slightly, shedding the leather coat he'd lent her, and reached for the door catch. He leaned across and undid it for her. While there, unthinkingly he pressed his lips to her cheek. She didn't recoil but he heard her breath expelled.

'Don't you like being kissed?'

'I think it's – unnecessary.'

'I only meant to be friendly.'

'Well, that is all right, I suppose. We are friends perhaps.'

'And partners. We'll get this thing sorted out. It's just a question of hanging on till half-term. Is that possible, do you think? If so, I'll have it all set up.'

'So that nobody ever knows.'

'Secretly and safely.'

'Safely, oh yes. It must be absolutely safe.'

'Don't worry, little doll. Big Brother will fix everything. Just you go and sort yourself out with your family now.'

She climbed out, easing the door shut herself. Watching her walk away down the lane towards the bright lights, growing smaller and shadowy in the darkness, he sensed a vacuum.

Then, returned through some kind of time warp, he was again the adult sceptic, leaving the world of children's best party manners he'd briefly been dropped into. Regretted that he hadn't thanked her for what she'd so willingly done, unquestioning, like a circus dog trained to jump through flaming hoops. Yes, he should have been equally party-host correct, at least saying, 'Thank you for coming.'

He waited until she disappeared in the gloom, overshadowed by the ragged winter hedgerows; waited three minutes more until he judged she would be somewhere near civilization. Then he let off the handbrake and coasted quietly down after her.

The two local police had driven off soon after the woman detective from Thames Valley turned up. On Elizabeth's insistence she ran her unmarked car through into the rear courtyard. A CID sergeant with a Polish-sounding name, she struck Elizabeth as both sensible and sensitive. Undeniably pretty too, with her soft brown eyes and curly mop of dark hair. A free woman, she thought bitterly. This one hadn't tied any irrevocable knots or found herself hobbled from birth.

But she brought no further news of Mayumi; was even hoping that Elizabeth might have something cheering to tell her.

Z peeled off her sheepskin coat and ran a hand loosely through her hair. Mrs Matsukawa, visibly shattered, had made no offer towards her comfort although she must know she'd driven there non-stop from the school. Uninvited, she seated herself opposite.

'Your husband has been informed by telex. He was catching the next flight out.'

The woman sat hunched over her lap, hands tightly clasped, knees closed, silent. After a few seconds she raised her head. 'If he hasn't had her snatched, at least by now he must realize she's my child too!'

'What do you mean?'

'He used to call me his Free Spirit. When we were students together. Young, and in love.'

It was hard now to remember how that had felt. After seventeen years of marriage they'd become two different people entirely.

She went on wonderingly. 'Perhaps that was what first attracted him to me, because then, at heart, he wanted to be free too and found he couldn't be. But one glimpse of it in me and he had to capture it. So I was trapped.'

Madam Butterfly in reverse, Z thought: a Japanese

31

Pinkerton who went sailing on to larger issues, leaving the Western wife to be engrossed by her child.

Elizabeth moved impatiently in her chair. 'May will find her way to me here. Dr Walling had no need to drag her father into it!'

'The school has to cover itself.'

'I suppose so.' Elizabeth sighed wearily and straightened. 'At least if he comes running it means he isn't involved. I'd been dreading that he'd taken her by force and she was already out of the country. But why isn't she *here* yet?'

'She couldn't have got far last night. It was too late when she left. She'll have rested up, or maybe stayed over with friends somewhere.'

'What kind of friends would let a girl of fifteen stay away from school and home without notifying someone?'

'You've had nothing by phone?'

'Only that message from Dr Walling on my answering machine. When I heard your car I started thanking God . . .'

'I'm sorry.' Z moved over beside her on the settee and took her hand gently between her own.

'She's all I have, you see.'

'Yes, but you mustn't assume the worst.'

Elizabeth pulled her hand away, rose and walked stiff-legged up and down the room, her fingers biting into each upper arm. For a while she fought with her emotion then turned almost viciously to say, 'He won't come here. I wouldn't want him to, anyway. He'll book in at some luxury London hotel. I must get ready for my summons up there.'

'I think you should go on waiting. This is the one place Mayumi is sure of. She'll come to you.'

'To her mother. I hope you're right. Oh, I do hope so.'

'Is there anyone you would like to have here with you? Some friend from the village?'

32

'I'd rather wait alone. With you, that is. You don't have to go?'

'Not just yet, I think.'

Elizabeth Matsukawa stared around as though the mellow room with its familiar shabby comfort were strange to her. The peach-tinted walls and dark beams lit by shaded lights were reflected back in the large windows gaping now on black night. The second night that May had been missing.

She went across and leaned her forehead against the glass, trying to see past the reflection. Somewhere out there Mayumi was trying to get to her. Elizabeth closed her eyes. For a moment she seemed to see the girl walking alone, her face inscrutable. Then huddled asleep in the passenger seat of a car. But the face of the driver beside her was hidden; just a dark, shapeless mass.

Perhaps it was better to imagine her quite alone.

The girl leaned foward and wiped steam from the train window with the back of her sleeve. She should be close now. It was hard to tell in the dark. Country people didn't seem to need lights in the same way town folk did. Just occasionally a cluster appeared, tucked into a valley; or bright farmhouse windows whipped past in the middle distance, veined with the black silhouette of bare trees. Nothing identifiably familiar as yet.

Pressing her cheek against the cold glass she could cut past the repetition of the carriage interior, to make out a paler skyline over barrow-shaped hills. It was starting to cloud over, which meant less frost than last night, but it was cold all the same. Out in the open the formal little flannel suit had been inadequate, but her overcoat was locked away with all the others in Cavell House, for distribution only when authorized by Matron.

Suddenly quite close there appeared the corner of a stone barn lit by a halogen lamp high under the sheet-iron eaves, and a flash-photo still of a gaping interior with the comfortable backs of cows secured in their stalls. For an instant she seemed to smell their sweet-hay breaths, the corned-beef smell of their urine. There'd be a steady munching against the hiss of warm milk striking steel buckets, the gasping pulse of the suction machines. Evening milking. All normal and reassuringly safe. It seemed momentarily possible that in her world too, things could turn out all right.

She closed her eyes to hold back the tears and opened them to catch the bright stare of the man in the corner seat boring into her. She switched her gaze back to the window, and there, blazing like a beacon on the Fire Hills, was the house on the skyline, every window ablaze. As if some very grand party was in progress.

The little local train slowed and, brakes squealing, shuddered to a halt. Mayumi slid the strap of her bag over one shoulder, stood to brush creases from her skirt. The man with bright piggy eyes took down a rucksack and followed her to the door. When she found it too stiff to open he leaned over to drop the window and wrapped his huge paw over the handle outside.

The Halt was unmanned, as always after 4 p.m. and of course there was no taxi waiting on the off-chance of passengers. But it was only half a mile's walk to the end of the driveway. She was so nearly home.

The young Jap-looking girl hadn't recognized him so he didn't speak. Best not alarm the lass. He knew her all right, Miss Beth's littl'un, but they oughtn't to let her travel alone.

He dumped his rucksack by the station wall, gave her a couple of minutes' start and then followed, although his own home lay in the opposite direction.

She'd made good progress, walking steadily uphill. At first he couldn't make her out against the tall hedgerows, but then his countryman's night sight took over and he caught her movement. He followed as far as the old brick pillars with the white stone balls on top, and there he halted.

From the gateway the long drive dipped into black trees at the half-way point, then the rise began again, topped by the bulk of the manor house ablaze with lights like a luxury liner lying offshore. He continued waiting, and at length a small figure moved blackly across the uncurtained glow of a window by the central entrance.

Miss Beth's littl'un had reached home safe. And it was time he wasn't there.

Four

'I did try phoning,' the girl said. 'But there was no reply.' Once her mother had let go of her she stood there stiffly, her face dough-pale, her shoulder bag on the floor beside her trailing from one hand like a toy dog on a leash.

Elizabeth looked stricken. 'I've been out all day. Over at Alison's. Don's gone abroad again.' She gestured dismissively as though abroad lay just outside the windows. Abroad was something she'd had and wholeheartedly rejected. 'Why didn't you leave a message on the machine?'

Mayumi's green eyes were unfathomable. 'I wasn't sure who'd get it.'

'But there's only me here!' Her mother sounded exasperated.

'I'll make us fresh drinks,' Z offered. 'Something hot.'

'There's soup,' Elizabeth said vaguely. 'Oh, we'd better all go through to the kitchen.' She was suddenly cold and angry and tired. There was something wrong with Mayumi. She hadn't run into her mother's arms, but *submitted* to being hugged and wept over. Elizabeth was harshly reminded of her own recent passivity in bed. Bodies sometimes spoke more clearly than words.

It wasn't just the policewoman's presence that made the barrier. Nor the strangeness that May had had her beautiful long hair cut short. Something had happened. She wasn't sure she wanted to know what it was. Despite that, she couldn't stop herself demanding, 'But where have

36

you been? Why on earth did you run away? I've been half out of my mind with worry!'

'I wanted to see you.' It couldn't have sounded more detached.

Z watched them together. Maddie had been right about May's doll-like perfection. She was really lovely. Even exhausted as she must be, there was an untouched freshness about her, an exquisiteness of line and texture to the curved cheek and the dark lashes lying on it.

But the girl's calm was unnatural. Or unnatural for an English girl of that age. Z had to remind herself that Mayumi was the product of another culture. Even her mother seemed to find her alien at the moment.

She put a hand on Elizabeth's arm. 'Why not run her a hot bath while I phone everyone to say she's safe. Then I'll see to the soup and butter some toast. There'll be time to talk later.'

But when Mayumi came back, scented with cologne soap and in a fluffy white dressing gown a size too small for her, she was so clearly tired that there could be no inquisition, no recriminations. Z, accepting the offer of a bed overnight, suggested that next day she should drive Elizabeth and her daughter back to school. But not too early. They would all benefit from a long lie in.

'Or I can borrow a pony from Graingers', and we can go riding first together. You'd like that, May, wouldn't you?' Elizabeth said, suddenly eager.

'If you like, Mother.'

'It's not as *I* like at all. It's whatever *you* want, May.'

There was a note of desperation in the woman's voice, as if she knew there was little time granted her and too much to get straight in it.

Z replaced her soup bowl thoughtfully on the tray. It didn't matter what the two of them decided. Tomorrow Matsukawa *père* was due to fly in. It seemed likely he'd be the one to impose decisions.

*   *   *

37

The three met again at breakfast. Z was down early but Elizabeth was before her, looking as though she hadn't slept at all, her fine skin almost transparent in the morning light. Mayumi slipped into her place at table wearing jodhpurs, a floating white cotton shirt and short brocade waistcoat, registering acquiescence and little else.

She was almost in time to catch Elizabeth's protest to Z: 'What I don't understand is *why?* I mean, she's made no attempt to explain . . .'

'Good morning, Mother; Sergeant,' May said, taking her seat. She kept her eyes on her hands as they reached for a bowl and the milk.

'I met your headmistress yesterday,' Z told her, pausing over her cereal. 'It's a beautiful school.'

'Yes,' May agreed tonelessly. 'Was she – is she very upset about me?' At last she looked up and her voice betrayed concern.

'Dr Walling was anxious, of course. In case you came to some harm. But, in a way, she seemed – unshaken.'

'Is there a reason then?' Elizabeth asked the police-woman sharply. 'That she wasn't surprised, I mean. Has May been in trouble before?'

'I certainly didn't get that impression. The Head spoke very well of you, May. It was more as if nothing one of her girls did would actually astonish her. Maybe she remembers being young herself.'

May had frozen, staring down at her plate. 'I didn't want to – disappoint her. She won't send me away, will she?'

'That's not for me to say. If it worries you, you could ring her now. She'd probably appreciate that.'

'I spoke to her last night,' Elizabeth interrupted hurriedly. 'She just sounded very relieved. She asked me to tell you she's left this afternoon free, if you'd like to talk to her then.'

Incredible, Z thought. No summons from on high, frowning dignitaries, rebukes for rebellion. An *invitation*, for heaven's sake, to a meeting of minds. Showing so much restrained civility, had Dr Walling something to cover up? Was May actually in a position to spill some pretty stinking beans about her high-class establishment?

'I just wanted to see my mother,' May said tentatively. It sounded almost a rehearsal for the forthcoming interview.

'It was my fault; that letter I wrote,' Elizabeth said miserably. 'I'm afraid you read more into it than I intended. What did you think I meant?'

May laid down her spoon and considered. 'Father was busy with restructuring the firm. So you'd come back here for a while. I was to join you later, for Easter.'

'But you'd guessed, hadn't you? I'm never going back to him. It's the end of our marriage. May, I want you to have a proper chance yourself . . .'

An insistant drone from outside had increased to a heavy clatter as a shadow sliced through light from the window. Elizabeth started from her seat and ran to peer out. The helicopter was circling behind the home farm, seeking a flat surface to land.

'He *has* come,' she groaned. 'It's too soon. We've had no time to talk.' She seized her leather coat from its peg in the scullery and ran out by the back way, leaving the other two pushing back their chairs.

'What will he do?' May asked wildly. At last she seemed to lose her nerve, her fingers biting into Z's sweater sleeve.

How the hell would I know? Z asked herself. But he couldn't be a total tyrant, could he?

'Does he – I mean, is he cruel to you, May?' she demanded.

'Cruel? He doesn't mean to be. It's just that he decides everything. He's right up there above us all. He thinks I'm a small child, to follow orders. He can't see . . .'

Z put an arm round her shoulders. At least the girl *had* parents; unlike herself at this age.

'He does what he thinks is best for you. Your time will come. If it's any consolation, I didn't enjoy being young either.'

The girl pulled away. The green eyes defied her own. 'But you are a whole person,' she accused with passion. 'I am in two pieces that don't fit.' She thrust her hands in the jodhpur pockets and, coatless, went out to follow her mother, her shirt-tail blowing in the wind.

The yellow helicopter alighted on the field, scattering the dairy herd and flattening the grass. The clatter slowed as the rotors flagged. Before they had quite stilled, a little ladder slid over the side.

Elizabeth Matsukawa watched the black-suited legs step down and the man come forward, briefcase in hand, ducking under the slicing blades. He put up one hand to protect the thin hair streaming from his high forehead and came forward bent under the down-draught. Not until he stood erect did she cry out and recoil.

Not the moon-face of her husband Yasuhiko, but the long hatchet features of his number two, Imura. The Mikado had not troubled to come himself. Instead he had dispatched his Lord High Executioner.

Following more slowly, Z watched the two adults approach and their formal bowing, then Mayumi moving forward to give the same greeting. The man began speaking, but not in English. Elizabeth looked appalled, took a few stumbling paces backwards over the tussocky grass half-turning to Z in protest.

The Japanese ignored the woman detective. It struck her she could be taken for a servant. She flipped out her ID. 'Detective-Sergeant Rosemary Zyczynski of Thames Valley Police, working in parallel with Wiltshire County force.'

He bowed to her in turn and fixed her sternly with cold eyes. 'I am authorized to return Mr Matsukawa's daughter to her school.' He produced from an inside jacket pocket a faxed letter which he handed over. Z passed it to Elizabeth for confirmation of the signature. The woman nodded slowly.

'I understood that Mr Matsukawa would be coming in person.'

'There was a change of plan. An urgent matter came up. Because I was already in Frankfurt, I have been directed here instead.'

'Dear God,' Elizabeth murmured. 'An urgent matter? Business – before his child's safety!'

Imura spoke sharply to Mayumi in Japanese.

'What did he say?' Z demanded.

Elizabeth's face flamed. 'He told her to tuck her shirt in.'

The girl unzipped her jodhpurs and began to obey. They were still grouped together on the edge of the makeshift heli-pad and the wind was biting. 'Go back and get a coat on,' Z advised.

'I – I can offer you tea,' Elizabeth faltered, but apart from another bow the man was unmoving.

'You will please fetch the coat,' he ordered her.

'I'll go.' Z turned away. 'Elizabeth, can I get anything for you?'

'No. He said I can't . . .'

'I have instructions to take Mr Matsukawa's daughter. That is all. There is no room for another person.'

So that was that. His the authority. Unless Elizabeth made some strong objection there was nothing she could do to prevent him loading Mayumi in and taking off for God knows where. Perhaps back to school as he claimed, but perhaps not. And Elizabeth was in no fit state to fight such obduracy. She looked as though the next gust of wind would fragment her.

'I need to fetch my uniform,' May said staunchly. 'And my shoulder bag. I can't go back dressed like this. It wouldn't be proper.'

That seemed to leave the man uncertain. Etiquette was obviously a consideration with him.

'Ten minutes,' Mayumi decreed. She turned back without waiting for his agreement, and the two women followed together.

'May, we have to talk,' Elizabeth begged when they reached the house.

'There isn't time.'

Z put a restraining hand on Elizabeth's arm as the girl went upstairs alone to change. 'Have you any doubt he'll do just as he said? Deliver her to school?'

The woman's face creased with worry. 'Surely he will. No, I don't think he'd lie to me. On my own I'm hardly important enough for that.'

'Then let me give you that lift we'd intended. I have to get back now that my part in this is done. We'll only be an hour or two behind them, and I don't think you ought to drive yourself at present. Maybe you can be there when May sees Dr Walling. Then everyone will get a fair hearing.'

'Yes, you're right.' Elizabeth was clutching at any hope. 'I'd like that. I'll just pack a bag. In case I stay over.'

Mayumi came downstairs, again in her school's Sunday uniform, and insisted on saying goodbye in the kitchen. 'Stay here, Mother. I'd rather walk out there on my own.'

There was a glint of something like anger in her eyes. 'It's a bit less like being arrested.'

So they watched from the window and, when the helicopter had taken off, Elizabeth fetched the house keys to lock up and followed Z miserably out to her car.

It must be obvious to her, Z thought, that there had been room enough in the helicopter with Mayumi. Her exclusion had been insulting, and her failure to protest must indicate she was accustomed to being discounted.

Fortunately on the longer journey by road there would be time for Elizabeth to recover from the humiliation of Imura's rebuff, and it did seem that the encounter had set her mind on another tack. Relieved of an immediate confrontation with her husband, she spent the breathing space on trying to make sense of Mayumi's actions. While Z was curious to know how the girl had spent the lost twenty-odd hours, Elizabeth was more puzzled by her reason for running away.

'She said she wanted to see me, but then when we met she had nothing to say, wouldn't properly discuss my letter when I brought the subject up. So there was something deeper behind what she did. She's not stupid; far from it. Perhaps – perhaps she thought that if she did something wild, her father would be obliged to come running. That must have been her intention: that he and I should come face to face in some effort to protect her. That could be why she stayed away so long before getting here. It was to give him time to come so much farther. And for worry to soften him for a reconciliation.'

Her drawn face quivered with emotion. 'And Yasuhiko let her down. He failed her. Business was more important. Instead of dropping everything and rushing to make sure she was safe, he sent that – that *automaton* to deal with the situation. The *situation*, not his daughter! God, what has happened to the man I once knew? What is Mayumi to make of a father like that?'

'Suppose he had come.'

'Ah, then it would all have depended on him – how much he could remember of what really mattered: whether he still valued our family life together. But no, even if—' Her face, briefly lit by hope, set again in its lines of despair.

'You would have had to make a decision. It's not too late, is it? You could still go back with them both?'

'I would have tried, with May's help, to persuade him that we all belong here.'

Not a wax cat's hope in hell, Z decided. It was a case for the judgment of Solomon. Hadn't Mayumi herself said, passionately, 'I am in two pieces that don't fit!' She hadn't meant only her genes. There were two opposing worlds, and she was precariously balanced between them.

*   *   *

43

Julia Olney-Pritchard had slipped away from the others after morning church. She stood now at Miss Goss's door in Cavell House, one hand raised to knock. But first she listened for voices. There was just a dull thud as though a disturbed book fell to the carpet, then a few barely audible footfalls. Closer she heard a decisive tread on the stairs behind her: Matron, bound for the linen room. She mustn't find her here.

Without knocking, Julia twisted the doorknob and slid into the housemistress's room. She caught Miss Goss, red-faced, straightening with a book in her hand. There was no shelf or table near her. She must have thrown the book across the room in a temper for it to land by the hearth.

'Julia!' the woman protested.

'Matron's just outside,' the girl warned. 'But I had to come and see you.'

'You know you shouldn't return here until after lunch.'

Julia's shrug meant, *So what?* 'I was watching you all the way through assembly. You looked so worried.' She went close and touched the woman's arm pleadingly. 'I want to help. Can I come tonight?'

'Of course I'm worried. It's that wretched Matsukawa girl. She's put me in an intolerable position. Now her parents will imagine she was unhappy here.'

'I know. I wish I could do something.'

Miss Goss slid into a chair. Julia perched sideways on the arm and brushed her fingers over the woman's forehead, but Goss impatiently pushed the girl's hand away. 'Haven't you any idea what she meant to do?'

Julia looked sulky. Under the thick sandy lashes her eyes were resentful. 'I'd say if I had. But Maddie's in on it all right. I think they were hatching something up together.'

'Well, Maddie is hardly likely to confide in me, Julia. Can't you find out from her what May is up to? You used once to be so close.'

'That was before Mayumi came.'

Miss Goss considered her coldly. 'Well, we shall know soon enough. She's due back at any time now. I hope for your sake you hadn't done anything to drive her away.'

'Not me.' Rebellion smouldered in Julia's eyes. With sudden spite she turned on the woman. 'How about you? Not unkind. Oh no, just the reverse. She's pretty, isn't she? The Doll. And clever! You'd be so nice to her. Maybe you scared her, went too far with all that lovey-dovey, mother-substitute stuff! Came on too fast.'

'Julia! You don't know what you're saying!'

'I know all right. I've watched you with her. You had her in here two evenings this last week. Once with Stella, and the second time alone. Do you think I don't know what you're up to? You can't do this to me!' Tears of anger rolled down her cheeks.

'Julia, my dear. I do believe you're jealous. Oh, my dear! Is that it?' She reached for the girl and folded her close. 'Try to understand. I'm worried for the school, not myself. She is just one of my young charges, a foreign girl, so we need to be especially careful of her. It's absurd if you think she could mean anything more to me than that.'

'So long as it's still me you love. Say it, Gossamer. I need to hear you say it.'

The woman gazed at her long seconds before answering in a low, fervent tone, 'I love you, Julia. And I always shall, my dear. We are so – right together.' She folded her more tightly, kissing the girl's forehead and the closed eyelids.

'Then I can come tonight?'

'Tonight, no. I really don't think it would be wise. Not for the present, my darling. And you must realize I'd scarcely any sleep these last two nights over the wretched child. I'm quite exhausted.'

'But soon then?'

'Very soon. Once everything has quietened down.'

Julia watched from the corners of her eyes as the woman disengaged herself, stood and smoothed her short hair back, braced on dumpy legs, head slightly tilted, her cheeks smiling as if there were invisible loops that lifted them towards her upper back teeth.

But the smile didn't reach her eyes. Poor Goss looked so upset still, even downright ill. Julia wasn't convinced by her assurances.

It could be that Goss was fearful of what Mayumi would report back to the Head. If there *had* been something special between the two of them. She wished she knew, however much it would hurt. But she wasn't much good at reading people. Sometimes she'd believe she did understand someone, and then she'd discover she was just being made a fool of.

The noise of the rotor blades made prolonged conversation out of the question. For which Mayumi was grateful enough because she had no intention of explaining her conduct to her father's deputy. She gazed down as the chequered fields below spun dizzily and the chopper lifted, circling. Settling into a steady north-easterly course, she thought, checking it against the toy track of the railway line. Which should be the right direction for school. But he could still mean to trick her by overflying and then turning off for Heathrow. She had to know for certain.

'Where are we heading?' she shouted, using English so that the pilot too was likely to understand.

Imura regarded her severely. She had difficulty catching his sour reply. 'I take you to your school. Your headmistress will know how to deal with you.'

She twisted her head away to hide her relief. He would be thinking of a Japanese school, enjoying the prospect of some harsh punishment awaiting her. She kept her eyes off him for the rest of the journey. There was another question nagging at her but she dared not put it to him. Was it expressly by her father's orders that her mother had been ignored and left behind? Or had the man decided for

46

himself that she was a subject of scandal by having returned to this country on her own?

There had been no chance in these past few hours to get a complete picture of how things stood between her parents because she'd needed to stay aloof to avoid being questioned herself. In a way it was an advantage being whisked away by Imura, because the longer car journey would have given that alert policewoman a chance to pick holes in her story. She hoped that Dr Walling would be an easier person to face than a professional interrogator.

Five

Imura ignored the cabbie's outstretched palm. 'You will wait here.'

He straightened, blinking in the sharp winter sunshine, and waited for Mayumi to come round from the cab's far side. She marched ahead of him up the entrance steps, her head high.

Sprinting back to School House, Julia had glimpsed the taxi through gaps in the shrubbery. Now she thrust her way in, forcing herself through stiff-branched rhododendrons, to peer at Mayumi rigid in her Sunday uniform, her face as inscrutable as ever.

She looked no different. For some reason Julia felt let down: there should be a special mark on the girl to set her apart now.

With difficulty she extricated herself from the branches, rubbed at the dark stains they'd left on her sleeves, and resumed her dash for the dining room.

Cavell House line had already gone in and grace had been said. Her absence, noted at table, hadn't yet been reported to the mistress on duty. In the scurry of servers jostling for positions at the kitchen hatch she managed to take her seat unobserved by authority. And the news she brought crowded out any curiosity about where she had been.

'What kind of man?' one girl asked, relishing possible scandal.

'Old,' she had to admit. 'And Japanese. Could have been her father.'

'What'll the Head do?'

Julia shrugged. Since May's disappearance she'd been incessantly demanding this of Maddie, who'd made little response beyond biting one thumbnail down until the quick bled. From the opposite corner of the table she was scowling across now. 'Wasn't May's mother with them?'

'No. Just the man. He's left the taxi waiting. He could be taking May away again once they've seen the Head.'

'He can't! He mustn't!' Maddie leapt up, making frantic gestures, clapped one hand across her mouth, scrambled backwards over the bench and fled.

'Shall I . . . ?' Julia hesitated.

'Best make sure she's all right,' Stella advised as head of table. 'She's looked groggy ever since May left.'

Julia caught up with her in the toilets. 'So you actually were sick?' she accused.

Maddie gave a sour grin. 'An old trick. Fingers down the throat. You should try it.' She wiped her mouth, blinked her eyes clear of water. 'Hang in here. I've got to try and see her.'

Mayumi was seated on a straight-backed chair in the upstairs corridor at some distance from the Head's room. Maddie called to her through the banisters and she came quietly across.

'It's going to be all right. At least I think so. Here, take these.' She shed her jacket and bundled it, with her shoulder bag, through to her friend. 'Go back now. Don't worry.'

The Head's sitting room door began to open. 'So I leave her in your hands,' Imura was saying with a stiff final bow. He revealed a double row of formidable yellow teeth to commend himself further, still disconcerted by having interrupted Dr Walling's lunch. This was due to the pilot's refusal to land on the school's frozen lacrosse pitch. Summoning a taxi to transport them from Denham airfield had unconscionably delayed his handing over of the Matsukawa daughter. As a meticulously punctual

49

person, he found only one thing more irritating than being behind his self-appointed schedule, and that was finding himself obliged to make excuses for it.

Dr Walling disguised the astonishment she felt at his haste to be relieved of his charge. He had been in the room for barely two minutes.

'We have received a fax addressed to you here, Mr Imura,' she said, equally formal and distant. She turned back to hand him an envelope from her desk.

'It remains for me to thank you for your assistance in returning Mayumi to us. I shall, of course, be in touch with both her parents after I have spoken with her.'

She walked with Imura to the stairhead where her secretary waited to take over. Passing where Mayumi sat she expected him to pause and take his leave of her, but he strode on and the girl kept her eyes downcast.

Head tilted, Dr Walling stood watching her as downstairs the man's footfalls reached the hall tiles and the heavy outer door sighed shut. 'Have you had any lunch, May?'

'No, Dr Walling.' The girl's voice was low.

'Then you're one course behind me. We'll have something sent up on trays. Your mother has rung to say she's on her way here, so we can leave talking until she arrives, if you'd rather.'

Z dropped Mrs Matsukawa off at the school's front door. They had made only one stop on the way back. That was for her to check in at the Crown Hotel in Amersham. While Elizabeth took her bag upstairs and made some necessary phone calls, Z had ordered sandwiches and coffee for them both in the lounge.

'I really don't want to waste time,' Elizabeth protested when she came down refreshed.

'It won't be wasted. Let's give everyone a chance to cool off before you go in.'

The woman gave her a wry smile. 'That's standard police

policy, I suppose. Well, maybe you're right. But since I'm not driving I think I'll go for something stronger than caffeine.' She lifted a hand and ordered a large brandy off a passing waitress.

When it came Z noticed that although she hugged the glass for comfort she only sipped. It wasn't a customary crutch.

She checked her watch, aiming to deliver May's mother to Dr Walling on the dot of 2.30 p.m.

Although she felt deprived of the policewoman's support, Elizabeth's main anxiety on reaching the school was relieved by Imura's absence. She had fully expected him to be with Dr Walling, sourly sitting in judgment on Mayumi, the school, and herself as an ineffectual mother. But it seemed that his return to Frankfurt was of more vital importance to the Matsukawa interests. She couldn't resist remarking as much to Dr Walling.

'I understand he is to stay on locally overnight,' the Head countered. 'If you should need to contact him you could ring his hotel at Beaconsfield. A fax arrived here for him saying that the firm had booked a room for him at the Bellhouse Hotel.'

'Does that mean he'll want to see May again?'

'No. I'm sure it doesn't. He seemed to regard his part in the affair as completed with her return.' She hesitated. 'Perhaps I shouldn't mention this, but the fax was in English, so presumably not a specially private matter. It may relieve you to know that he is to travel tomorrow to North Wales.'

'Ah. Business again, then. Which leaves to you the matter of May's—' Elizabeth frowned over finding a description that wasn't too damning.

'Unofficial absence?' Dr Walling suggested.

'Thank you. Has she given any reason for going off like that without a word?'

'Not to me. Her friend Maddie had suggested it was a

spur of the moment need to see you. Following a letter she had received that morning.'

'I blame myself for that. I thought I had been discreet, but apparently not. Reading between the lines she must have realized that I'd made a final decision and come home to England for good.'

Dr Walling stayed silent, waiting for more.

'Which meant, of course, that my marriage to her father was over.'

'And this distresses her.'

'It must do, but she doesn't say. In fact she hasn't said a thing. Just turned up on the doorstep like a waif, kept whatever she was feeling to herself. No burst of affection or reproaches, no weeping, nothing. Of course, that policewoman was there, but I don't think it was that which kept her silent. If anything she seemed pleased that the woman stood between us. I'm afraid she blames me entirely for any – er, coolness between her father and me, and can't bring herself to face me out with it. Dr Walling, is there any way you can get her to unburden herself? Perhaps to you?'

'I'll do what I can, of course.' She rose and came across to Elizabeth's chair and laid her hands on the bowed shoulders. 'This isn't the first of my girls in this unhappy situation. Nor are you by any means the first mother to share such a confidence with me. Now, shall we ask May to come in and join us? She may be imagining all sorts of horrible prospects while we leave her outside.'

The girl came in and stood, hands linked behind her back, eyes still downcast, and if the mother hadn't been under such strain Dr Walling would not have suppressed the ironic little smile she felt inside. Really Mayumi was too good to be true: Superlamb to the Slaughter.

Invited to explain herself May conceded that she had felt an urgent need to consult with her mother on their future. She could see now that it was stupid to go off

52

without permission or leaving any note of explanation. She was truly sorry for any anxiety she had caused and promised it would never happen again.

Watching Elizabeth, Dr Walling appreciated that she believed her daughter unconditionally, because she needed to. The Head's own options were more open. 'You seem to have covered most angles,' she remarked mildly. 'But not the outcome of your original purpose. What conclusions have you arrived at with your mother? About your own future, for example? Do you feel your recent conduct may have some effect on this?'

May looked up with sudden alarm. 'I hope I haven't – I don't know. What does my father— ?'

Dr Walling leant back in her chair. 'Impulsive acts such as yours can have unforeseen and unwelcome results. The ripples spread widely. In this case as far as Kobe perhaps. Fortunately for you it does seem that your father is satisfied for the moment that you should be returned to my care. But for how long I and my staff will be considered competent guardians no one can say. Your action could well have shaken his trust in us. You may feel you should write to him, suitably contrite. His final decision can have considerable impact on your future.'

And that was all she was prepared to say for the moment. Let the girl work it out for herself. And she should be granted an exeat until nine that evening, to give the mother every chance to get their misunderstandings ironed out.

Not that the consequences of a broken home life seemed fully to have struck Mayumi as yet. She had merely seized on her mother's letter as a convenient cover. No; whatever lay behind her taking off as she did, it was for some more personal reason, the Head acknowledged. And Mayumi had no intention yet of confiding to anyone precisely what that was.

Unless to that imp Maddie.

Dr Walling sighed, rang through to Matron and asked

53

her to bring along the girl's winter overcoat. Then, watching from her window as mother and daughter were driven off in a taxi, she stood immersed in thought. In her long experience with adolescents she had learned to wait for truths to surface. However deep and complex the girl was, she must eventually respond to others' sympathy.

The Crown Hotel was bright, warm and buzzing with life. The room Elizabeth had reserved had low beams and a four-poster double bed, almost an echo of her own room at home. 'I wish you could stay over with me for a few days,' she told Mayumi.

'Yes, it's cosy here. Very English.'

'Maybe we could stay on a while when I come for you at half-term. It's less than a fortnight away. Shall we spend it here? Go for drives round the countryside?'

'If you like, Mother.'

Back behind shutters! Elizabeth felt like shaking the girl. 'May, we've just a few hours together before you have to go back. Can we talk? At least tell me what you would like to do with the time we still have.'

'I think – as Dr Walling suggested – write to Father. It may stop him coming across. I don't want him taking me away from school. Not yet, certainly.'

'You may be too late to stop him making alternative arrangements for you.'

'Not if we take the letter to Mr Imura. He can have it faxed out immediately. I'd rather that than have to talk to Father by phone.'

'You're probably right. There's some stationery on the writing table.'

'That won't do. It's got the hotel address. I wouldn't want him to get the wrong idea. Could you get me some plain paper from a shop, while I think out what to say?'

Such a clear-headed child, Elizabeth marvelled: she's way ahead of me. Takes after Yasuhiko in that. She stood up. 'Yes, I'll go right away. And I'll need to hire a car for getting home.' Then she hesitated, apprehensive. 'May, you will be here when I get back?'

'Of course I will. You heard what I promised Dr Walling. I won't run away again.'

She sounded fervent, even a little fond. Or am I wrong again about her, Elizabeth wondered. Is she just impatient with me because I don't understand?

When she returned, breathless from haste, May was reading through the letter she'd drafted on the hotel paper. 'What do you think, Mother? Will this do?'

Elizabeth scanned it: a model of formal apology written in English. Even for Japanese requirements there was adequate self-abasement. Studied words. Completely right for the occasion.

And curiously disturbing. The girl wrote merely what her father would expect to receive. But that couldn't have come from the real May who could be spontaneous, at times even impetuous. It was as if she could separate out the two sides of her, and at present the Western one was quite suppressed.

She is more foreign to me just now than Yasuhiko himself, Elizabeth marvelled. Because she's an adolescent too, complicated, and a little beyond adult understanding.

When the letter was copied Elizabeth insisted its delivery should be put off until after an early dinner together which she ordered for 6.30 p.m. Until then they could wander round the Old Town and window-shop the boutiques. Perhaps, sweetened by the promise of some teenage fashion item, May could be persuaded to open up over their meal.

Nothing could be more rural-English than the wide-streeted village with its Norman flint-faced church and irregular houses, Georgian jostling with Stuart and the occasional Tudor in a huddled row. Bow-fronted shop windows with bull's-eye glass were tricked out for year-round tourists, enticingly lit as if for a weekday as the dusk turned to chilly dark. Bright pottery, wicker furniture, model dresses, glittering haberdashery, belts and accessories drew would-be shoppers with the lure of bold sales notices, still competing for the stimulated after-Christmas custom.

Mayumi had finally responded with a slight ethnic shift, allowing Elizabeth to promise her an outrageously expensive French patchwork shirt in purples, blues and hunter's green.

The olde worlde tea shops had closed, but beyond the solid Market Hall which blocked off half the thoroughfare, a sweep of cars double-parked to either side advertised the popularity of the restaurants and pubs. Yet for all their evidence of the modern world, there was a contagious sense of calm and uncrowdedness throughout the little town.

When they returned to the hotel the Avis rep had delivered the hire car, a red Vauxhall, and there were papers to fill in. While Elizabeth saw to this Mayumi took a leisurely shower.

The relaxed mood lasted with them through most of their meal, until Elizabeth felt it safe to ask, 'May, how do you feel about me leaving your father?'

The girl didn't look up. Just for a moment her fork was suspended, then she resumed eating her dessert.

So the question wasn't unexpected.

'It's your decision,' she said at last.

'I asked how *you* felt about it,' Elizabeth repeated, unusually persistent.

'How do you expect I would feel?' Mayumi's eyes were angry when they met her own. 'Do you really have to?'

Yes, to survive, Elizabeth wanted fervently to answer. 'You think it's unnecessary then?'

'It looks that way to me. You seem to get along all right. And it's not as though you both have to spend much time together. I mean, you're always saying he's never at home.'

'Perhaps it's more the country than the man that I'm leaving. There's no place there for me, regarded as a foreign freak. I was never accepted, just an onlooker unable to influence what went on. Even in my own home. It was other women employed to look after you, in case I made mistakes, gave you wrong values. And I don't suppose you ever knew they were your father's comfort girls'.

'How could I know? I barely ever saw him there.'

'No. He neglected them almost as badly as he did me.'

'So why did you stay with him this long?'

'What else could I do? You were all I had, even the little I was allowed to have of you.'

'You found them as strange as they found you.'

'I don't want to be judgmental. It's just that we are totally different races, have different blind spots, different standards of behaviour, hygiene, culture. They regard all Westerners as clumsy, overgrown barbarians. And Japanese men - to me they seem more like cruel children, treating their women like talking dolls. It's no country to be a woman in even yet. And in private I think most good little Japanese wives despise their tin-god husbands.'

Elizabeth gave a bitter laugh. Having gone so far she might as well unload completely. 'And I hate the cities, so teeming and noisy and brash. What a mockery, those contrived little gardens of peace squashed into the teeming hell of everyday existence. Just like the hysterical way the men play when work's over, then drag themselves back from their excesses and again kowtow to formality. I can't live any more among masks. I want living faces, real people.'

'We have a nice home. And the garden's lovely. That's peaceful enough.' Mayumi sounded doubtful.

Her mother sighed. 'It's not as though we could be all the time in Hokkaido, where it can be quite pleasant. And then of recent years we've been able to spend at least six months in the UK, but it seems that's over now. Yasuhiko has restructured the British end with new senior management, and he's going to spend all his time overseeing the rebuilt Kobe factory.'

She shook her head. 'It's a question of – balance, I

suppose. I just can't be a Japanese wife. I've tried. God knows I've put a lot into it. Until I've lost touch with the sort of person I really am. Was.'

'Why did you marry Father, then?'

Elizabeth was at a loss how to answer. It must be the worst question a child could ask any parent. 'Because I – thought I loved him. I was very young and I believed life had to go on being as good as it always had been up until then. I suppose I saw myself as the heroine of an ongoing romance. It was an adventure.'

'And now you wish it hadn't happened, any of it?'

'May, I wouldn't for the world have missed having you. You were the most wonderful thing that has ever happened to me. You must know how much I love you.'

'You might be mistaken again, about your love.' The girl's face was impassive, inquisitorial. 'Like you were about Father. Was it just because you were young you were wrong before?'

Elizabeth felt humiliated. She sat hunched at the table, unable to speak, her mind in a turmoil. She knew she had been less than honest with herself, as well as with May. But must the child be so brutal?

As her eyes brimmed with tears she managed to get out, 'I did love him. In a way I still do. It's just unbearable the way that things are now.'

'You're pulled apart,' said May. 'You imagine you can go backwards in time and get free. Perhaps you can. But I can't. I'm here and I'm stuck in the middle.'

What was she trying to say? That if her parents parted she'd be destroyed herself, lose them both? 'Nothing's definite yet,' Elizabeth pleaded.

'Do you mean it's just a trial separation? You might possibly get together again?'

'I'm not sure. I don't know. It's too early yet,' Elizabeth whispered, cowardly and without complete honesty.

Mayumi stared round the room, everywhere but at her wretched mother.

'What does he think about it, my father?'

'We haven't discussed it.'

'But already you discuss it with me. It's not fair!'

'*Marriage* isn't fair!' Elizabeth said, suddenly passionate. 'And a mixed marriage is even worse. How could you know what it's like? How could anybody know but the two people trapped inside it? And then even they—' She raised her thin shoulders, hands gesturing helplessly.

'It's time we delivered my letter,' Mayumi said abruptly. She pushed back her chair and stood beside her mother's. Her face had its too-calm, closed-up look.

Elizabeth was the outsider again. Maybe, she thought with sudden enlightment, I seem a foreigner to her too. And I thought it was only Yasuhiko!

On arriving at the Bellhouse Hotel, Mayumi, still wooden and unnerving, insisted that her mother should stay in the car while she saw Mr Imura alone. Well, she was schooled well enough in the social niceties he'd require. Elizabeth, abashed, left her to it, resigned to waiting.

But as twenty minutes passed Elizabeth became nervous and followed her in. She went straight up to the room which was always reserved for her husband, and knocked, ignoring the 'DO NOT DISTURB' notice hung on the doorknob. With her head close against the panels she thought she heard a noise of movement from inside, but nobody came. Perhaps she had missed Mayumi by using the stairs. She could imagine Imura's cold disdain if he was obliged to open up when wearing his night clothes. She waited just a minute more then stole away.

There was no sign of Mayumi in the foyer which was crowded with people in party dress. Elizabeth went back to the car and about five minutes later Mayumi opened the passenger door and slid into the seat beside her. She offered no account of the interview with Imura.

'Did you see him?' Elizabeth ventured.

May belted herself in, staring straight ahead. 'No. He'd

hung a DO NOT DISTURB notice on his door. So I slid the envelope through underneath.'

'He may not find it until tomorrow.'

'In Kobe it is tomorrow already.'

Which wasn't conclusive either way, but Elizabeth let it ride. She wondered what else Mayumi had done in the time she was absent, but the girl was in no mood to be questioned.

'So shall I drop you off at school now? We've half an hour before your exeat expires.'

'Might as well,' May granted. It sounded loutish and a trifle sullen. Totally English schoolgirl for once.

Six

'There was no need for me to see Dr Walling again. So I dropped Mrs Matsukawa off at the school at 2.30 p.m. and came on,' Z completed her verbal report.

Yeadings looked up at her, over his coffee mug. 'Not getting personally involved, I hope?' he enquired cannily.

'No, sir.'

'But— ?' He had picked up her unspoken reluctance.

'I feel there's a lot been swept under the carpet. It makes me think there's more to come.'

'The girl's back where she belongs. You responded promptly, saw her into the right hands. End of story. It's up to the parents and the school to sort the rest out between them. We aren't social services, Z.'

'No, sir.'

'I think you mean "yes sir" but never mind. I have a new inquiry for you. High Wycombe: another missing schoolgirl, would you believe? Seventeen years old, so a borderline case for Child Protection Unit. An Asian family this time. So – softly, softly, with the parents.

'The school's anxious about her absence and a neighbour believes she's being held in the house under restraint. Cries of distress heard two days back; nothing since. I've arranged for a uniform constable to go with you. Collect the details from DI Mott.'

'Right, sir.'

Not really the same kind of case, missing schoolgirl or not, Z thought. Almost the opposite, in fact. Mayumi, feeling distanced, could be trying to pull her family together around her: this new girl, possibly trapped inside, could be frantic to get free.

Or was she wrong about the Japanese girl? It was Elizabeth Matsukawa's suspicion that Mayumi had staged her flight in the hope of getting her parents back together. But the girl could have been working on them with something else in mind, drawing Matsukawa back to England for some quite different purpose.

The girl herself was an enigma, giving so little away; just a momentary panic on being confronted – as she'd thought – by her father in person. And that alarm hardly squared with her mother's theory.

Give it up, she told herself. As the Boss said, it was now a closed file; although if he had met these people himself he might have felt differently.

It still left her dissatisfied, always uneasy with open-ended stories. She needed to follow them through. When she'd read a novel she'd often ask, 'and *then*?' It was the same now, because, although Yeadings might write the case off, the human problem remained. For Mayumi and her mother a fresh phase of the dilemma was surely just opening.

But theirs, not mine, she reminded herself finally. She picked up the new case sheet from Angus Mott and went to look up the Wycombe address on a large-scale map.

It was a drab Victorian terrace house of scarred dark-red brick, its downstairs windows masked with heavy lace. The small garden space at its front was concreted over and two bicycles, far from new, were chained under the sill to a heavy staple in the wall. The doorbell had lost its central button. PC Aziz raised the stiff iron knocker and had to exert some pressure to bring it down, which it did with a thunderous crash, startling them both.

Doubtless only family came and went here, probably by the house's rear. Z was prepared for the twitching of the nearby downstairs curtain as someone unseen checked on the callers. There was a substantial pause before a shuffling behind the door was followed by the sounds of a key being inserted and two bolts drawn. The door then opened a mere three inches on its chain and the shadowy face of an elderly Asian woman appeared.

Z stepped forward, smiled reassuringly and wished her good afternoon. The woman was unresponsive. As if slotted in a wooden mask, her eyes switched to the Asian constable who spoke to her in Gujerati. She answered at first falteringly, then volubly protesting. Suddenly animated, she was flicking bony brown fingers in front of her face. It was unmistakably a demand that they should withdraw.

'She says,' Aziz told Z, 'that we must wait until her son and grandsons are home. It would not be right to let us in.'

'Is she alone?'

The two spoke again. 'Her husband is here. He is old and sick, she says.'

'Ask her whose bikes are outside if her menfolk are away.'

A discussion followed, patient on his part, passionate on the old woman's. They were clearly at cross purposes. Finally Aziz sighed. 'She thought we were going to take the bikes away. She says it cannot be against the law to leave them there.'

'What about the men?'

Aziz tried again. 'They work until six. For them Sunday is not a rest day. They leave the bikes behind because today there is no room in the van. They do decorating and electrical work.'

'Tell her we'll be back later, about seven. No, make that six on the dot. If they're late we'll camp outside. I don't want them smuggling the girl away in their van.'

'I go off then,' said the constable. 'And we're not allowed overtime.'

'Just tell her we'll be back.'

At Division she learned that the only Asian PC available for the time she specified was a girl probationer. 'Not on,' Z said shortly. 'We'll be dealing with young male Asians and she may find them overwhelming. I need Aziz.'

She met expected reluctance but eventually got her way. The abortive first visit had augured badly. Without their getting a foot in the house yet, it threatened to be a protracted and unrewarding exercise.

They returned to the street, parked two houses down, and it seemed the old lady hadn't phoned any warning to the men because on arrival they took no special interest in the unmarked car, beyond the driver's normal cautionary glance across while locking their van. Whether he was on the lookout for potential customers or a threat from racist louts, wasn't clear.

There were four of them: a father with sons ranging in age from their early twenties to early thirties. While the others made for an arched passageway between the central houses of the row, the older man approached the front door which promptly opened unbidden.

'They do seem on the defensive,' Z murmured. 'Who's the supposed enemy? They've no record. Do you suppose there's been trouble with neighbours?'

'Just uneasy because everything's new in this country,' Aziz surmised.

'Not so new, surely. They've had time to set themselves up in business.'

'It could have been ready waiting for them.'

Z grunted, admitting that there was a pattern; with one family member having qualified as a Brit, the others could get in on the strength of the relationship. The problems of immigration, legitimate or otherwise, fortunately weren't her affair. All she wanted was to identify and speak with a seventeen-year-old girl, presumably daughter to the man who'd just entered the house. One must presume she was officially British and entitled to the usual freedoms which that implied. Once it was established that she was present, at liberty and in good health, Z could pass on the information and get shot of the inquiry.

She granted the family a few minutes to hear the story from Granny, then nodded to Aziz who followed her to the door. This time it was the man who answered their knock, and he spoke adequate, heavily accented English. Z introduced herself and the PC, holding out her warrant card for the man to read through slowly.

'There is some trouble?' he asked, frowning fiercely.

'I don't think so. I should just like a word with Yasmin.'

'Yasmin?'

'This is the address the school gave as hers.'

He gave her a hard stare. 'I have a daughter, Yasmin. I speak for her.'

'We need to see Yasmin in person. She hasn't attended classes for nearly two weeks. Is she unwell?'

The man screwed up his eyes. Square-jawed and with a deeply lined brown face under coarse, greying hair, he looked a tough customer. 'She finish school now.'

'Then perhaps we can come in and speak to her.' It wasn't a question. Z was already moving forward, brushing against the man who almost filled the narrow hallway.

'No! I do not invite you!' His raised voice brought two shadows forward from the kitchen end of the passage; the two older sons.

'Just as you please. Constable Aziz can wait outside while I fetch a warrant to search the house.'

'You can do that? You can come in my house?'

'By notifying a magistrate and getting a written order with your address on it. It does mean that your name will be recorded—'

'You come in then. But there is nothing here.'

'Your daughter, Mr Patel.'

'She goes away. To visit family in Gujerat.'

'I see. Then I will check her room. She does have a separate room to sleep in?'

He made no move, barring her way to the staircase.

'Perhaps your wife would show me?'

'My wife die. I take you.' The man's conceding tone was too sudden a change. He was up to something.

'Stay here,' Z ordered the constable. If anyone tried to leave the house while she was upstairs he would pick up on it.

The room she was taken to was a small one at the rear. When Patel switched on the light a feeble central-hanging bulb showed there was nobody there. A low truckle bed sagged in one corner, covered by a multicoloured shawl. A similar one was haphazardly pinned across the window. The only other furniture was a rush-bottomed chair, three greasy cushions and a free-standing wooden cupboard painted orange. This Z opened to reveal a metal rod with five or six wire hangers holding women's garments redolent of stale cooking spices. Under the row of baggy *shalwars* were two pairs of down-at-heel slippers with snagged embroidery uppers. There was no school uniform, nothing that a teenage girl would want to wear, no books.

'These are her grandmother's clothes,' Z accused.

'She share the room,' the man said quickly. 'I tell you my daughter go away. She take everything with her, everything.'

It might be true. He could have shipped her out. Maybe it was time – more than time at seventeen – for her to go back to wherever they'd come from and bring back another immigrant as her husband.

'Thank you, Mr Patel.' She made it sound as if she was satisfied, but she had picked up a muffled sound of voices through the partition wall. Two sons below, and the grandparents glimpsed together in the sitting room; that left one other son. So had he a wife upstairs here or did he talk to himself?

She followed the man out, turned abruptly and threw open the next door. If anything, this room was even narrower than the first. Here the window was similarly

66

masked. Light from the landing slanted across the young man seated on the side of a low single bed. He was too thin for his bulk to hide the outline of someone behind lying under the covers. Z reached alongside the doorway for a switch and the scene sprang alive.

'Yasmin?' Z queried. The covers squirmed.

'Get out,' Z ordered the brother. And to Patel, 'Send my constable up.'

The girl had been in a terrible state, covered in old bruises, one cheek split open and suppurating, her wrists chafed where ropes had tied them. As she struggled to sit up the finger-marks came up red beside her mouth where her brother had stifled her efforts to cry out.

'Ambulance required,' Z snapped at Aziz, 'then get transport and back-up to sort this lot out. I'll question the father myself back at the nick.'

The man was shaking with rage, his fists beating the air as he stormed, but he knew enough not to launch a physical attack. Cuffed in Z's car he still managed to scream at his daughter as she was carried past on her stretcher.

'What was all that?' Z demanded of Aziz.

'Threats. What he'd do to her if she opened her mouth.' He sounded ashamed. They were his kind of people after all. Or once had been.

At the nick the questioning went on into the night, all the males – except the sick grandfather – pulled in for interrogation separately. The general version was that Yasmin was wilful and disobedient. She had been restrained because she had threatened the good name of the family. They were responsible for her. Discipline was the right and duty of the males she was subject to.

Which depressed Zyczynski, while she admitted that alien culture couldn't be put across in a few short months. We're their foreigners after all, she told herself in a break for coffee. It's hard on newcomers who've lived by their own values for generations.

Roll back three or four hundred years and women were regarded in much the same way in this country. And still we need refuges for battered wives and abused children.

Fortunately this was a story she could write up and then hand over for others to deal with. Maybe it wouldn't even reach court. Instead, a caution, then professional counselling, because, apart from roughness in restraining her it would be hard to prove the family had intended a vicious assault on the girl. As the Boss had said only this very day - no, it was yesterday by now – our job isn't social welfare.

Belting herself into her car, she looked out at a watery pre-dawn and decided there was one thing more she must know before she could take her rest. Wycombe hospital was only across the way. In it Yasmin Patel would be facing the first day of the rest of her life. But she needn't wake to it alone.

It was the hour of bedpans, wash-ups and the early tea trolley. Her warrant card got Z past Sister's clipboard and the bustling nurses to where the uniform constable sat on guard. Yasmin's bed had a notice above it: NIL BY MOUTH. She was due for surgery that afternoon. X-rays had confirmed a broken radius and ulna in the right arm, and the opthalmologist was to investigate a sharp foreign body in her left eye.

'You don't need me bothering you at this point,' Z told the girl. 'I've just dropped in to wish you a quick recovery. There'll be a chance to talk fully later, but if you can give me some idea now what set this all off I'd be grateful.'

'They don't like my friends,' the girl whispered.

'Ah. Anyone special? Some boy you met through school?' This sounded like a familiar story: the fear of contamination from Westerners with looser sexual habits. She could see both sides. These days native Brit standards fell a long way short of stricter cultures.

Yasmin turned her head away. She was trying to force back tears.

'Can I give anyone a message? Is there someone you'd like to have visit you?'

'Nobody. I don't want to see anyone.'

She was closing up, as she'd been instructed. It was disappointing. But when she felt better her courage might return. If she stuck by her newly acquired outlook, surely she wouldn't choose to go back for more of the same treatment? But it was up to others to present her with an alternative.

'Right. I'll say goodbye then, for the present. You're in good hands here. Get well soon.'

No progress there. And it would have been nice to be thanked. Only life wasn't like that most of the time.

Early morning traffic was beginning to build up as Z drove back. Wycombe was always a pig to get in and out of. Even when traffic was no more than a trickle drivers kept down to 30mph in the 40 area from sheer habit.

Within half an hour she was putting her key in the lock, stumbling upstairs to her cosy flat, bed uppermost in her mind. She almost resisted a red light blinking on her answerphone unheeded for nearly two days, then relented. She pressed the button to let the messages drivel on while she dropped her skirt, and tore off her shoes and tights.

It was not all inconsequential, though: after the local bookshop announcing the arrival of a paperback she'd ordered a week back, there came the Boss's voice calling her to a 9 a.m. meeting of DI Mott's team at Charlie's Caff. Which could only mean that they'd a new violent death.

'I need you in on this, Z,' the Superintendent said, 'however tied up you are with the Wycombe schoolgirl.

'We've a rather important body, and you had the advantage of meeting the subject when alive. It's Mr Hiromu Imura, the director from Matsukawa's. He's been found dead in his bedroom at the Bellhouse Hotel.'

Seven

Z stood back in the hotel corridor to watch the SOCO's team of experts at work, from long practice not crowding each other as they puffed dark powder on, lifted dabs, searched, and took photographs. A local police surgeon had already attended, confirmed death – not a difficult decision in the circumstances – and had gone below with Mott for a stiff drink.

What sickened her at first sight was the blood. Arterial jetting. It had sprayed in all directions. The mattress and bedclothes dragged across the floor were dark with it. A wide crimson arc flung across the nearby wall grotesquely dangled red spider's legs down the cream distemper. On the beige carpet a trail of elongated drops led back to the bathroom.

Not that the dead man could have caused these. With such blood loss he'd have been past it. The killer must have been drenched. Even staying on to shower, how could he get away unnoticed in that state? Been naked when he struck? Or brought a change of clothing with him?

But then perhaps he hadn't needed to go far, having a room nearby, on the same floor.

Another option would have instantly suggested itself if she hadn't come here direct from twenty-four hours' duty without sleep. But, despite her slowed reactions, training was taking over, with adrenalin flowing at the promise of a murder chase. Her eyes panned the general scene, then lit on nearer details.

Just inside the room and to her right the sliding wardrobe door gaped open. She saw Imura's shiny black Oxfords neatly stretched in metal shoe-trees on its floor. A jade-green, patterned silk dressing gown dangled from one end of a hanger, still held by the neck loop over its wire hook. A prim, methodical man, Imura: he'd seemed to like things in order. Which they certainly weren't just now.

A jumble of underclothes lay below the tipped hanger. There were no top clothes, no shirt. So was the body still wearing its suit? In bed? Because certainly it was on the bed that the man had been killed. She craned to see and confirmed that the suit wasn't on him.

The body wouldn't be nice on nearer sight. But she had to make sure it was the right man. She moved forward, leaned sideways for an unobstructed view, and the civilian photographer working on close-ups straightened, saw her and called out a warning, 'Zyczynski, you'll not care for this one.' It was Newman from High Wycombe, as hard a nut as they came. And scornful of squeamishness.

The body was wearing some kind of silky peach-coloured gown. For a brief second she thought it must be a woman lying there and that Imura had made off after killing her. But then, closer, she could see that the assumed identity was correct. These were the unlovely remains of the Japanese she had yesterday seen stepping from the helicopter sent to take Mayumi back to school.
The same long, lantern face with the sparse dark hair receding above a bony forehead. And now, in the rictus of death, so much grimmer.

What he wore was some elaborate kind of embroidered nightshirt. Maybe that was traditional. It was long, probably would be almost floor-length when he stood, but was rucked up now so that the scrawny legs and the bloody stump of his penis were exposed, the gaping belly shining red-black.

How could anyone—?
She turned away, steadied herself with a few deep

breaths, then forced herself to consider the circumstances. Before retiring to bed, a formally correct man – as Imura had seemed to be – would have hung up his suit. Since it was apparently not in this room, the chambermaid could have taken it for valet service. But more likely the killer had been wearing it when he left.

And the tell-tale bloodstained things he'd worn for the killing? Removed and hidden, or smuggled out under cover.

Luggage: what kind of bag had Imura brought with him? There was none on the luggage rack or in the wardrobe cupboard. She'd have to find whoever was on duty when the Japanese checked in, to get a description of luggage and suit.

Did she remember his suit herself? Dark. She'd had the impression of near-black with a sort of expensive-looking shine to it. Fine worsted and mohair? Cashmere? With it a white shirt and sombre blue tie with a pattern of gold diamonds not unlike the Renault car logo. If he'd had an overcoat it had been left inside the helicopter while he got out.

She'd go straight down to Mott now and get a shout put out with the man's description as she remembered him from yesterday. But first formally confirm identity.

'Want a closer look? I've finished here.' Newman had stood back and was waiting for some comment.

Tight-lipped she spent five more seconds taking in the dead face for permanent recall, then nodded. 'That's him.'

She laid a hand on the lower jaw, then the exposed arm and tried lifting it by the wrist. The flesh was cold, rigor clearly setting in. It confirmed what the congealed blood had implied: this man had been dead for some hours. Pathology would have fun working out how long. Someone would need to check whether the hotel heating was turned down overnight.

'You knew him?' Newman was taken aback.

She nodded. 'Done the bathroom yet?'

'Finished all the background while the doc was with the body.'

'Including inside the wardrobe?'

'Nuh. D'you need that?'

'I want photographs showing all contents. That's important. There are things missing there. If I'm needed I'll be with DI Mott downstairs.'

Newman treated her to his ugly grin, tombstone teeth stained at the roots with nicotine, as he surveyed her from her crisp brown curls to tidy ankles. 'Right, missy.'

She gave him a cold stare. 'The word is Sergeant, Mr Newman.'

'So – *Sergeant*, missy.'

She turned on her heel, carrying away with her a vivid image of the murder scene. She could visualize it under other circumstances as a pleasant enough room with the inevitable blankness of a hotel facility, neutral, with no lingering trace of any one person's existence – no accumulation of gadgety junk, books, litter of children's or adult toys. As correct and impersonal as the unsuspecting Japanese who had walked in to take temporary possession.

But fair appearances – of both man and place – could lie. You needn't be in the job to encounter equally bland rooms as a setting for grim events. Hotels were like the false façades of a film set. Impeccably smooth running front-of-house, while coffins were sneaked out by the rear, courtesy of the service lift.

And there was not only this kind of violence. While briefly working undercover in a hotel* she'd picked up some hard facts. A guest with no luggage beyond a spirit-store's carrier bag was a red-light warning for Reception, and barmen were schooled to recognize a drinker with the hopeless, dogged eyes that determine they shall never open on another day. There were lost souls enough who

* See *First Wife Twice Removed*

came to such places seeking anonymity, to shield those who'd known them alive from the shock of their discovery dead.

These promiscuous rooms, once tainted, faked ignorance of the mugging, rape, murder or suicide committed in them. Routinely sanitized and impersonal again, they were ready to deceive the next unsuspecting innocent to move in.

This man too was as false, the grisly reverse now of the passionless image he'd seemed earlier. What had become of all that chilling power and self-sufficiency? He was another's victim. Unless his destroyer had happened upon him by accident, his inscrutable surface had concealed a secret which earned him a hideous death. That was the buried reality which she must dig for.

Still shaken, she managed to conceal her feelings on encountering DI Mott at the lift. He nodded. 'Ah, Z. Did you get a look at the body?'

'It's Imura all right, Guv. Or was.' She passed on her observations about the missing suit and luggage.

'Yup; I'm not blind, Z. I've been asking around. Nobody remembers seeing him last night after he came up from dinner, and I haven't got a good description yet of his clothes. Dark suit, the waitress thought. Not much help there.'

She obliged with a rundown of the man's outfit as she'd seen him. 'If the killer was wearing those things to leave, with his own bloodstained clothes hidden in Imura's bag—'

'He'd be instantly sussed carrying luggage out. The girl on reception would be alert for any supposed guest flitting without settling his account. And after she left, the night porter sat in the foyer until everything was locked up out front just before 2 a.m.'

'So, unless he's resident here, the killer probably left by another door. Or window.'

'Their security's pretty good, and with a silver wedding

party hanging on late there was constant activity in the kitchen area. No one could have gone through there unnoticed.'

'It wouldn't be the first time luggage left by a window and then its owner wandered out for a moonlight stroll.'

'Probably not by these windows, but I could be wrong.'

'How about other guests?'

'Beaumont's doing the rounds with a WPC, knocking on all doors. We've also got a list of guests who attended functions downstairs. And today's duty manager is helping to check on staff.'

'So what's left for me, Guv?'

'Briefly hitting the hay, Z. As the Boss doubtless instructed, once you'd identified Imura. But our meeting's moved on to 9.30 a.m. Make good use of the time between.'

Back home again she kicked off her shoes and lay flat on the bed staring up at the angled ceiling, her mind by now too stimulated to permit sleep. A sunburst of ideas was crackling in her mind: directions to follow, inquiries to make, individuals to interview. She reached for a notepad, turned on to her stomach and scribbled furiously until the words slowed, ran together, tangled and stretched into faces mouthing silently, fingers flicking in dismissive gestures.

The vision blurred. Her last fully conscious thought was surprised recognition of the old Asian woman at the door in High Wycombe.

Nothing to do with the case, she told herself. Like 'the flowers that bloom in the spring, tra-la'.

That was Gilbert and Sullivan. But she'd got the wrong opera. This was *The Mikado.* Hadn't Elizabeth Matsukawa said something about it? The Mikado not coming in person. He'd sent his Lord High Executioner instead.

Yes, that was it. Ironic: the executioner executed.

And, muzzily half-satisfied, she let sleep roll over her.

*   *   *

The team meeting was held over a late breakfast in a secluded corner of Charlie's Caff. An ex-sergeant of the Met, invalided out after injury in an affray, Charlie could accommodate them at almost any hour of the day or night. The Boss even carried the Caff's doorkey on the ring with his own. In the brightly lit diner with its formica tables and hissing coffee-makers, truckers were welcomed, the press permanently barred, and invasive strangers eyed with guarded suspicion.

This was to be a short meeting, to discuss the initial briefing at the Incident Room at Gerrards Cross nick. Angus Mott explained he'd be controlling it remotely, with a slightly hobbling Beaumont sitting in as assistant to the Office Manager. The previous night he had taken a brief ride on the roof of a ram-raider's car and was lucky not to have ended in hospital. Now, with his ribs strapped and moving stiffly, he refused to absent himself totally from what promised to be an interesting case.

Initially there'd be twenty working on the active Inquiry Team while the expected first rush of info came in: all of DC rank except Z as sergeant. DI Mott and the Boss would share overall control of briefings, both having other serious crime inquiries on hand elsewhere. Basically all interrogations would fall to the DCs and the DS, who were, after all, the experts at that.

'We old-stagers,' Yeadings put in drolly, 'being a bit out of practice at chatting with chummy.'

The PR office at Kidlington would cover press handouts in the probably vain hope that the core team might then be left free of mobbing by microphone and camera.

In the Caff, Superintendent Yeadings, seated beside Mott with his back to the mirrored wall, said little, putting away a plate of mixed fries despite having breakfasted properly (according to Nan) on grapefruit and bran cereal at home. Mott gave less attention to his bacon omelette than to his words. The two sergeants sat opposite, content with black coffee.

'So,' Mott said to round up, 'we run a check first on who knew that Imura would be there, who saw him arrive, other guests booking later, absentees, casual visitors who might have mingled with the silver wedding guests, and all hotel staff. And a check run on local nutters with a known taste for knifing. Further checks on access and exits, with searching of all rooms for traces of bloodstains or presence of clothing and baggage unaccounted for.'

'That should keep uniform branch busy,' Beaumont approved. 'What's CID tasking?'

'Z, you've met the Matsukawa women already. Better get off to see the mother before she ups and gets back to Hampshire.'

'Wiltshire, Guv.'

'Whatever. Where was she putting up locally?'

'The Crown, Amersham. I'll go there now.'

'Another coffee if you want,' Yeadings offered.

'Thanks, but I'm awash already. Relied on caffeine to come awake this morning! And I still haven't put in my report on yesterday's business in Wycombe.'

Mott looked up again from his plate. 'Domestic abuse: right?'

'That's about it. The girl's booked for orthopaedic surgery this afternoon: uncomfortable, but it seems there's no serious permanent damage.'

'As yet,' Beaumont suggested sombrely.

'Not really our concern,' Z quoted across at Yeadings, grinning. 'Family Protection Unit, Social Services and the NSPCC have taken over. In the end the father will probably get off with a caution.' She pushed back her chair, re-energized, seized her shoulder bag and nodded goodbye.

Yeadings watched her go, wishing he was twenty years younger. No, not for that old lascivious cliché: he wasn't phallocentric. But to set off on the new trail as fresh and vibrant as young Zyczynski.

He sighed, visualizing the case translated for himself

into reams of reports and static desk-hours. Still, in the detecting lark there was something to be said for experience, if you didn't collapse into wearied cynicism first.

Z was still mainly untried in her rank of sergeant, but a natural for all that. With Beaumont immobilized, it would be a chance for her to make good as senior on the inquiry team. Women seemed to have a talent for poking into details.

And that included Nan, he considered comfortably, remembering her that morning dangling a tired sock under his nose. Accusing: 'This has blood on it. Let me see your toenails.' Scanning the contours in the bagged woollen mixture: 'Fourth toe, left foot, I think.'

He recalled himself sharply. Indictable offence: mind disorderly while in charge of a murder case. Back to hard realities. Their body. Male; late forties to fifty; a foreigner, so there was no background as yet. All they knew was that Imura represented the powerful Matsukawa empire. A lot of punch behind that mighty organization. Considerable pressure could be brought on the team from above.

Thank God it hadn't been The Man himself.

Belting herself into her Ford Escort Z reflected on the obvious omission from the suggested agenda: Imura's background. Out of direct reach seemingly, since he was Kyoto-based and had come only recently to this country via a Frankfurt conference. He wouldn't be easy to research from this end, but she had no doubt who would shortly have his thumb plunged up to the oxter in that choice pie! The Boss himself. And what was the betting that he had some police contact on his information debtor list even in that far corner of the world?

At Amersham the lounge of the Crown Hotel was filled with large, genial, middle-aged Americans drinking coffee, a group from Seattle intent on seeing the original venue from the film *Four Weddings and a Funeral.* Staff on duty were getting hard pressed and it took a few minutes to find out that Mrs Matsukawa had already left.

'On the road early,' Z said ruefully.

'Seems so.' The receptionist was scanning a bunch of carbon receipts. 'It's got Sally's signature. She was on last night. The B&B's paid up, plus extras, so the lady must have settled in advance for an early morning departure.'

'Who would have served her at breakfast? Maybe she mentioned where she'd be going from here.'

'I can find out if you don't mind waiting.'

It took over ten minutes during which the milling visitors threatened to adopt her, and she was treated to an enthusiastic commercial on the delights of the north-west coastline of the US of A.

The girl from reception came back with a puzzled air. 'It seems the lady didn't have breakfast in the dining room, so I checked with room service. A blank there too, so I thought I'd ask housekeeping. The room hadn't been used overnight. I guess Mrs Matsiwhatsit just changed her mind and left soon after dinner last night. But she settled up as if she'd stayed over.'

'How can I contact this Sally who was on reception?'

'I'm sorry. We don't give out addresses and phone numbers of staff.'

'I've explained to you, this is a serious police inquiry. Don't mess me about.'

'I'm sorry. Look, I'm new to this. Would you like to speak to the duty manager?'

'It would be quicker if you rang Sally yourself, then handed the phone to me.'

The girl was reluctant, darted a quick glance in the direction of the camera-laden scrum, who were now lining up for exchange currency, and relented.

Sally did remember the lady. After an early dinner last evening she'd gone out with her daughter, came back alone, then must have gone out again unnoticed because she came back a second time at about 10 p.m. She seemed a bit upset and asked for her bill, said she'd changed her mind about staying over. When Sally had asked whether she had a complaint about her accommodation, she said certainly not but things hadn't turned out the way she'd expected. She hadn't demanded any reduction of the account, settled it with her credit card, picked up her overnight bag from her room and went off. No, she hadn't given any indication of where she was going.

Home, Z assumed. And since her car was back in Wiltshire she'd have needed a taxi to the station. 'Did she phone for a cab?' she asked Sally.

'No. She went out to the car park. I happened to be looking from a back window and saw her get into a car.'

'So someone was waiting for her?'

The girl was silent, remembering. 'No-o-o-o. She unlocked it and got in on the driving side, put her overnight bag on the seat beside her. So she had to be alone, hadn't she?'

Z thanked her and rang off. 'If I wanted a hire car locally where would you recommend?' she asked the receptionist and was given a list. Just as well to know, in case Mrs M had gone elsewhere than straight home. So that query, it seemed, was what she'd better clear up next.

As she left she found that the earlier desultory snowfall had thickened and was now floating down in large feathery flakes which pricked coldly at her upturned face. With head bent she made for her car and almost collided with someone making for the hotel entrance.

Startled, she looked up, half-way through an apology before she recognized the woman.

'Dr Walling?'

'Sergeant Zyczynski, I didn't expect to run into you so soon.' Something had disturbed her customary composure.

'There's nothing wrong, is there, Sergeant? With Mrs Matsukawa, I mean?'

'Were you hoping to see her? I'm afraid she's already left. I've been disappointed too.'

'Really this is too bad of her. I had expected better manners.' Two bright spots of colour showed on the headmistress's cheeks. 'She might at least have told me she was taking Mayumi away. It puts me in a most difficult position. I'm sure May's father will disapprove.' Snowflakes were creating a white snood over the woman's faded blonde hair.

'Look, let's go inside,' Z suggested. 'There are things we need to sort out.'

Eight

'What did you mean, about Mrs Matsukawa taking Mayumi away?' Z asked.

Dr Walling explained. She had overlooked May's absence until that morning.

'I knew Mrs Matsukawa was staying at the Crown, and when it was reported to me last night that May hadn't returned at 10.30, when we had agreed on nine o'clock, I took it that they had mistaken my p.m. for a.m., assuming that I had granted an exeat for her to spend the night with her mother. Inexcusably slack of me not to check further then, but I'd taken painkillers and had been asleep when the report of her absence came from Cavell House. Miss Goss had assumed until then that Mayumi was with me.

'I wasn't clear-headed, and at that hour it seemed unreasonable to disturb them at the hotel, but again when May failed to turn up for house assembly this morning I tried ringing through. The line was busy so I got in my car and came over. And now you tell me that Mrs Matsukawa has already checked out.'

'But that was last night,' Z told her. 'And she was alone.'

They stared at each other, both reaching the same conclusion. 'It looks . . .' Dr Wallinger began.

'. . . as if May's done another runner,' Z murmured.

'. . . as if May has gone absent again,' Dr Wallinger said at the same time. 'But she'd given me her word!'

This last was so vehement that Z felt sorry for the woman. 'And you believed her?'

'I believed her, certainly. I thought I knew her that much. She has always been a girl who would stand by her word.'

'And her mother? Could you trust her as easily?'

They had reached the cosy lounge inside the hotel and the older woman was shivering at the sudden change in temperature. 'Let me order you some coffee. Maybe something stronger,' Z offered. 'I'll join you when I've made a phone call.'

Mott was unobtainable by pager or mobile phone. She had to go direct to Superintendent Yeadings. 'Sir,' she reported, 'both Elizabeth Matsukawa and her daughter appear to be missing now. Separately, according to a witness at the hotel. The mother last night, probably in a hire car, making for Wiltshire.'

'Leave that with me, Z. You'd better contact the school, make sure—'

'Sir, I've got the headmistress with me at the Amersham hotel. She's been trying to make contact herself. May was expected back last night and didn't show up.'

'I'll see to the Wiltshire end. You'd better have another go at those study-mates at the school. Get their reactions. Don't ease up on them if they seem to know anything. This is starting to look nasty. There may be a connection with what happened to Imura.'

Z felt a chill grip her. He couldn't seriously believe that a fifteen-year-old schoolgirl had committed that ghastly carnage in the hotel bedroom? Or did he fear that something of the same kind might overtake her? Was some unknown maniac setting out to destroy anyone connected with the Matsukawa family or firm? A savage campaign of vengeance, perhaps linked with incidents in Japan?

Ever since the first gas attack in the Tokyo subway a quite new viciousness had surfaced out there. Japan, once the safest country in the world, had become a hostage to religious and political fanatics. Were they now moving in on specific targets, a sort of Eastern supermafia running a protection racket?

She went back to Dr Walling who, refusing refreshments, sat stiff and apprehensive. This morning she was clearly a sick woman, perhaps mortally so. Z felt instant sympathy. For this well-intentioned woman, if for no other reason, she must get Mayumi safely back at once.

'I'd like to follow you back to the school,' Z told her, 'to have another word with Maddie and Julia. There's just a chance they may decide to talk more freely now that May's gone for a second time.'

Even with that hope in mind, Z was startled by Maddie's reaction. The girl was horrified. Suddenly white-faced, she appealed to Dr Walling. 'She can't have! She never meant—'

'Maddie, have you been in touch with her since the first time she disappeared?' Z demanded.

'I – no, of course not.'

'I'm not sure that I believe you.'

Maddie looked defiant, but almost sick with worry.

'You were expecting it the first time, weren't you? But this is something different.'

They were interrupted by a knock on the Head's door. A woman looked in and came through at a nod from Dr Walling. 'What is it, Matron?'

'I found these things in the girls' study. Mayumi's shoulder bag, her jacket and the underclothes she took away last time.'

'So how did they get there?' Dr Walling confronted the two girls. 'May must have passed these things to one of you when I was talking privately with Mr Imura or her mother. Which of you was it?'

There was a short silence, then Maddie shuffled her feet. 'At lunch time I saw her waiting outside your room. She stuffed her bag and the jacket through the banisters to me. But we didn't talk. Not really talk. She just said everything was going to be all right.'

'Well, everything is far from all right now,' Z said grimly. 'It will probably reach you through the media anyway, but I have to warn you that the man her father sent to bring her back has been killed, and no one has any idea where May has gone. If either of you knows anything at all that may help us find her, it could be very much in May's interest that you speak out. It's possible that she could be in some danger herself.'

'No,' Maddie said vehemently. 'I know nothing at all, truly. If I did I wouldn't hesitate. She's my friend. I'd do anything I could to help.'

'Julia?'

The girl was sniffing. She shook her head dumbly.

'Dr Walling, could I speak to Maddie for a moment alone?'

The Head rose slowly from her chair. 'If you think it will do any good.' She nodded to Julia to follow her and went out, closing the door firmly behind them.

Z stared at Maddie, letting the silence build uncomfortably. This wasn't the same cocky imp of their first meeting. Something was gnawing at even her superb self-confidence.

'Maddie, you know and I know that your friend May took French leave that first time as part of a pre-planned exercise. You were in that with her. If anything discreditable happened as a result it leaves you in the role of conspirator. You must share responsibility. I want you to tell me what she was up to, and if in my opinion it has nothing to do with the present situation I will respect that confidence. But you must understand that I am dealing now with the most serious crime I'm ever likely to be faced with, so peccadilloes are of no importance. Be open with me. Even petty crime can be overlooked when we're considering murder.'

Maddie shivered, tightened her lips and shook her head. 'I can't tell you, I just can't. It was something very personal, between her and me. Nobody else is involved at all. It can't have anything to do with her father or mother or that Japanese man who brought her back.' Her chin went up defiantly. 'You can tear out my tongue but I'll never tell you what it was.'

It sounded ridiculously childish. Maddie was no longer the streetwise sophisticate who knew exactly where she was bound for. But she was still stubbornly loyal and close-lipped. Z was tempted to leave it there, admitting to herself that adolescents' secrets have little adult reasoning in them. Molehills were Himalayas to an innocent. Or a comparative innocent in Maddie's case.

'Can you give me your solemn word that it was something purely personal to you both? No more than that?'

'Yes.'

'Right. And you've no idea why May should decide to break her word given to Dr Walling that she wouldn't go off again?'

'No, I haven't.' Maddie frowned. 'Did she really, though? Did she promise that?'

'Yes. That's why Dr Walling's so upset.'

'But that's awful. May had a thing about promises. And she would never lie. I've never met anyone so honest. So she can't have chosen to go, can she? This time someone must have snatched her.'

Zyczynski looked in at the Incident Room. It was buzzing. Beaumont claimed that statements were coming in like a machine-gun backwards. Four indexers were hard at work entering information from witness statements. In the next room the Incident Analyst was setting up a cleared wall for the computerized and colour-coded Progress Chart. Four telephonists were taking calls simultaneously. But no eye-witness had yet appeared with a sighting of anyone leaving the Bellhouse Hotel wearing Imura's clothes.

A request to Wiltshire force had resulted in a negative on Mrs Matsukawa. She was not at her home. Telephoned inquiries regarding a car hired in her name had turned up particulars of a red Vauxhall supplied to her by Avis of High Wycombe. A general search for this was being made throughout Thames Valley, so far without result.

'Make it countrywide,' Z ordered. Obviously the lady had something in mind other than returning home. Could she be lying low in some hotel, having arranged with May to meet up with her there? Not if Maddie was right about the girl's rigid honesty. So where was Elizabeth Matsukawa likely to make for on her own? Had she some special friend-confidante she would run to when in trouble? And what was this supposed trouble – a murder committed in passionate anger, or distress at a daughter likely to be wrested from her care?

Had she even picked up flight tickets to go and reason with her husband, and the car would be found parked at Heathrow or Gatwick? Time would tell, but in the interval what fresh horrors could occur? Z went back to see what new items were being logged in the Incident Room.

'A bite of lunch,' Beaumont ordered, rising stiffly and reaching for his walking-stick. 'We can't function indefinitely powered only on black coffee.'

He was right, of course. They slid their trays round the cafeteria rails and filled up with hot shepherd's pie and baton carrots. Beaumont was half-way through his strawberry yogurt dessert, with Z as spectator, when her pager called her to the phone. The headmistress again.

'Dr Walling?'

'We have some fresh background about Mayumi which I should like you to see, Miss Zyczynski.'

She wasn't giving more away on an open phone line, so Z had no choice but to drive out again to the school. It was still midday break there, and girls in overcoats and scarves were stomping about in the lying snow. Taken by the maid up to Dr Walling's sitting room, she passed Julia seated on a chair in the corridor. She had evidently been crying. So had the girl decided to come clean about her study-mates' goings-on? If so, it would be the end, Z guessed, of any remaining trust between her and Maddie.

The Head went straight to the matter concerning her. 'I thought you should see these,' she said, opening a folder and spreading over her desk a number of eight-by-ten glossy prints in black and white. The paper was slightly curved as if they had been kept together in a roll.

Z bent over to look. They all showed a beautiful Japanese model posed provocatively in the scantiest of clothing.

'I can appreciate why Maddie prevented us seeing these. I sincerely hope Mayumi isn't looking like this at present. For her own safety.'

They were exotic poses, minimally draped. Nothing porno, but certainly in the girlie-art class.

'I should have kept in mind,' the Head regretted, 'that Maddie's grown-up brother is a photographer in the fashion world. I must assume that these were taken during the Christmas holidays when May was staying with the Coulters. It seems that Maddie has been leading her into areas her parents would certainly disapprove of. In showing you these photographs I really must ask you not to release them to the press.'

'Does Maddie admit that these were taken by her brother?'

'I haven't spoken to her yet. They came from Julia. Under pressure Maddie will try to lie herself out of any uncomfortable situation. I am not ready to risk that until we have enough proof to convince even her that it would be pointless. But these photographs are of a highly professional standard. Technically, that is. And the Christmas vacation was the only occasion when Mayumi would have had the opportunity to pose.'

'But can these photos have any bearing on her recent behaviour? Maddie has assured me—' Z caught the gleam in Dr Walling's eye and halted. The Head's words still hung in the air: 'She will try to lie herself out of any uncomfortable situation.' Admittedly this *enfant* was pretty *terrible.* A compulsive liar – or at any rate a determined one – didn't pass on the most reliable statements.

'I take your point, Dr Walling. But when she assured me that May's earlier disappearance was concerned with some strictly personal matter between the two of them, I did believe her.'

'She can be very convincing. And disarming into the bargain, I'll admit.'

'Suppose,' Z suggested, 'that the two girls had some plan for Mayumi to model for more photographs. That could rightly be described as a personal matter, don't you think? Could May's first disappearance have been for some such purpose?'

'I hardly think so. Mayumi is a serious student. To behave like this during the holidays is one thing – though even that is unexpected – but I am sure she wouldn't have contemplated breaking into term time. I could more easily accept that she was away attempting some move to reunite her parents.'

'But possibly having a further motive,' Z said, half to herself. She shared the Head's suspicion that May had been hoping to manipulate her parents. But if Maddie had set up a term-time meeting for her with the brother – Greg, was it? – this could explain the considerable time missing between the girl's leaving school on the Friday night and her arrival in Wiltshire next evening; a period she had managed to avoid accounting for. It wasn't beyond possibility that she had been for a photo session in between. Or had she, ingenuously, been swept into a romantic entanglement with this older man? Greg Coulter was certainly worth taking a look at.

His studio, she found, was in Rathbone Place, West London; less seedy than some of the Soho set-ups, but not that far distant. Just a hop across Oxford Street. Z went there with a DC from the Met who obviously fancied an extension of the connection.

They climbed a double flight of stairs to reach a large brilliantly lit room by way of an untidy and deserted office. Greg Coulter was in mid photo session with two assistants and a girl model posing on a dais. The spotlights were dazzling, picking out a muzzy scenic backcloth in romantic sweet-pea colours. Equally unseasonable, the subject was in full Ascot or Henley garb, frilled parasol and all.

The police duo's arrival was observed but not commented on. Z was content to stand back and watch operations.

Behind the camera a dark-haired man was ordering the poses. 'Right. Lovely. More snooty. Throw your chin up. Do some come-hither over your shoulder. Per-r-r-rfect.'

'Hang on,' ordered the girl assistant, bespectacled and harassed-looking. One of the sunshade's spikes had caught in the chiffon draperies. While she ran forward to disentangle it Z had a glimpse of the photographer's face. Slightly under average height, the man was compactly formed, with a dynamic dark-browed, animated face. Something challenging about him, she decided. Curving, rubbery mouth. Sexy. Maybe dangerous, but fun. Yes, an unwary schoolgirl might well find herself out of her depth with him.

'Look,' said the taller blond man lounging against the wall, 'you've got to change the lighting there. See how that move's altered your composition. With a great blob of shadow now where the dress detail is. That's what they want to sell, dammit. The girl's just the cherry on top, but the outfit's the cake. And our bread and butter.' He sounded tetchy, almost waspish.

Instead of bridling at the interruption, the photographer gave an expansive grin. 'Whatever you say, Greg.' Totally obliging.

Greg? So she'd confused the two men's respective identities, because the smaller one more resembled Maddie, and he'd been handling the camera. She took a second look at the tall fair man. Artificially fair, she was almost sure, as was the close-trimmed beard. A single ring in the left earlobe; an open silk shirt to expose pectoral muscles that spoke of regular workouts; the eyes pale blue and deepset; a general healthy Viking image. But there was something about the moist red mouth, just visible between moustache and beard – a touch petulant perhaps?

'Gregory Coulter?' Z addressed him formally.

His eyes took her in from red-brown curls to slim ankles. 'Who sent you?'

He'd assumed she was from a modelling agency, touting for a job. 'Thames Valley police,' she told him, displaying her warrant card. 'I'm Detective-Sergeant Zyczynski and this is Constable Jeffreys, Metropolitan CID. Could we have a word with you in private?'

The man's eyes switched rapidly to his colleague's in silent communication, then back for slow consideration of the visitors. 'I hope you don't bring bad news. Don't make me kill the messenger.'

'That shouldn't be necessary, sir. In the office, perhaps?'

He swung round on the cameraman. 'Carry on, Danny. You're nearly there. Another ten minutes, then pay the girl off.'

In the office he sank into a chair behind the desk, waving a languid hand towards a padded bench against the wall. 'Do sit down. If you'd hoped to catch me taking blue piccies you've chosen the wrong man. I don't.'

'I'm glad to hear it.' Expressionlessly. 'I should like you to tell me the date when you took these photographs.' She spread the glossies of Mayumi over his desk, between bulging files, two used wine glasses and the greasy foil container from a takeaway lunch.

Greg Coulter glanced casually at the prints. 'Ah yes. Sometime over Christmas. Couldn't say which day exactly. We just did the one trial run. Black and white gets the essentials. Photographs well, don't you think? Just a kid, but she's got that something it takes; dormant, ready to spring awake at the right touch.'

'And *did* you actually touch, sir?' insinuated DC Jeffreys.

Coulter considered him for the first time, coldly. 'No. She's not to my taste. I photograph women day in, day out. An under-age female? It would be professional suicide, *mate.*' Coulter smiled insultingly. 'And if you're making me an offer, Constable, thanks but no thanks. I already have an ongoing relationship.'

Z ignored the DC's tight-lipped anger. 'Mr Coulter, was that the first time you'd met Mayumi Matsukawa?'

Coulter turned back to her and assumed an expression of caution. 'Ye-e-es.'

'And since then?'

'Since then what? She's a school kid. I imagine she'd not get the opportunity, even if I had the whim.'

'Let's leave your imagination out of it, Mr Coulter. Have you seen her since?'

'To that, the plain answer's no.'

He was playing with a slim gold propelling pencil, reversing it between elegant fingers and tapping each end lightly on the desktop. All the while his pale eyes held her own and the red lips inside the blond beard were smiling with mockery. Z remembered Dr Walling's warning about Maddie's tendency to lie. It could be a family trait. She resisted the urge to say his denial could easily be checked. Let him think she was satisfied. Then he'd not bother to cover up.

'Is that all, Inspector?'

'Sergeant, sir. Yes, thank you. Good day, sir.' While Coulter lounged on in his chair she let DC Jeffreys open the door for her and follow her out. On the landing he gave his crooked grin. 'Left him purring at his own wit, didn't you?'

She grinned back, counted silently to three, reopened the door and poked her head in. 'Oh, there was one other thing, Mr Coulter.'

If she had hoped to catch him off guard she was to be disappointed. His blond calf cowboy boots were up on the desk, ankles crossed. He was stretching languidly.

'Speak on, Superintendent.'

She let it go this time, refusing to let him rattle her. 'Where were you on Friday night? From 8.30 onwards?'

He stared at her coldly. 'That, surely, is my own business.'

She let a silence build, forcing him to go further. He shrugged. As he elegantly withdrew his feet from the desk and tipped forward she caught the quick glance thrown past her.

It should have been the DC standing at her back but instead it was Danny, leaning against the wall. She remembered he'd been shooting in his sock soles for greater mobility. He switched on a dazzling smile for her.

'Since you find my private interests so fascinating, Commissioner,' Coulter was offering, 'I will confess. Our weekends begin at noon on Friday. And last until noon on Monday. I was at my flat with Danny throughout. Do you require a blow by blow account of our actions? I believe there's a great market for such things among the sexually deprived, but I hadn't imagined that you . . .'

Of course Danny backed him up, openly fed the information while she stood fuming at the way her subtlety had been side-stepped.

'Where the hell were you?' she stormed at DC Jeffreys when she caught up with him at the car. He had the grace to look uncomfortable. 'Thought you'd finished with the questions. How was I to know you'd do a Columbo retake? Did it matter?'

'Just gave Coulter's boyfriend the opportunity to latch on to his extempore alibi,' she said viciously. She didn't look forward to explaining to DI Mott how she'd blown that one.

She used the car phone to contact Beaumont and her spirits fell even lower at the news he had for her.

'We've caught up with Mrs Matsu. Well, sort of, if you know what I mean. Bit of a dead end there. See you back at base for details, Z.'

Nine

Elizabeth Matsukawa wasn't dead as Z had feared.

'In the John Radcliffe Hospital at Oxford, with con-cussion, broken ribs, multiple bruising, internal bleeding. Involved in a single-vehicle RTA,' Beaumont told her succinctly.

'The Radcliffe? What was she doing near Oxford?'

'On the M40 motorway, heading north.'

'Going where?'

'Anybody's guess. Birmingham and beyond. Who does she know up that way?'

'Wiltshire's where she originally came from, but wasn't she in North Wales with her husband for some time? There's a Matsukawa factory near Wrexham.'

'Possible, I guess. We've nothing on record, but the M40 is the route I'd have started on to get there. Best follow that up.'

'Is there any chance she had a passenger with her? We still haven't located her daughter.'

'She was alone when found. And probably had put her overnight bag on the seat beside her, because it went through the windscreen. We're waiting for Traffic's detailed report.'

Z hummed. 'Lucky she was still in our area. But we should have had a positive on the car earlier.'

'It was towed off by a local garage. The officer dealing with the RTA had been ten hours on duty and hit the sack before his report was on computer. You want to go up there?'

Z shook her head. 'If she's unconscious it can wait.' She flopped on to a chair. 'Where's Angus?'

'Our indefatigable DI is now on the trail of the double rapist over at Bicester. Meanwhile the Boss is trying hard not to look surplus to requirement. Try using him as a sounding board.'

'Why not? It could be embarrassingly useful: I've a horrid feeling I've goofed up something important.'

Superintendent Yeadings wandered in while she was catching up with the Analysis Chart in the next room. 'Hope you're not having recourse to that drinks machine, Z,' he said lightly. 'I'm perking, along the corridor. Drop in when you're free.'

She was glad to. With the steaming fragrance of a mug of mocha between her fingers she found it easier to sort her impressions. She kept nothing back.

'It sounds as if Mrs Matsukawa isn't going anywhere for the moment,' Yeadings led off as she reached the end of her summary. 'So we can leave her to the medicos. And there's nothing in on Mayumi. Which leaves us just two queries to work on. This Greg Coulter, as a possible to Mayumi's whereabouts, and Hiromu Imura who is total enigma.'

'The Met are looking into Coulter's background for us,' Z offered, 'and they'll send someone round to his home address in Kensington. They're already running a check on the alibi he gave for last night and also for the twenty-four hours that Mayumi first went missing. It's a pity I muffed his statement on that. Now he's on his guard he's sure to produce further witnesses to his alibi for that Friday/Saturday.'

'Let's hope you wrong-footed him enough for any such alibi to have holes in it. We need only one independent witness to his being elsewhere over the crucial period. Are you expecting results with him?'

'I'm hopeful,' she allowed. 'He was so smarty-pants answering my questions. There had to be a reason. Preening himself on acting so laid back.'

She shrugged. 'But there was no real underlying unease; so even if we find Mayumi was somehow involved with him over that weekend, I doubt it has anything to do with this later business over Imura.'

'Did you believe his claim to be homosexual?'

'Yes, he was so condescending about it. The ongoing partnership he spoke of has to be with the man I first mistook for him; Danny Bevan. But that doesn't rule Coulter out from chasing personable young girls as well. It really depends on whether . . .'

Yeadings waited, watching her mobile face as he stirred sugar substitute into his coffee.

'. . . on whether he actually keeps professional and personal life separate,' she concluded.

'So, with Coulter too put on the back burner,' Yeadings said equably, 'let's switch to our murder victim. Any bright ideas on him? I'm still waiting for definitive information from a contact in Tokyo, but what I'd like right now is some hint of his connections with this part of the world. Just run your mind back through the murder scene as you walked in on it, Z. What struck you most forcibly?'

Zyczynski sat silent a moment, then, 'The blood,' she said shortly. 'So much of it. A really frenzied attack.'

'I attended the post mortem,' Yeadings said quietly. 'Do you want the preliminary details? Seventeen stab wounds, plus numerous defence injuries to the hands. But the main injury, and what killed him, was the slit throat. Virtually from ear to ear, running from his left side to his right. Which implies a right-handed attack from the rear, or – less likely – a left-handed one from in front.

'Death wasn't instantaneous, hence the huge amount of arterial blood. The dying man must have turned back to face his murderer, attempting to defend himself, and was probably still hanging on to him as he collapsed back on to the bed. The photographs show bloody marks from both the unknown's hands on bed linen to either side of the body. It seems there's not much hope of getting

96

recognizable prints off the creased cotton, but the lab is trying to enhance them.'

Z nodded. So much for the blood. What else had struck her at the time?

'The gown he was wearing,' she wondered. 'Was he a cross-dresser?'

'It was a nightshirt,' Yeadings explained. 'A very fancy one and must have cost a pretty penny. I've seen similar in menswear shops in Hong Kong. They're cool for summer wear; and some Eastern men prefer them all the year round. I don't think it necessarily had any sexual connotations.'

'I see. Being so elaborate, it made me think he might have had a woman or a call boy with him, and either they had a disagreement which led to a knife attack, or it happened in the course of an attempted robbery.'

'Well, certainly some of Imura's stuff must have gone away in the bag which the killer took, but there were personal things of obvious value left behind.'

Yes, she recalled now the silver-backed brushes and an intricately carved ivory photo frame. This last came from a time when tusk-dealing wasn't frowned on. The picture in it had been of two little boys, perhaps twins, of about six years old. So had the stern-faced Imura been a father? It seemed poignant now. At the time she had merely listed the photo in her mind without comment. Shock, she accused herself: she had let the horror get to her, all that blood. So what else had she missed?

'The night staff are adamant that no service existed to supply call-girls, or -boys,' Yeadings said thoughtfully.

'Well, they wouldn't admit it if there was one.'

'Angus questioned them himself. If he's satisfied, I am too. But there was quite a bit of activity in the hotel that night. It wouldn't have been impossible for a sneak thief to gain entry to Imura's room while he slept. If he was armed with a knife, and Imura woke, turned away to grab the phone . . .'

Z could picture it. When she'd seen the room the phone had been on the floor, the receiver trailing from its flex, the bedside table overturned. Yes, she liked the sneak-thief scenario. Anything that cut out Elizabeth Matsukawa and her teenage daughter.

As if he recognized what was in her mind, Yeadings recalled her to other options. 'Leaving aside the chance intruder, I want you now to draw up a list of everyone who knew that Imura was to stay at that hotel.'

Yes, that was the overlooked intention that had hovered in the back of her mind, worrying her. She had been getting around to working on it when Dr Walling set her off on another tack with the news of Mayumi's second disappearance. She attempted to tackle it now.

'Dr Walling certainly knew where Imura was staying, and so did whoever took the message off her fax machine. The Bellhouse booking had been made direct from Japan and the hotel name notified to Imura through the school. Elizabeth Matsukawa was told that. Apparently she and her husband had always stayed at the Bellhouse when they brought Mayumi back at the start of each term.'

'But this time Elizabeth Matsukawa booked herself into the Crown at Amersham. Why was that?'

'Obviously she wouldn't want to run into Imura again, but she had actually checked in on the way back from Wiltshire. I was driving her, so I know. And at that point she had no knowledge of where Imura would be staying, or whether he'd be flying straight back to Germany.'

Reluctantly she had to admit, 'Of course, she could have assumed that he wouldn't leave at once. In which case the firm would almost automatically have booked him in at the Bellhouse. But for herself anyway, the Crown would seem more attractive, cosy and olde worlde; very English-village.'

Yeadings was watching her, aware where her sympathies lay. 'So, if the mother later learned from the fax where Imura would be staying, did she tell the daughter? Isn't it natural that there'd have been some mention of it between them?'

That was pure supposition, and Z saw no reason to comment.

'So what's your next line of inquiry?' Yeadings demanded.

'Unless any lead comes in on Mayumi, the Radcliffe hospital, I think.'

'Mmm. Before that, have yet another word with Dr Walling. See if she'll release the full text of the fax from Japan. And bear in mind, Z, that whoever sent it was also aware of where Imura would be holed up for the night. Dr Walling may not be the only person that information was passed to.'

Z hadn't given the fax much thought, and even now she was reluctant to bother Dr Walling again. However, if the Boss wanted the whole fax, then the whole fax he must have. She just hoped the text was in English. She doubted that Thames Valley ran to an Anglo-Jap translator.

By now the Head was sufficiently disturbed to hand over the original message without demur. And it was easily readable. Within a covering message to Dr Walling, the memo addressed to Hiromu Imura informed the Matsukawa director that he was booked overnight into the Bellhouse Hotel, Beaconsfield, and should proceed on the following day by air to the factory at Wrexham in North Wales.

'By air,' Z repeated aloud. 'What was the hurry, I wonder?'

'He'd hired a helicopter from Denham airfield to pick up Mayumi,' Dr Walling reminded her. 'It may be the normal Matsukawa means of business travel.'

'May I use your phone?' Z had left her mobile in the car, to avoid interruptions.

Dr Walling handed her own to her. 'Do you need the airfield's number?'

'If you have it.'

The Head flipped open a leather-bound pad, ran her fingers down one side and read out the code, then 833327. 'That's the flying school. One of the instructors takes passengers. Girls' parents sometimes use him.'

A woman answered the call but hesitated to release flight information. Assured that it was a Thames Valley police request, she said brightly, 'Hang on. I've got your chopper pilot right here. Does he know you?'

She waited while the man took the phone over. 'Who's this?' he demanded cautiously.

Z told him.

'I've never had the pleasure of meeting you, but you're much quoted. Would you mind spelling your name out for me?'

She complied, and heard his answering chuckle.

'If you can run it off that fast it has to be you. What information were you after?'

He grunted when Z told him, and was absent for a short time checking on the airfield departures.

Imura, he told her on his return, had rung through last night to confirm 8.30 a.m. for his piloted plane flight to Chester next morning, but had failed to turn up at the airfield. A call to the hotel had informed them that he was seriously indisposed. The flight had therefore been cancelled but the charge remained against Matsukawa UK's account. Was that all the info Z needed?

'What time is logged for his phone call to the airfield last night?'

'19.47 hours.'

So at that time he'd still been alive, still intended carrying out his instructions from Japan. Z thanked the pilot and rang off.

Dr Walling was nervously standing by the window. 'I have spoken again to Maddie about the photographs. She now admits that her brother took them at Christmas. She was furious with Julia for showing them to us, particularly as she thought she'd hidden them away somewhere quite safe.

Obviously our search of their study hadn't been thorough enough.

'She said Mayumi did it for a lark, when the brother boasted he could pass her off as a professional model at any time she cared to try.'

'I see.' Z nodded. 'It's just possible she did follow that up. Officers of the Met are checking now whether anyone saw her at or near Coulter's studio on the night she first disappeared.'

Dr Walling ran a hand through her hair. 'I can't believe I've been so mistaken in her.'

'Perhaps she had what seemed to her a good reason. Needing money maybe for travelling to see her mother?'

'She had adequate in her pocket-money account here. She had only to ask her housemistress for any extra.'

But doubtless she'd have had to give a reason, Z thought. And Miss Goss might not be the easiest person to approach for private expenses. Explanations would probably have been demanded.

She thanked Dr Walling for her help and left. By car phone she brought Superintendent Yeadings up to date on what she had learnt. 'So next I'm off to the Radcliffe,' she told him. 'And afterwards to the factory in North Wales, because maybe that's where Elizabeth Matsukawa expected to catch up with Mr Imura.'

'Right,' said Yeadings. 'But leave it to tomorrow. And not by air in your case. Travelling by road, mind you take greater care than the poor lady you're checking up on. We're thin enough on the ground as it is, Z.'

Next morning there was little to be learnt at the Radcliffe. Elizabeth Matsukawa, with padding strapped to her head, lay pale and dead to the world in a narrow white bed surrounded by the sighing and ticking impedimenta of coma therapy. The woman constable seated outside the unit's door gave Z directions on how to locate the Traffic officer who was handling the case. He was at home on his free day.

Z found him in the garden of a Kidlington semi, muffled to the ears against the slicing north-east wind and tenderly making some adjustments to an impressive Yamaha motor-bike. He wiped his fingers on an oily rag and prepared to entertain the personable CID sergeant indoors. His mother produced her best Worcester china with tea and home-made almond slices, confiding that Norman worried her whenever he was out on that great bike of his. She'd be so relieved when he transferred to a patrol car.

'Right Ma. Thanks, but you can buzz off now,' he cued her. 'She fusses,' he explained unnecessarily to Z. 'With a bike I get places quicker. I like to be the first on the spot.' And he gave a succinct rundown of the accident scene as he'd come across it.

Elizabeth's car, it seemed, had struck black ice and spun from the road, careened off a lamp standard, run up a bank and overturned against a tree. There were burn marks from the tyres where she'd been braking. Closing up too fast on an articulated lorry, according to an eye-witness travelling behind.

She'd been fortunate the car didn't catch fire. The passenger side had torn away like the lid off a sardine can and the roof was depressed to within two feet of the seat beside her. It had taken the fire service almost two hours to extricate her.

'I spoke to a houseman,' Z said. 'They're hopeful of her eventual recovery. Apart from the concussion the injuries wouldn't be life-threatening for a fit person. My real interest is to make sure it was a genuine accident. Are you satisfied there was no other vehicle involved?'

'No tyre marks apart from her own. Sudden braking would have intensified the skid. The eye-witness has given a clear description of what happened. Fortunately he had a mobile phone and got emergency services there promptly.'

'This witness is entirely reliable?'

'A local doctor going home after a house visit. No connection with the injured woman, except indirectly, through the Radcliffe itself. That's where he used to work before entering general practice.'

'Well, I'll accept that he'd not be touting for custom. How about the car? There are connections with a known murder, so I want that car examined for pre-accident defects.'

'It's already been bagged,' he told her. 'On its way now to Accident Investigation Unit.'

'Good, so now I'll have to check on where we assume she was going.'

The Traffic constable nodded. 'Heading north.'

'Towards Birmingham.'

'Or beyond. There was a road atlas in the wreck. I pulled it out. A bit messy with blood, but it had a blank postcard tucked in as a bookmark, between pages 46 and 47, which reach as far north as Mold and Congleton, if I remember correctly.'

'And I'm sure you do.' Z couldn't suppress a note of excitement. Mold must be about twelve miles from Wrexham. It did look as if Elizabeth had set out overnight, by road, for the very place where Imura would be heading next morning by air.

She could have intended seeing him there to make an appeal on behalf of Mayumi. With the girl duly delivered back to school, Elizabeth might have hoped to work on Imura, to modify his report to Kyoto. But he'd been killed before she could reach him. And Elizabeth had ended almost as badly.

Or had she been meaning to head him off from some meeting in Wrexham? To make sure she delivered her own version of her daughter's escapade before he did?

Either option was preferable to supposing that her accident was the outcome of frenzied flight after murdering the man at his hotel!

Since neither he nor Elizabeth had reached Wrexham, was there any point now in continuing her journey? Z sat pondering the question as she lunched on a cheese and pickle sandwich in the car. At least she could check on what business would have taken Imura up there. His purpose could hardly be relevant to Mayumi's disappearance, but would at least serve to flesh out the scanty knowledge they had of the man's function in Matsukawa UK and his standing with his boss's family.

While Yeadings waited for a reply from Tokyo, she just might come up with some pearl of information herself. There were hidden advantages to being given a fairly loose rein in the inquiry team.

The North Wales force took her quest seriously enough to allocate a CID sergeant to accompany her to the Matsukawa factory, a modern, rurally sited complex of brick and stone-clad buildings. These were assembled round a central piazza with a sunken garden where the theme was minimalist Zen, with a pergola, a pool, a trickling cascade and attractive smooth stepping stones of black Welsh slate. The skeletal willows which overhung it were limned with silver. The frost had hardened as she went further north. As they left the warmth of her escort's Granada, their breaths hung mystically in the air. Already the sun was sinking, blood red, behind darkening hills, leaving the sky barred with horizontals of black and crimson.

She stood taking in the scene: the toy-like precision of the buildings and the dramatic natural setting. Such unexpected beauty; and all this for toys, she thought inconsequentially. No: correction. Actually, all this for money. There were benefits for the Japanese in proximity to an ever-spreading European market and a ready workforce unaccustomed to high wages; for the locals, a welcome escape from prevalent unemployment; for the county authority, a huge tax boost to help provide costly social amenities. It was money, after all – not love – that made the world go round.

So could it be money linking the seemingly separate elements of the case she was now dealing with? Was Elizabeth Matsukawa simply concerned with financial freedom from her husband for herself and Mayumi? Had even Imura's death some monetary value to it?

It struck her then that this place – one of Matsukawa's sources of great wealth – could provide a common answer to all these questions.

Ten

On Wednesday morning Beaumont reported to Superintendent Yeadings that he was officially declared fit for active service and rarin' to go.

'You don't consider the Incident Room activity enough?' the Boss demanded.

'Clerical's fine, but I'd get libido cramps if I sat much longer at a computer. Not that I haven't learnt a fresh dodge or two in there. Like how to bring defunct files back from limbo.' He glowed with pride at the achievement.

Yeadings' famed eyebrows twitched. 'Well, don't get above yourself and start raising the dead.'

Beaumont was caught open-mouthed. 'Sir.'

His gaze drifted past the Boss's head to the window where blown sleet was turning the previous day's snow to slush. It might be a thought to try walking on water first. But he wouldn't risk mentioning that hope aloud for fear he got charged with blasphemy. The Boss was a bit particular at times and there were some quaint old laws still on the statute book.

'Rosemary Zyczynski is staying on at Wrexham for a day or two,' Yeadings mused aloud. 'And DI Mott's still hung up on that double rape. We're reduced to fifteen DCs at present on the main inquiry. I can certainly do with another sergeant back on the street.'

'Is there anything through from Japan on Imura?' Beaumont asked hopefully.

'Mmm.' The Boss was evidently not going to share it yet.

'Came in an hour back. It'll be indexed when I've had a moment to consider it. I'd like you to have another go at the school end. They've seen your face already. I want them to be aware we're still giving them a long, hard stare.

'Something wrong with that?' he demanded, looking up swiftly and catching Beaumont's grimace of distaste.

What was wrong was that the place was packed with females. But there again he couldn't complain because that would imply he barred cases involving roughly half the world's population.

'I thought we'd just about wrung that source dry, sir,' he suggested.

'There's juice in it yet.' Yeadings slid a handful of papers under a heavy glass paperweight. 'And blood from a stone is something you might well set your loftier sights on, Sergeant, since you're now into minor miracles. Exploit, if you can, the situation between those two lasses who shared a study with Mayumi Matsukawa. The one who's started coming clean will be feeling the draught by now from the one who's stayed stumm. Give her a bit of sympathy. Maybe she'll try to justify herself and come up with something fresh. It's worth trying.'

Beaumont scowled. 'Julia something.'

'Olney-Pritchard.'

Yes, the hyphenated little darling. It wasn't just the femaleness of the place that raised his hackles: it was the rarefied, upper-class, reeking-of-wealth aspect. Until now Z had made the necessary contacts, he'd just stood by and reacted to the vibes. If the headmistress was anything like that built-as-a-battleship woman Goss he was in for a bad time. And as for showing sympathy . . .

'So? What's keeping you?'

An invisible thread to a computer, he told himself. Because anything – technocrap included – was better than women in bulk. Even the modified one he was legally tied to was sometimes more than he could take.

But by the time he had got that far in his inner mutterings

he had reached the outer door and was faced with a car park flooded by overflowing gutters and leaf-choked drains. Splashing across, he verified that his weren't the right shoes for walking on water. Now he was going to spend the best – worst – part of the uncomfortable day on audibly squelching soles.

On entering Dr Walling's study, the first sight of her silhouetted against the window – small and frail, nearing retirement age – reassured him, but her direct glance warned him she was nobody's fool. He must watch his step, act purely according to PACE, and treat her as the lady she clearly was.

She in turn observed the questing nose, the quirky mouth and the mock-innocence of his round eyes, and wondered why he had been sent when surely Miss Zyczynski had covered all the material facts. 'Is there some development, Sergeant?' she asked anxiously.

'I think I'd better be the one that asks the questions, Dr Walling.'

'I'm sorry, but I'm worried. You must understand that I am wholly responsible for my girls while they're here. And I cannot believe that Mayumi would run away a second time.'

'What alternative is there? That she's hiding in the buildings or grounds?'

'No. Your police and my staff have searched thoroughly. She isn't anywhere here.'

'Then where is she? You've heard about her mother's accident? Mrs Matsukawa was alone in the car when it crashed.'

Dr Walling slowly drew herself up and the movement seemed to cause pain because she slumped slightly with one fist clenched against her chest before she could answer. Then, 'I won't beat about the bush, Sergeant. I am afraid she may have been taken against her will. I fear for her safety.'

'Kidnapped? Have you any reason to suppose that? Were there earlier threats, or a demand for ransom?'

'Nothing.' Her voice sounded hollow. 'It's just that I believe I know her.'

'You were mistaken in her the first time.'

'But when she explained her need to see her mother, I understood why she'd gone. This time. . .'

'There may be an equally understandable reason you don't yet know of.'

'I think that after our talk she would have confided in me.'

It was pointless to go on disagreeing with the woman. OK, so the Jap girl was an innocent wee lamb. Some naughty person had snatched her. But then that wasn't so unlikely, since some naughty person had also made serious fretwork of the man sent to bring her back the first time. And both incidents had occurred within a few hours of each other.

'Do you suspect anyone in particular who might be responsible? Do you connect this with the likely break-up of her parents' marriage?'

Dr Walling hesitated. 'It couldn't be her father. That wouldn't make sense. He has every right to take her away openly. And Mr Imura, as his representative, could have obliged me to pass over responsibility. No, I can only assume it is some outside move against the Matsukawas, possibly with ransom in mind, and that they will shortly hear from the kidnapper.'

There was sense in that. But, with Mrs Matsu unconscious in hospital, how would a kidnapper make contact with May's absent father? Maybe by fax through his firm, since it had featured already. This wonderful modern hi-tech world! Get your victim on the network! E-mail your enemies!

A glance at the woman's shadowed eyes abruptly made him serious again. She looked quite ill. 'Can I get you anything?'

'I'm perfectly all right, thank you.' She put out a hand backwards, feeling for a chair, missed it and almost fell.

He was quick to grip her shoulders and guide her into it.

'Not perfectly perhaps,' she allowed with a faint smile of thanks.

'The brave are allowed to exaggerate a little.'

She ignored the probe in that. 'Is there any way I can help *you*, Sergeant?'

'I'd appreciate a chance to talk in private with Julia. There may be something more she knows which she doesn't realize is important.'

'I'm afraid there's little privacy to be had in a school. She knows that, and even being seen in your company would be instantly flashed through the grapevine.'

'And she's in trouble enough with her friend Maddie?'

'Because of the photographs, yes. But perhaps . . .'

He waited hopefully.

'It's irregular, but if you were to drive away, leave your car past the curve in the drive and cut through to the tennis pavilion, I could send my secretary down with the key to let you in. If you can wait a short while with her, Julia will join you. Miss Maddox will stay out of earshot while you both talk together, then escort Julia back to class.'

'Thank you, Dr Walling.'

'I'm sorry it sounds so cloak and dagger, but I must protect everyone's interests. Julia is a very outdoors sort of person and will probably feel more relaxed if you both take a little walk in the spinney. It isn't overlooked from the school.'

Kindly meant, he was sure, but then she didn't know the state of his socks. He could be on the way to growing webbed feet.

The headmistress had known her girl. Once free of the secretary's sceptical eye, and beyond observation from her schoolbound contemporaries, she seemed to breathe more deeply, trudging heartily through the slush, hands dug deep in the pockets of her navy duffel coat, woollen ski cap pulled low over her eyes.

And she talked. Nothing about Mayumi or Maddie. Absolute zilch on the kidnap-murder front, just beefing on about what a lousy term it had been, everything gone wrong and everyone against her.

It didn't seem to matter that he was a policeman and a stranger. Maybe it made it easier for her, because she was hardly likely to come across him again.

'Half-term soon, isn't it?' he consoled.

'Another twelve days. If I last out that long. I'll be – *bloody* glad to get home.'

He smiled at the slight hesitation before the explosive word, and the sense of victory it gave her to voice it: a girl not much used to swearing. Not so very different from his own son a few years back. There was no mystery about kids really. After all, they were only part-made people.

'Your parents coming to collect you?' He was just making conversation, having given up on any hope of gathering useful facts.

'Nuh.' More gloom. 'Dad's always too busy with the business, and Mother's never at home. She's a solicitor. The brains of the family,' she added resentfully.

'What does Dad do?'

'He owns Floradora. It's a chain of nurseries and garden centres. We live at the first one he opened just after he and Mother were married. It's at Shrewsbury.'

'So who looks after you? D'you have brothers and sisters?'

'There's just Gran and Poppa. They brought me up mostly. Gran's a sweetie. Poppa was in the army; a Major. Only he's a bit past things nowadays. Dad says the war finished him really. And that was over fifty years ago.' She sounded uncertain, as if she suspected there'd been some attempt to fool her about it.

'One of the unsung heroes,' Beaumont said helpfully.

'That's what Gran says.'

The path was turning back on itself and the informal interview had done nothing for him. Except help him

111

decide to jettison his shoes the moment he got home. What he needed was something like young Stuart's 'bonfire' boots. He'd laughed enough when his son bought them – bright blue and shiny – but they did have the soles welded to the uppers; ideal for conditions like this.

'I didn't tell you anything, did I?' Julia demanded almost belligerently as Miss Maddox materialized to take her back.

'No,' Beaumont admitted. 'But then I didn't really expect you would. Have a good break at half-term.'

He arrived back at the Incident Room in time to take the tail end of a call from Zyczynski on arrival at Wrexham. She had already reported to the Boss on her visit to the Radcliffe.

She listened without comment to his nil score from the latest visit to the school. Surprisingly Julia's remarks about her home life seemed to interest her.

'I passed a Floradora on the way here. It could be the one she lives at. If I come back the same way I might drop in on the offchance.'

'Of getting a few cheapo plants on the strength of the connection?'

'Don't you think Granny might be the very person Julia would let her hair down with? Just because she's familiar background but clear of the action. And if Maddie was getting under Julia's skin, or she really resented Mayumi's presence – two being company, but three a crowd, sort of thing – she might have beefed about it in a letter home. It's worth a try.'

Beaumont didn't think so but forbore to discourage her enthusiasm. After all, the longer she was away the better chance he had of hitting the jackpot himself back in the murder zone.

Much as he liked Z, it was uncomfortable having her as a sergeant alongside, especially with a policy of negative discrimination to bring up the numbers of women with seniority. (Or was it positive discrimination? Bloody semantics! Both euphemisms for injustice.) The truth was

112

he'd been quite content to remain at the present rank until Z had been promoted from DC. But if she got upped again it would be a real slap in the face for him.

At Matsukawa UK, Z was penetrating the upper echelons. 'Sergeant Rosemary Zyczynski,' she articulated carefully, expecting the usual embarrassment as the addressee tried to master the name.

The little middle-aged Japanese turned her warrant card between his fingers and read it through before returning it with a slight bow.

'Miss Jijinski.' He made a passable attempt at the pronunciation. A better first try than most Brits. 'How can I help you?' His face was as bland as a round Dutch cheese, the eyes hidden by thick lenses which threw back the room's bright strip-lighting.

So how could he? Or, more likely, *would* he? She felt herself the foreigner. A non-Matsukawa person, irrelevant, unless it turned out that she would provide a vast order for electronic toys.

The sergeant from the North Wales force who accompanied her sensed her awkwardness. Son of a local farmer's daughter and an incoming Manxman, Gareth Quilliam considered himself the equal of any foreigner. 'This young lady,' he stated solidly and sounding very Welsh, 'has come all the way from the Thames Val-ley Po-lees force to ask you some ques-tions. She is em-*pow*-ered –' (making the most of the three lengthened syllables) – 'to inquire into the death of one Hiromu Imura, a member of your com-pan-y.'

'Headquarters Director of Commercial Operations,' breathed the manager, correcting him in clipped syllables but reverent tone.

Z suppressed an urge to giggle. Thank heaven Beaumont wasn't present, with his irrepressible humour. Just a flicker from his puppet eyes and she'd hear inside his mind, 'There was a Welshman, a Jap and an ethnic Pole . . .' Some version of the hoary three-nationalities joke.

113

'The *late* Hi-ro-mu I-mu-ra,' said Quilliam, to make sure there was no confusion.

'We are – desolated,' said Mr Ichikawa. 'Everyone here, the whole workforce, we are appalled.'

'How did you learn of his death?' Z enquired, sitting where the female assistant had placed a chair for her, facing the manager across his desk.

'From UK television, and then later there was a message from our headquarters in Kyoto.'

'It appears that after attending to a family matter for Mr Matsukawa in Thames valley, Mr Imura was to travel here on business.'

'I believe that is so.'

'You were not informed by Kyoto?'

'Not directly.'

'Then how did you know about it?'

Mr Ichikawa's face remained impassive, but she sensed his resentment. 'There have been messages arriving for him. All yesterday afternoon.'

'Concerning whatever business he was to attend to here?'

'I assume so.'

'Only assume? You have not had access to these messages?'

'They are in his personal code.'

'I see.' But she didn't entirely. Unless it meant that Kyoto had lost confidence in their manager at Wrexham. Or was this normal Japanese business practice? She wished she knew something more about this new industrial culture.

'Does the Kyoto office use separate codes for all its senior executives?'

She thought she caught a gleam of sweat on the smooth brow of the man opposite. 'Only for Mr Imura. It was so when he came before. That is all I know.'

All he was prepared to say. She could read that in the single-line, down-turned mouth. All for the present, maybe. But she would come back for further answers when she had poked around a little and listened to whatever gossip

114

was to be had. If Mr Imura needed to be briefed in code his function was one of some importance. And important people had a way of ruffling up those they dealt with. With any luck she would get to hear what it was he came about last time. There could be those willing and eager to voice their complaints if he'd been stirring up wasps' nests. And she remembered Elizabeth Matsukawa's bitter reference to him as the Mikado's Lord High Executioner. Presumably he'd be responsible for anyone's getting the chop.

This time she made sure the local sergeant was still within earshot as she casually turned back at the door.

'One more thing, Mr Ichikawa.'

'Miss Jijinski.' Another polite half-bow.

'Did you know that Elizabeth Matsukawa was also on her way here?'

The man's round cheeks shuddered as he suppressed his surprise. Or was it alarm? But his voice was under control. 'I did not know.'

'Then you hadn't heard that she was involved in a car crash and has been taken to hospital?'

Now he groaned aloud, shaking his head and beating one fist inside the other's palm. 'No, no. Poor lady. Is she badly injured?'

Not so inscrutable after all. Plainly upset by Elizabeth's accident. And he hadn't really been bothered that Imura was dead.

Outside, in the chilly dark, Quilliam was unlocking his car. 'Look,' Z said suddenly, 'there could soon be a surge of press interest and I don't really want to get caught up in it. Is there any alternative to this hotel they've booked me into?'

'Somewhere quiet?'

'Somewhere more private.'

'Ah.' His mouth puckered with thought. 'How about a B&B? There's Mrs Benyon, a PC's widow. Kind lady, very discreet. And she's a great cook into the bargain. Does little parties for us sometimes. Birthdays and that. Nice little cottage, and she'd find the money useful.'

It sounded ideal. Quilliam drove her there now and introduced Z to a sharp-eyed lady in her late sixties with apple-red cheeks and a mass of white hair like fluffed-out cotton wool. They agreed a daily rate before Z was driven back to Wrexham police station to pick up her car and luggage.

Her evening ended with a brief pub meeting, as Quilliam's guest, with the local CID inspector, Frank Henderson, who broke off from serious drinking to inform her on the incoming Japanese and their effect on Clwyd customs. It sounded as though the natives, although initially suspicious, had been willing to adopt new work conditions in preference to long-term unemployment. The newcomers were now generally accepted as an eccentric part of the Welsh scene, if not over-warmly welcomed.

'They don't mix with locals,' Henderson complained. 'At least, not easily. When they do try to, you can guess there will be ructions.'

But he didn't choose to define these ructions and Z, guessing from his tone that he spoke from uncomfortable personal experience, promised herself to question his sergeant about it next day.

In the event she forgot to do so for some time, because the wind was somewhat taken from her sails when she was next shown into the General Manager's office. Mr Ichikawa was not there. Even the engraved nameplate on his desk had disappeared. In his place a rather younger Japanese rose to offer his hand. He was lean, with an attractively curved mouth and deepset dark eyes in a flat but firm-jawed face. Above it his black hair stood up stiff and thick in a hedgehog effect. No horn rims but, aged somewhere around forty-five, he possibly wore contact lenses. His grip on her hand was strong and his gaze direct. None of this scraping and bowing business.

'Sergeant Zyczynski,' he addressed her, and his voice was staccato. 'I am Yasuhiko Matsukawa. I understand that you have been in personal contact with my wife and daughter.'

Eleven

Superintendent Yeadings received the news of Matsukawa's presence in the UK on arrival at work. He played back Z's taped phone conversation with Beaumont which the latter, in a sudden fit of rivalry, had left prominently on his desk, since it didn't leave the girl in the best light possible. She had clearly been wrong-footed by the Big Boss's appearance when she was armed solely with a list of questions for Ichikawa probing the Matsukawas themselves.

Accustomed to wielding authority, the Japanese had taken the initiative and demanded a rundown of the police role in his daughter's original escapade. Z seemed to have extracted herself satisfactorily from the situation but only after including a defensive account of her own part in accompanying Elizabeth from Wiltshire to the school. This, Z admitted, he had found intrusive and somehow insulting. But then they had been confronting each other as aliens, each fixed in a rigid code barely comprehensible to the other.

When he had pressed her for details of her meeting with Imura she simply regretted that she could not give more information since the inquiry into the man's death was an ongoing police matter.

'Um,' said Yeadings on a buzzing note as though it were a mantra. He leaned back in his chair, staring at the ceiling.

'What strikes you about that, Beaumont?'

'About Z's statement?'

'About his sudden appearance on the scene.'

Quite a lot of things did actually. Why hadn't the man come sooner, when his daughter first went missing? Or had he actually arrived in England before Imura's death? And it seemed he wasn't clued up on recent happenings: he'd heard that Imura was dead, but it was left to Z to tell him of Mayumi's second disappearance and that his wife was seriously injured in hospital. So what had brought him now? And why to North Wales, when all the action seemed to be down here in Thames Valley?

This last query was the one he voiced to Yeadings.

'Um,' said the Boss again. He tried tipping his chair on its back legs and its refusal reminded him that it was a replacement for the old one and only spun on its axis.

'He'd have been informed by Imura that he'd found and returned Mayumi, so he could assume the danger was over and he went on to more pressing business.' Yeadings dropped his sardonic tone and spun to face Beaumont glumly. 'Perhaps he's safer up there.'

'Sir?'

'Something interesting came out of my inquiries to Kyoto. The booking at the Bellhouse Hotel wasn't actually made for Imura. It was in Yasuhiko Matsukawa's name, who at the last minute cancelled and had Imura fly in from Frankfurt to replace him.'

'So you're saying that maybe Imura's death . . .'

'. . . was a mistake, and someone who didn't know one man from the other got the wrong victim.'

'A British hit man!'

'A knife man who was available locally; that much is certain. But also someone who was informed about the name used for the booking.'

'Well, at least that clears Mrs Matsu and the girl, because they knew who it really was at the Bellhouse.'

'Unless, expecting her husband to visit the school, and knowing where he always stayed, Elizabeth Matsukawa set it up in advance and never had a chance to cancel the instructions once she discovered who it was stepping out of the helicopter!'

'And Z was with her from then on. For how long, though? And would she know if Mrs M was trying to make phone calls to stop the hit?'

'Find out,' Yeadings ordered. 'Get through to Z at Wrexham nick. Tell her I'm waiting for the answer.'

But Z wasn't available at the police station, nor at the hotel where she had been provisionally booked in. So Beaumont left messages in Yeadings' name at both, to ring his number as soon as she came in.

It hadn't struck Z that Matsukawa could be ignorant of Elizabeth's accident. Since it had had such a dramatic effect on Ichikawa, it seemed inevitable that he would mention it when his Chairman unexpectedly turned up.

But the two men never met. Suffering from jet lag, Matsukawa had sent a handwritten note to Ichikawa's house. He was to take the morning flight from Manchester to replace Imura at the international convention of toy manufacturers at Frankfurt. Ichikawa's reply to this, which included respectful sympathy for Elizabeth's misfortune and fulsome wishes for her rapid recovery, still lay unopened on Matsukawa's office desk when Z arrived. She therefore witnessed the full force of the man's first reaction when, asking for the latest bulletin on Elizabeth, she discovered she must break the news herself.

'Elizabeth?' he repeated, unbelieving. 'Injured? But how? Where is she?'

Alarm certainly. Perhaps real distress. Elizabeth was, after all, still his wife. And Z had only her opinion that the marriage was at breaking point.

Z explained how, instead of delivering Mayumi back to school after an exeat allowed by Dr Walling, Elizabeth had apparently decided to travel northwards overnight. The car had struck a patch of black ice and ended upside down against a tree.

'I must go to her,' Matsukawa snapped. 'She has concussion, you say. That is serious. And I need to collect Mayumi from the hospital. Poor child, she will be alarmed and confused. Did she escape injury herself?'

So that was another item of news that he hadn't caught up with. 'I'm sorry,' Z ventured, uncertain what kind of further outburst to expect. 'Mayumi isn't at the hospital. In fact nobody seems to know quite where she is at present.'

It stopped him in his tracks. The experienced controller of an industrial empire, he seemed incapable of dealing with both shocks at once. She watched all colour drain from his sallow cheeks as he leaned with clenched fists on the desk.

'Imura, Elizabeth, Mayumi,' he said in a low growl. 'What is this? I cannot believe . . . This could not happen in Japan.'

Well, lucky old Japan, Z thought, suddenly angry: the innocent country where no crime exists and no accidents happen. Only the mafia-type *yakuza* flourishing, and safe little things like earthquakes which kill thousands. And to be really up-to-date, how about Aum Supreme Truth religious fanatics? It was time Matsukawa and his like removed their rose-tinted spectacles and realized that disorder was universal. The old days of disciplined control were gone.

He stared at her, fiercely accusing, jaw muscles taut and fists bunched. But then she saw the raw pain behind the baffled anger. For a brief instant she recognized the fleeting expression she had seen once before, in Mayumi's eyes as she faced going out to confront the helicopter.

'We are making every possible effort to find your daughter,' she tried to reassure him. 'And to solve the death of Mr Imura.'

'His *killing*. He was murdered.' Matsukawa stood ram-rod straight again, sufficiently in control of himself to demand the correct terms.

And to respect niceties, he was right, she agreed: death itself can't be solved. It's just the who, how, and why of vicious crime that we police have to cope with.

'Superintendent Yeadings is in charge of both inquiries,' she told him. 'He needs to talk to you as soon as you can reach Thames Valley after seeing your wife.'

By the time Yeadings' message reached Z, Yasuhiko Matsukawa had been borne off towards Oxford in his maroon chauffeur-driven Daimler; a gesture to English tradition from a national of the world's highest producer of anything on wheels. The man might not bow and scrape like some of his compatriots, but he observed a strict protocol, Z noted.

'Sir,' she said, returning the Superintendent's call, 'I've been in touch with Mr M again and he's on his way to the Radcliffe now.'

'Right. I'll arrange VIP protection for when he gets there. And we'll be prepared for a Demon King entrance later here.' Then he put to her his theory that Matsukawa was probably the killer's intended victim.

'And there was a reason for all that blood, Z. It seems Mr Imura was a karate black belt and well able to take care of himself in unarmed combat. A pity for him that there was a knife involved. But the killer could have been injured too before Imura finally passed out. Mr Matsukawa might have proved an easier target, despite being younger. His main exercise is golf.

'What I'm curious about is whether the killer knew at any point that he was attacking the wrong man. A hired hit man might not have known one from the other, even if he'd been shown a photograph of Matsukawa. All he'd be expecting was a Japanese businessman. And that's what he would have found.'

She picked up quickly the importance of whether

Elizabeth could have tried to cancel a killing once she discovered a substitute was in place for her husband.

'She didn't get a chance from home,' Z claimed. 'She was so knocked back at Imura's taking May off, and I hustled her out too fast. But she had an opportunity to ring from the hotel at Amersham. As soon as we arrived she went up to her room to tidy up. Next day I noticed phone calls entered on the carbon of the bill she'd settled.'

'Right. I'll see if we can get the numbers traced.'

Z thought a moment. 'But if the calls were charged to her it means she actually got through. Yet the murder went ahead. So I don't think that scenario fits, sir. Her calls must have been innocent ones.'

'We'll know better when we've discovered who they were made to. It might have been necessary to pass on a message, and in the event it didn't reach the right person in time.'

'Sir, do you want me to continue up here, follow Mr Matsukawa, or return to base?'

'I've made arrangements for Mr Matsukawa, Z, and anyway I'm hopeful he'll be coming this way very shortly. Beaumont is running the inquiry team on the murder, with sideline visits to the school. Satisfy yourself over Elizabeth Matsukawa's intentions in her dash north, then come back. It's not beyond the bounds of possibility that Imura's death and her husband's survival required some vital change of plan which only she could be trusted to carry out.'

'But sir, if she set off from Amersham the same evening that I left her there, how could she have known that Imura was killed that very night?'

'That's the point, Z. Only if she'd been party to setting it up, and not able to call it off!'

With Ichikawa already dispatched elsewhere, Z expected Matsukawa's prompt departure for Oxford to leave the factory in some disarray, but when she was shown into the now familiar, airy office she found a new framed nameplate on the central desk. Beside it stood an exquisite harlequin doll as advertisement for the company's products. The man who rose to shake her hand was a towering six feet two, and British.

'Mr Robinson,' she bluffed readily, 'I understand that you are empowered to give me all the information I require.'

'If I can help you in any way, please ask.' The words were cautious, the handgrip firm, the grey eyes assessing.

She began with an inquiry after Ichikawa, and the stand-in explained his rapid departure. A stopgap for Imura had to be found immediately. The Frankfurt convention was of prime importance, dealing not only with Euro-Japanese trade restrictions but also international patents and licensing. Failure to represent the firm's position fully could have an undesirable effect on the next few years' sales. There were plenty of rivals eager to squeeze out the considerable Matsukawa slice of the market.

'Yet Mr Imura was called away from that convention to act for Mr Matsukawa in a family matter.'

Her point was rather lost as the harlequin doll suddenly began emitting soft electronic beeps. Robinson said, 'Thank you,' and the beeping stopped, but the doll's left eye continued to blink.

'I'm sorry,' he said rather smugly. 'Pagliacci's a new kind of answering machine. I'm trying him out. Now, you mentioned Mr Imura's withdrawal from Frankfurt: I'm sure you'll agree that a daughter's sudden disappearance must come even before business.'

It didn't sound like the priorities Elizabeth had quoted as her husband's. Japanese businessmen, she'd complained, had little time for their families.

Robinson settled his large bulk back on the fragile-looking chair. 'Hiromu Imura was to step in temporarily, until Mr Matsukawa could come and take over in person.'

It sounded reasonable, but didn't explain why Imura was then instructed to come on to Wrexham, leaving his convention seat still empty. But Z could sense Robinson's patience wearing thin on the subject and she wanted to keep him obliging. More casually she followed up with inquiries about the length of Ichikawa's service at Wrexham and his family circumstances.

It appeared he was a widower, lived here with a teenage daughter, and had been with the firm since university; first in Kyoto, then in the Kobe factory. He had been sent to Wrexham some seventeen months earlier to take charge. Robinson himself had been one of his first appointees, headhunted from a British firm in the Midlands.

Robinson showed no reluctance in offering this information. By now an emaciated Japanese woman had provided a tray of pale tea and tiny rice cakes. The cups were oriental and without handles, but it seemed Z was to be spared any lengthy ceremony in the serving. She waited until the woman withdrew before mentioning Elizabeth's intended visit.

'Her home's here, just outside Wrexham,' Robinson pointed out. 'It's down by the River Clywedog. She took a great interest in its decoration and furnishing. There's a local couple who live in as caretakers, but no doubt she was coming to check that everything was in order.' On Z's request for the address he wrote it out on a sheet of the firm's headed notepaper.

So that was to be her next port of call, she decided. To interview Mr and Mrs Gryff Lloyd.

She found only the husband at home. A fit-looking man in his fifties with greying dark hair cropped close and the appearance of an ex-soldier. He was limping about, checking potted plants in a heated greenhouse but stood to attention when she told him who she was. He regretted his wife wasn't there to receive her. Gillian had gone to Chester, shopping for a hat to wear at a niece's wedding. Yes, the Matsukawas had a lovely house and he was sorry that his instructions were not to allow anyone to enter during his employers' absence.

Z briefly considered threatening a warrant to search for a missing minor, but realized that Matsukawa's own arrival here would show up any person concealed in his house.

Had Mr Lloyd been forewarned by Elizabeth that she was on her way to Wrexham? she asked. Apparently not, but he remained unmoved by the prospect: everything was left prepared for unannounced visits by the family. His wife had matters firmly under control and could rustle up a four-course meal at the drop of a hat. He sounded so complacent that Z was satisfied news of the car crash and Mayumi's disappearance hadn't yet reached him. Imura's murder in Thames Valley, announced by the media, would hardly touch him personally. Nevertheless she wondered aloud what difference it would now make to the Wrexham end of the firm.

Gryff Lloyd stiffened, and he deliberately turned away to avoid her eyes. 'There's some'll not be broken-hearted,' he said tightly.

But that was all he was prepared to say, and he ignored her next questions, moving farther down the duckboard path, busy with temperature readings.

'There, I've finished now,' he said abruptly. 'Best lock up here and get back to tasks indoors. I'll say goodbye, miss. You'll want to be moving on yourself, like.'

So, back to canteen gossip at the local nick. And follow up the hint of ill-feeling against the murdered man. When had he previously been here, and what was the likely purpose of this proposed visit which he was prevented from making?

And there, elbow to elbow round a table with the beat and patrol men, she thought maybe she'd struck pay-dirt, because it turned out that Imura's name had been connected with something she remembered Elizabeth briefly mentioning. A young man in the accountancy department had disappeared after a sudden swoop by auditors. His landlady had been upset because he'd left for work one morning after breakfast and never even came back for his things. A nice lad, she'd said, for all he was a foreigner.

Z checked with the Welsh policemen: did foreigner mean English or Japanese?

A Jap, yes. That's why they couldn't do much except raise a query. His rent had been paid in advance, so the landlady hadn't any complaint once the firm had had the lad's luggage collected for redirection. Funny thing was there was no evidence that he'd actually left the UK. So there was a bit of talk at the time. A police check failed to find his name on any outward flight, but a couple of weeks later there'd been an air-letter from him posted in Kyoto, thanking Mrs Benyon for her kindness and apologizing for not having said goodbye.

'Benyon? Not the good lady I'm staying with at present?' Z said without much hope, the surname being pretty common in Wales.

But for once her luck was in. It was the same woman, and Z looked forward to a cosy chat with her over a shared pot of tea when she returned.

Gwyneth Benyon's famed discretion was fortunately limited to police matters. The invading foreigners were a curiosity well worth a wagging tongue. Not that she hadn't grown quite fond of Yoshio in the two years he was with her. Very polite young man, if a bit stiff to begin with. He'd picked up a few words of Welsh along the way and, unlike the rest of that bunch, used to enjoy the odd night in local pubs, swopping stories with tradesman and poacher alike. She'd never believed that story that he'd been fiddling the books.

'He was really straight. Just crossed the wrong people, I always thought. If he'd had a fault it was an over-fondness for alcohol. And maybe for young girls,' she added as an afterthought.

'In general, or anyone in particular?' Z asked, sounding casual.

Gwyneth Benyon halted in the middle of refilling the

teapot. 'Both, I'd say. In particular there were two. Young Libby Davies, the bank manager's daughter, and a pretty little Jap girl, couldn't have been more than fourteen, more's the pity. There was some wild talk she'd got pregnant, but nothing came of it. Only, since then, she's gone quiet as a mouse. Isn't allowed to go out alone; her dad pays an older Japanese woman to accompany her. No smoke without fire's what I think.'

'And her father works at Matsukawa's?'

'That's right. Top man locally, so I'm told. Even funnier sort of name than most of them, and that's saying a lot. Itchy Something. Still I suppose they find some of our names a bit hard to get round too. Like yours, love, if you don't mind my saying so.'

Their gossip was interrupted by a phone call for DS Zyczynski: DI Frank Henderson from the local nick with an invitation out to dinner. His emphasis on the hotel at which she'd originally been booked was surely to impress her that the occasion was formal. Best bib and tucker stuff, she registered. Well, she'd packed her coral silk blouse with the scoop neckline and huge sleeves. It could team up with her black skirt.

She accepted the invitation and thanked the DI, agreeing to meet him there at 8.15 p.m.

It was more than time they compared notes on her case. At the nick he had displayed a deal of involvement with more important matters and she'd written him off as a probable male chauvinist.

In the hotel she was referred to the bar where she found him, leather-patched elbows on the counter, tweedy shoulders hunched as he leaned in to catch the words of the blonde who was pulling his pint. Not his first, Z reckoned. She took note of the broad gold band on his wedding finger. His hands, large and pink and covered with sandy, almost invisible hairs, reminded her of pig's flesh. She accepted the bar stool alongside, letting him order her a vodka Martini.

127

Henderson eyed the coral blouse appreciatively. 'So how ya doin'?'

'I wish I knew. I've been gathering more impressions than information. It'll take a deal of sorting.'

'Nice part of the country,' he offered inconsequentially. 'Stay on a few days and we'll offer you some skiing.'

She hadn't kept in touch with the weather forecasts, and anyway she wasn't here on holiday. A waiter hovering close with two leather-bound menus saved her from having to reply. She selected her main course and starter while the DI resumed his chat with the barmaid. As the waiter hung on he turned back dismissively. 'I'll take the game pie. Scampi first.' He obviously knew the menu by heart.

Over their meal, accompanied by an indifferent Rhône wine, Z tried to interest him in the Imura killing. 'You must have come across the man sometime,' she suggested. 'An oriental in a small place like Wrexham, he'd stand out like a—'

She'd intended saying 'sore thumb', but in time realized the cliché was uncomplimentary.

'Like a tart's titty,' Henderson offered. 'Yuh, I saw him about. Got wind, so to speak. Sour old bugger. They're a tight-arsed little bunch in general, don't mix with us mere natives. Anyway he only made short visits.'

'With some spectacular results?'

The DI stopped munching and looked hard at her. 'What have they been telling you?'

'Dismissals among senior management. And then that young accountant getting the chop. Wasn't Imura behind that?'

Henderson's fork chased an unwanted lettuce leaf to the edge of his plate and he considered his last morsel of scampi. 'Imura would have been here at the time, yeah. You seriously think staff sackings provide a motive for murder?' His voice was heavily sarcastic.

'Give me some better motives.'

He pushed his plate away, drained his wine glass and

128

refilled for them both. Z had barely sipped hers, too aware of the low blood content of her own slim body compared with the man's bulk. Even with his head start she knew the drink would get to her faster. And he was certainly in better practice with the stuff.

'Look, darling,' he said, leaning across familiarly. 'Your case has nothing to do with us. I'll hang a tenner on it, some wise guy's getting it all sewn up down south while you're drafted off up here.' The leer in his eyes was echoed in his voice.

'You think so?' she asked coolly, seething inside. 'My boss has a notion it wasn't Imura the killer was after.'

The DI's knife hovered over the butter pats. 'Tell me more,' he invited sarcastically. 'How many Japs have you got running loose in Thames Valley?'

'It's come to light,' Z told him, plastering the last of her really good pâté on some Melba toast, 'that it was Mr Matsukawa the hotel originally booked in. By fax from Kyoto. Someone within the company could have accessed that fact and acted on it. No correction was made in the booking when Hiromu Imura was sent instead. A hired hit man would never have questioned who it was he'd killed. Simply the Japanese man in room 14.'

Henderson seemed shocked into sobriety for a moment. Then he shrugged. 'Load of bollocks. Far-fetched as—'

'As faxes from Kyoto?' Z grinned. 'Well, I never said that's the sole premise we're working from. Could be Imura, could be Matsukawa as the intended victim. It just means more work for the infantry, chasing up two sets of enemies instead of one.'

'Who would want to wipe out the Big Boss?' Henderson demanded loudly. 'They're all too bloody busy kowtowing.'

'Sacked employees with a grievance; power rivals from other firms; even his wife?' she tempted. 'Wives do kill husbands quite a bit these days. Often with good reason.'

Neither spoke while their plates were removed and the main course served. Z regarded the soft pink of her marinaded lamb with satisfaction. Chernobyl memories or not, this chance to taste the local delicacy was not to be missed.

The DI ordered more wine and waved the waiter in to pour, without tasting it first. Then both dealt with their loaded plates. There was no more discussion of the case until Henderson, wiping his mouth after a chocoloate cheesecake dessert, said finally, 'You could waste your time considering Matsukawa. The simple solution's often the right one. If it was Imura got killed, it was Imura someone meant to snuff.'

Over coffee, which Z took black and unsweeetened, the DI made his last clumsy throw. 'Good meal?'

She agreed it had been splendid.

He leaned close. There was still a smear of chocolate on his lower lip. 'That room we booked for you. It was here. You really missed out on something.'

He leaned back luxuriously. 'As it happens, I somehow overlooked cancelling it. Number thirty nine. Why don't we pick up the key, take a looksee, darling? Get an idea what they provide. All mod cons. Real cosy.'

She smiled distantly. 'A pity to run up needless expense. I'll cancel with reception on the way out.'

She rose, picked up her shoulder bag and offered her hand. 'Thank you for a wonderful meal, Inspector. It's been – interesting to get your views on the case. Goodnight.'

He tried to rise but one chair leg was caught in the tablecloth. A wild swing with his hand overturned the cafetière which dribbled a dark streak across his plate and on to his shirt front.

Z's eyes lingered on it. 'Oh dear. Well, safe journey home, Inspector,' she told him in motherly tones.

Twelve

Back at Mrs Benyon's Z turned down the offer of a milky drink.

'Enjoyed your dinner out, then?' the landlady probed. 'I didn't expect you back this side of midnight.'

'Lovely meal,' Z admitted. She resisted the temptation to add, 'Pity about the company.'

Henderson's assumption of his own irresistible charm was nauseous. It left Z aware of whose company she would most have enjoyed. She was on the point of ringing Max Harris when she recalled that her lover was away in Amsterdam. The prospect of bed without him, and in the small unheated room upstairs, was uninviting. Instead, when Mrs B in her red fluffy dressing gown hovered at the door with a, 'Put more coal on, do, if you're sitting up,' she stayed on, staring half-mesmerized at the red embers and listening to their soft clicking as they cooled and sank into grey ash.

In her mind the sound became confused with the remembered beeping of the harlequin doll on Robinson's desk, then unaccountably was the gentle panting of the radiator in the CID office at the local nick. Not the DI's but Sergeant Quilliam's voice was pacing the same rhythm as he warned her that some wise guy was sewing the case up down south while she was drafted up here.

She started awake, certain that Yeadings hadn't ordered her trip with that in mind. There was vital information to be gathered here. She was suddenly convinced that she already had all that was needed, had met everyone who mattered. If only she could work out how it fitted together; which details were the main picture and which mere background.

Yawning, she steeled herself to brave the comparative igloo condition of the unheated bedroom, raked out the last ashes of the fire and went upstairs, turning off the light.

However wrong Henderson was about her being side-tracked into the trip to Wales, he had been spot on about the weather. She awoke to a sense of difference. The ceiling had a new lofty airiness. There came no customary hum of traffic from the nearby main road. Instead an eerie stillness and a strange white glow in the little room. She peered past the half-open curtains and saw there was snow to a depth of six inches on the windowsill. But there would be no skiing for her. It was time she made tracks for home.

She dug out the car's back wheels with a borrowed shovel and drove in to take her leave of the North Wales force. A phone call to the Radcliffe hospital brought news of no real change in Elizabeth's condition. Her husband had arrived and was even now in consultation with the neurologist in charge of her case. It was unlikely that the patient would be transferred elsewhere.

So, there being no point in a detour to Elizabeth, Z decided to break her return journey at the Floradora Garden Centre which was Julia Olney-Pritchard's home.

Even in late February it was impressive, the extensive showrooms packed with conservatory furniture and hor-ticultural equipment. The hothouses were brilliant with house plants, and under their white duvet the landscaped grounds showed humped with hardy shrubs and conifers.

As expected, Julia's mother was at her legal chambers, but Mr Olney-Pritchard was away too, at an expo of mechanical plant in the Midlands. It was his elderly parents who received Z in their modern bungalow and met her apology for the intrusion with anxious inquiries after Mayumi. They both had white hair and the permanent cigar-leaf colouring of northern Europeans returned from a long stay in the tropics, but where the woman appeared to have shrivelled, her husband's big frame was dropsically swollen.

Z took off her sheepskin jacket and loosed her collar. The pleasant chintzy room was pulsing with heat from radiators and an open log fire. 'You knew that Mayumi had disappeared a second time?' she asked them.

They did: Julia wrote regularly, sometimes twice a week. Not that she ever had much to say in the normal run of school life, but she was a good girl about keeping in touch.

When the housekeeper brought in coffee and sandwiches, Major Olney-Pritchard waved his share off to a far corner and moved stiffly across to a rattan and wicker chair there, where he settled in a half-doze facing a picture window.

'Poor darling, he does so miss the sun,' his wife whispered.

Her anxious smile created myriad tiny wrinkles in skin as fine as rice paper. White-haired, with eyes of quite startling periwinkle blue, she had small, soft hands covered with the flat freckles of old age. Once perhaps the proverbial Dresden figurine, now – Z thought, wildly imaginative – more like an apple stored too long, the inside shrunken, but the exterior holding together, folding in on itself, crinkling as it slowly dries out. Beauty transformed by old age. Except that when she smiles, real sweetness: beauty *in* old age. Physically the complete opposite of Titan-built Julia. But maybe the girl's impossible role model.

'Your granddaughter spoke of you to my colleague. She's obviously very fond of you both.'

'I actually brought her up,' the old lady said proudly. 'She's my little rosebud.'

133

'You must be very proud of her, doing so well at school and in sports.' Z hoped she wasn't treading on delicate ground. Julia hadn't struck her as an impressive student.

'I wish she wasn't so far away,' Granny complained. 'We see each other so seldom now. We sent our own little ones back to England to board, of course, but then there was no alternative really. I'm sure there are day-schools near here where she would do as well.'

She sighed and turned her hands palm upwards. 'When you get to our age you want to spend whatever time is left with the ones you love most.'

Her sad smile left Z guilty at taking advantage of her. 'I've met Julia and her study-mates,' she said. 'They seem good friends. I'm sure they really enjoy their schooldays.'

'Happiest years of one's life,' the old lady quoted forlornly. Her eyes focusing distantly, she seemed mentally to have floated off elsewhere. Z plunged in to recall her before, like the Major, she nodded off in the overheated room.

'Sometimes,' she suggested, 'friends know more about a missing person than they realize at the time. I've wondered if that was so in Mayumi's case. Do you think there could be anything in Julia's letters home to you that might serve as a clue to where the poor girl would go?'

'Letters!' The old lady came quite awake, sat up straighter and moved fluttering hands over her breasts as if she'd lost a handkerchief in her blouse and suddenly needed to use it. 'Julia's letters. Of course. I'll fetch them.'

They couldn't have been far. She was back almost immediately with a red japanned box painted with storks in gold flying over a mountain lake. The letters were still in their envelopes, bound together with white ribbon.

'There. Read them yourself. I'm afraid it's a little hard for me now. My eyes aren't what they were.'

Treasure trove, Z gloated silently, and took the nearest bundle. They were the latest letters, dated since Christmas.

But what information they contained about the two girls who shared Julia's study only mystified her further.

Do I really understand what she means? she asked herself. Or is this Julia's classic habit of getting things the wrong way round? A magic box for conjuring tricks? But nothing to do with Mayumi.

DS Beaumont had decided that although plenty of infor-mation had come in on the Imura murder, there was practically nil progress at present. As compensation he was conscious of some feedback from his other efforts: he was definitely getting the hang of the school.

He would never have admitted to anyone that the place had its good points, but he was already more at ease when coping with adolescent girls. They could be, he'd discovered, quite similar to their male counterparts: tetchy, crude, quick to take offence, forthright, and occasionally wanting the ground to open up and swallow them together with their shaming acne, bitten nails or whatever personal physical defect cast its gigantic shadow over their lives.

He now saw that the pernickety delicacy some of the girls displayed was often defensive, part of an image they projected as circumstances required. He no longer felt elephantine beside them. And any elitist pretensions they affected went over his head, being nothing new, since several of his own son's early friends who'd gone on to snooty establishments thought themselves no-goat's-toe as a result, but would drop their lofty poses when it came to the nitty-gritty.

What he had cannily to keep aware of was a dodge common to both sexes, but more subtle in females. This was the assumption of a worldly wisdom that was only tissue-paper thin, barely concealing the blank inexperience under it.

Regarded at first by the girls as a weird intruder and the butt for some mocking asides, he had become a commonplace sight barely to be considered. His keen ears picked up careless conversation through open doorways, and sniggers in the library as he browsed between the stacks. He was amused to discover that among themselves and in private they owned a bawdy repertoire of allusions in an argot which they imagined only the initiated could understand. Topics they considered adult (meaning sexual) were indexed under familiar school terms but accompanied by giggles and sideways glances. It was from this gauchely assumed raunchiness that he picked up some of their special vocabulary. The chemi block, for example, meant more than the yellow brick building that housed the science labs. It was their euphemism for a condom.

At the same time, although such words were confidently bandied about in the girls' conversation, he was aware that the objects themselves probably belonged to a world they hadn't yet entered. It was quite alarming, the careless way they exposed themselves to being misinterpreted, with their play at adult sophistication.

He was fascinated by the composition of the Maddie trio. Having yet to meet Mayumi, he was prepared to accept Maddie as the strong character to whom the other two had to give way.

And a threesome was provocative. He had noticed this among crooks, each slyly checking on the other two, competing to outshine them, fearing betrayal and then opting for it, to gain a larger share of the spoils or a lesser degree of punishment. He tailored his approach to Julia to induce just such betrayal.

She reminded him of a beginner at swimming, conscious of her own inaptitude but compelled to be forever in there bobbing about with the others. She was no great brain, but constantly pushed her half-digested knowledge to the fore in an attempt to stay intellectually afloat. And she did this with a blatant abruptness intended to cover her desperate need to be right this time; but too often instead she met with a scornful put-down.

Besides her reputation for getting facts arse-about-face, he recognized Julia's underlying resentment, built up from

136

constant hurt, which was never properly discharged. At school she was classed on the bottom rung. In an easier, less competitive world she might have been valued for her amiable loyalty, long-suffering, and a refusal to criticize what she admired.

And those virtues were the ones he must break down to get an insider understanding of the world Mayumi had run away from. So with Julia he needed the sympathetic approach, oiled with a little admiration to build her confidence in his good intentions.

He would have enjoyed his tussles with Maddie Coulter more if he hadn't been aware of real distress behind her reckless pertness. A streetwise kid, the urchin ever ready with the definitive comeback; sprung from a wealthy background certainly, but sometimes don't even the best families have them? And anyway, *was* her family one of the best? Substantial, and the father quite famous, but also – according to hearsay – an arty-crafty Bohemian.

In recall Beaumont always saw Maddie in the home clothes they were allowed to wear in the evenings: facing up to him frizzy-haired, her chin high, all in black, skinny and defiant in a diminutive tabbard over pipe-cleaner legs that ended in pixie boots. Tiny but tough. Gutsy and trying hard not to let panic show through.

Maddie had known well enough why Mayumi went missing that first time. But right now she was scared half out of her mind because she couldn't account for this second disappearance; yet resolute not to give away anything that might betray her friend.

No kid should have to take all that alone. His anger against her distant parents began to stir in him a desire to meet them on their home ground. And why not? Didn't Mayumi's Christmas stay with them mark the beginning of her disaffection, delinquency, or whatever?

He consulted with Superintendent Yeadings on the possible value of a trip down to Petworth. It seemed no outlandish project when they were already trawling information from places as far distant as North Wales and Japan.

The Boss, his desk covered in printout statements on the murder, saw little harm in Beaumont's brief absence from the Imura inquiry. A message from Z had assured him his other DS was on her way back. Despite the recent snowfall, she should get through on the cleared motorways.

He sanctioned Beaumont's request. 'But get back sharpish. Just as well to check down there before half-term sends young madam home. You'll get less hassle without her in your hair. I'll fix it with the West Sussex force.'

While Beaumont collected things from the detectives' office, through the opened doorway Yeadings recognized the tune his DS was whistling.

> Three little maids who, all unwary,
> Come from a ladies' seminary . . .

Ah yes, from Gilbert and Sullivan's *The Mikado*. Well, wasn't Mayumi the modern, commercial Mikado's daughter? And by now Beaumont was probably the best to judge just how unwary that trio of Maddie, Mayumi and Julia were. Or were not.

Rosemary Zyczynski drew into the parking area as dusk was falling. This far south the thaw had already set in. No dramatic horizontals of crimson, silver and black on this horizon of rooftops; just the dull blur of a less sombre disk sinking behind, overcast with a smudge of catarrhal yellow. The yard was puddled, greyish white mounds lingering at the base of angled walls for the next snowfall to join them.

Locking her car door she noted that the CID office was in darkness but the Boss's window still lit. Which meant that Beaumont was off hoovering up data, and she must report to Yeadings in person before getting anything down on paper. As she knuckled his open door Yeadings looked up. 'Ah, Rosemary.'

'Sir. I'm back.'

It sounded lame. Yeadings swung his chair round and got to his feet. 'Canteen,' he said crisply. 'You look half dead.'

He joined her at the cafeteria rails and they both opted for doughnuts and tea with lemon. 'My coffee machine's on the blink,' Yeadings complained. 'But I've another being delivered tomorrow. Have you got enough to eat there?'

'I'm not all that hungry; just thirsty, and cramped from driving.'

They unloaded their trays and sat opposite each other, ignoring the curious stares of uniformed men at other tables. 'Where's Beaumont?' she couldn't resist asking.

The Superintendent darted her a quick glance. She knew well enough that it was his place to put the questions. It struck him that she'd sounded wary, and he hoped he wasn't going to regret having two sergeants in parallel.

He brushed sugar from his fingers before answering. 'He's visiting the Coulter family home.'

'But the local police have looked there already.'

'He's not expecting to find Mayumi. Just to find out a little more about that Christmas holiday. Who she might have met there. Whether she learned of a suitable bolt-hole somewhere else. He's not staying over. Now, how about your inquiries? Anything that won't wait?'

'There's nothing urgent,' she said cautiously. 'I got a lot of information about a number of people who may or may not be of interest to us, but I shan't have it assessed until I've moved it around in my mind. One thing I'm sure of is that whatever Elizabeth Matsukawa's reason for driving there, no one I met at Wrexham was expecting her, not even her housekeeper or the head man at the factory. And I never heard of any special friend she had, although I asked around. It seemed as if, up there, she only existed as wife to the Chairman. And although there are other young Japanese, none of them seems to be at all intimate with Mayumi. I just don't see Wrexham as the place the girl would have made for if she was running to hide with friends.'

'What reaction was there to Elizabeth's injury and May's second disappearance?'

'They hadn't known until I told them. Mr Ichikawa was quite distressed, but I never got a chance to find out more about him because as soon as Mr Matsukawa arrived he sent him to Frankfurt to replace Imura. I wondered later whether his teenage daughter might have spent time with Mayumi during her summer holidays, and if in that way the two families were fairly close. There's an Englishman replacing Ichikawa at present; a Derek Robinson.'

'Are there many other British?'

'Most of the workforce. There's just a top layer of Japanese executives.'

'And Elizabeth is English. I wonder. If her marriage really is breaking up, could someone there be responsible?'

A lover? Z had only fleetingly considered this. 'I never met anyone who struck me he'd fit the bill. She'd have had to be be very discreet to keep an affair dark in a close community like that. And her husband struck me as pretty tough; the maker and breaker kind. He'd take it as personal dishonour if she looked elsewhere. I doubt if anyone inside the company would risk his future in that way.'

Yeadings grunted. 'Emotions aren't always subject to reason.'

'Robinson's the only person I could imagine being on Elizabeth's wavelength, and he struck me as having a reasonably tight rein on himself. And too good a job to throw away on a mad impulse. Outside the company I doubt if she'd have much chance or choice.'

'So what's Robinson's background?'

She gave a résumé of the man's recruitment, length of service, his previous company, his pretty wife and two children aged seven and five whose photograph had appeared on Ichikawa's desk alongside the toy harlequin.

'Not a prime candidate at first sight,' Yeadings agreed, 'but we don't judge a sausage by its skin. What did you make of Matsukawa's attitude?'

'He seemed genuinely upset at hearing that Elizabeth was injured. It made me wonder if he didn't properly realize that she wanted out of the marriage.'

'Possible, I suppose: nose to the grindstone and no eyes for anything else. Which in itself could accelerate her decision. Well, thanks for the rundown, Rosemary. Let me have it all on paper by tomorrow midday. Team briefing at 9 a.m. Get off home now and grab some rest.'

'Thanks, sir. I'll take a look in the analyst's office first, see how things are coming out.'

'Ah.' Yeadings rose, grimly smiling. 'Slightly pear-shaped I'm afraid. We're more than ready for a little slice of luck, to slap it into form.'

Thirteen

The Coulter house was a quarter mile outside Petworth, standing a hundred yards back from the country road, with a horseshoe drive to the porticoed front door. The woman who answered Beaumont's ring was in her thirties; a voluptuous red-head poured into a sweatshirt and stretch-satin leggings of olive green. Her black velvet hairband seemed to stretch her arched brows upwards from a hauntingly white face with heavily made-up eyes and lips. She stood still a moment to allow him to take stock of her, confident of his admiration.

'Mrs Coulter?' he asked, po-faced.

'I am. And you are?' The eyebrows went even higher. Cheekbones and teeth produced a smile which faded as he produced his warrant card and intoned his name and rank.

'Is this about my summons?'

'Not immediately. I should like a few words if you can spare the time.'

'Really, I thought I'd been questioned enough.' She sounded petulant, gestured towards the hall behind her and he followed her in, using the time needed in removing his car-coat to take in its details. Black and white chequered floor tiles with silky Persian rugs; walls covered in a dark plum brocade; four panelled doors and a rear passage approached through an archway; oil paintings and plants on jardinières ad lib; an oak staircase leading to a galleried upper floor, with a carved settle in its angle.

Past the door through which she led him, Victoriana gave way to lived-in brightness. Beyond giant bean-bag cushions and ceiling-hung wicker chairs the pale walls were all painted with outdoor scenes set in modern *trompe-l'oeil* arches. The woman gave him no time to take this in before she began defending herself.

'You realize, I hope, that this last lot's likely to cost me my licence,' she accused. 'How am I going to manage without a car, marooned out here at the bloody back of beyond? My husband is far too busy to be bothered with domestic runs. And it's not as though I'm the only one who exceeds the limit. Everybody does it round here. You should pick on some outsiders for a change instead of lying in wait to catch local people.'

'I'm a bit of an outsider myself,' Beaumont confessed with mock humility. 'Or perhaps you didn't catch what I said. Thames Valley force. It's not about what you think.'

'Something else?' That pulled her up. 'Thames Valley? My God, you're not going to accuse me of speeding there as well?'

Beaumont sighed. He took out his notebook and pretended to read from it. 'December last, you entertained a schoolfriend of your daughter Madeleine . . .'

'I haven't any daughter. She's Gilbert's, thank God, and I'm not responsible in any way for what she gets up to. Wait a minute, what's this about a schoolfriend?'

'Mayumi Matsukawa.'

'What about her?'

'You do remember her staying here with you over Christmas?'

'Look, we weren't here at Christmas. We went skiing.'

'Who's "we"?'

'Gilbert and I, of course.'

'Not Maddie?'

'No. Maddie stayed behind. Greg was here to keep an eye on her. They had some friends in, left over from Christmas Day. Maybe that's what you're thinking of.'

'I think,' Beaumont said faintly, 'we should get some details straightened out here,' and he offered her the version he'd had from Dr Walling.

Before it was sorted to his entire satisfaction Coulter came in from outdoors, a big, hearty man, red-cheeked from splitting logs in the rear flagged courtyard. He removed leather gloves and a shaggy pullover to reveal an open-necked shirt and a mat of grizzled hair. 'God, it's sweltering in here. How can you stand it, Steph?'

His voice was loudly confident but the glance he darted from shrewd blue eyes under craggy brows, was wary. Beaumont refused to be overwhelmed, delivering his ID in a studied monotone.

'Thames Valley? That's Bucks, Berks and Oxon, right?'

'Yessir. I am inquiring into the second disappearance from school of a friend of your daughter Maddie, er, Madeleine.'

'Little Japanese girl, wide-set eyes, lovely cheekbones? Only half-Jap, of course. That makes a difference. She was here at Christmas, you know. Did a couple of pastels of her after lunch. See if I can lay m'hands on 'em. They'll be around here somewhere.'

'I don't suppose the girl herself is?' Beaumont asked hopefully.

'Eh? No idea. Have you, Steph?'

'No, of course she isn't. There's nobody staying here at present. Anyway you told me Maddie phoned and said she'd returned.'

'So she did. So she did.' Coulter grimaced. 'But run off a second time, you say?' He turned to Beaumont again. For all his vagueness he seemed more capable of grasping essentials than his wife. Patiently the DS went through it again for the man's benefit, by which time he'd had a decanter waved at him and his assent assumed. A large cut-glass tumbler was thrust into his hand and it would have been boorish to complain because it contained some of the finest malt Beaumont had tasted to date.

He sat sipping while Coulter lumbered and bumbled

144

about the room like some myopic hippo, and it struck the Thames Valley man that if this was truly the father of the puckish Maddie, then the mother had been of a very different cast from either him or the present Mrs Coulter.

'What you want to know,' the man said, abruptly planting himself in front of Beaumont's chair, 'is what other guests we had in the house at the time she was here. Because you think somebody took the young lady's eye and she's gone after him. Well, we can only say who was here when we left. Just half a dozen, maybe eight. My wife'll give you their names. No good at names meself, I'm afraid. Could sketch 'em all if that's of any use, but what they're called God only knows that I don't.'

He had been staring fixedly at Beaumont's face for some minutes, and now he leaned forward urgently. 'I'd like to draw you. Hang on while I get a block.'

Maybe, Beaumont thought, artists are like alcoholics: the need comes suddenly over them and has to be satisfied. But he wasn't prepared for being a model. His face stiffened into its most Pinocchio woodenness, which delighted Coulter more.

It took no time. In a few strokes Coulter had the sketch finished and the DS had to admit that that was the face he saw in his shaving mirror.

He accepted the block from Coulter's hands and flicked back a few pages. Stephanie looking shrewish; a cruel study of her putting on the charm; another of her stripping off a sweater, the upreaching arms revealing lifebelts of fat where her bra edges cut in.

They weren't a fond lover's portrayals. He hoped Coulter didn't dislike his wife as much as the caricatures implied. Perhaps he'd grown detached enough to enjoy her as a comic character.

And the man was really clever with a pencil; an individual with a forceful mind. So that was where young Maddie got it from, even if she'd missed out on his big, clumsy body.

*　　*　　*

145

On Saturday morning Z read her notes through before joining Beaumont for a session with the Boss.

'I've had Mr Matsukawa on the phone twice,' Yeadings said, nodding them into chairs opposite his desk. 'I don't think he often finds himself out of his depth, but at the moment he's torn between sitting at his wife's bedside in Oxford and helping with the search for his daughter down here.'

Beaumont nodded sagely. 'It's like one of those personality teasers: your boat sinks, do you rescue your wife or your child?'

'Of course there's a third option.' The Superintendent looked grim. 'You could let the other two drown and save yourself.'

It took a moment for this to sink in, then Z leaned forward. 'What are you saying, sir? Do you seriously think Matsukawa set all of this up himself?'

'Not his wife's accident, but why not the rest? It's a possibility we have to consider. If for some reason he needed Imura wiped out, what better distraction than make it appear a mistaken attack on himself, and simultaneously have his daughter abducted to fog the issue? It would bring him into the picture as a potential victim, and any ransom demand that's made will only gain him extra sympathy.'

'He could know people who would carry it out for a price,' Z agreed cautiously.

'And with modern technology he's at the heart of things to control everyone's movements.'

'Except Elizabeth's. She was freeing herself from his hold on her.'

'You said yourself that we've only her word for that.'

'I wouldn't risk taking the job on,' Beaumont broke in, 'whatever he paid me or promised in return. Anyone cold-blooded and devious enough to create that kind of scenario wouldn't risk the paid killers getting caught. He'd exterminate them first.'

'Z, you've met him. What's your opinion?'

146

'He's formidable; a power person certainly. I shouldn't like to speculate what he might do. It all rests, doesn't it, on what kind of threat to him Imura represented? We've only heard of him as his boss's righthand man. And could it be worth Matsukawa's while to set up such a fantastic plot? He could always threaten to sack the man if he got out of hand.'

'What you mean is that I'm off my trolley to suggest it,' Yeadings said with a sudden fierce grin. 'Consider it the exercise of an over-fertile imagination. Sometimes, at this stage in a case, the possibilities seem limitless.'

He regarded them evenly. 'Let's go through it together, then, feet firmly on the ground, and restrain each other's wild surmises.'

He had fed his desk VDU with the analyst's information. 'SOCO's got only negatives for us. The only recognizable prints found were eliminated as Imura's own or the chambermaid's. The bloody handprints on the bed have been enhanced but are useless. The outer doorknob had only smudges and the imprint of a fabric glove's seam. Which could imply that the last person to leave the room, before the night porter went in, was dressed for outdoors. There were no traces of blood there. And to date there's only one blood source analyzed.'

'Happy about that night porter?' Beaumont asked.

'He's an established employee, has good references, had met Matsukawa twice before, but not Imura until that evening. He was constantly in the foyer while the wedding party was present, with absences of only three to five minutes at any time. At 5.07 a.m. a guest rang down for sandwiches and coffee, which he prepared and delivered approximately twelve minutes later. Returning to the lift he noticed the door of number 14 unfastened, knocked, got no reply and eased in to check everything was all right. Found it wasn't. When questioned about it, he remembered he didn't touch the doorknob; just pushed on the panels.'

'He was suffering from shock when I arrived,' Z offered. 'I'd be willing to bet it was genuine.'

'So what have we got on Imura himself?' Beaumont asked.

'Let's read it off the screen.' Yeadings tapped in the name and the data came up.

Imura, Hiromu: aged 54, domiciled Kyoto, widowed. Hobbies – squash, fencing and karate (black belt). Next of kin – sons Masanori, 29, and Takeo, 27.

'Try them,' Beaumont pressed, and Yeadings tapped in the first name. Masanori's age and address in Kyoto followed; marital status single. He was a junior manager with the Matsukawa company. Takeo's name produced the same for marital status and employment. But his address was in Kobe, followed by the terse 'Deceased, Kobe earthquake, 1994.'

'There was a photograph in an ivory frame in the hotel bedroom,' Z remembered. 'It showed two little boys. I took them for his grandsons, but it could have been taken years ago, of these two.'

'So dear to him that he carried the memory of them around with him,' Yeadings said sombrely. 'I think we need more on how Takeo died. We do know Matsukawa's factory in Kobe is under reconstruction. So was he killed there? Could any blame be attached to conditions at the original building, so that Imura held the company responsible? Was he a threat to them in some way?'

'That's what started you off suspecting Matsukawa,' Beaumont accused. 'But fear of reprisals isn't adequate motive. Matsukawa wouldn't have kept Imura on if the man was out for revenge. And anyway, what sane person would blame another for an earthquake?'

'Imura wasn't popular,' Z reminded them. 'He was the hatchet man, responsible for firing staff and terminating contracts. Elizabeth called him the Lord High Executioner. He must have had plenty of enemies inside the company, both here and in Japan.'

'So that is what I've requested from my friend in the Tokyo Police Department,' Yeadings threw in. 'A list of anyone who had a real or imagined grievance against Imura. Meanwhile, let's look at the known circumstances of the killing.'

He slotted colour scene-of-the-crime transparencies in the projector's carousel while Beaumont blacked out the room. 'I know you've all examined these, but let's see them magnified.'

As each image filled the opposite white office wall, Z fancied she again smelled the close, heated hotel room; the sickly sweet scent of blood mixed in with some unfamiliar soap and stale male sweat. The pictures were hideous, more so with the detailed wounds enlarged.

'He must have fought like a tiger,' Beaumont said, awed. 'The throat's cleanly cut, so that would have been the first injury, while he wasn't on his guard. But then he turned and tried to fight the attacker off with his bare hands and feet.'

'A professional attack by someone he'd taken for harmless.'

'Such as?'

'One of the hotel staff, or someone wearing their uniform.'

'Or?'

'A visitor he was expecting. Someone he invited in.'

'Ah. So who might fit that bill?'

'Unlikely,' Z cautioned. 'He was a stranger there and not the sort to make friends easily. Quite forbidding, in fact. I can't see him sharing a table at dinner and asking a new acquaintance up to his room.'

'Unless it was a woman,' Beaumont said flatly. 'He was in his nightshirt, after all. Or it could be a young man. And then the mutilated genitals. That vicious refinement happened after death. Whoever, they must have had a shock when they discovered the man's karate skill.'

'So, Rosemary. What's your opinion? Could a woman have carved him up?'

She hadn't missed the significance of the Boss using her first name. She was singled out to speak for her sex. She only knew she couldn't have gone blood-letting like that herself. Not unless it had been in a desperate attempt to escape with her own life. And the clean throat-cutting seemed to rule out that circumstance. They were both waiting for her judgement and she didn't know how to answer.

'I think,' she said at last, '*if* it was a woman then it had to be a very angry one – a very determined one who almost saw it as a mission.'

'And strong?'

'Not necessarily. Fit certainly, and nimble enough to evade him after the first cut. But, with the advantage of surprise and enough hate . . .'

'I would agree,' Yeadings said bleakly. 'So we can't instantly dismiss the two women already connected with the dead man. Given both motive and opportunity, plus a sharp knife, either Elizabeth Matsukawa or her daughter would have been physically capable of killing Imura.'

'Imura as Imura,' Beaumont said thoughtfully. 'Because neither of them would mistake him for Matsukawa. So what case can we make for them having sufficient motive?'

'So far,' Z offered, 'just the fact that, following orders, he'd removed Mayumi from her mother's care and returned her to the school. It would take resentment bordering on madness . . .' Her voice tailed away as Beaumont interrupted.

'So we look at opportunity. They were both close, and in each other's company at roughly the right time. Both knew where he was, but not necessarily in which room.'

'Hold it there,' Yeadings ordered. 'We have it from the hotel that Matsukawa always demanded the same double room, and being able to afford all sorts of extras he invariably got what he asked for: number 14. Twice his wife had stayed there with him in that room, and it's probable that Mayumi knew it too, arriving with them en route for school.'

'So neither of them would need to ask for Imura at reception or to look at the register. Simply slip in and take the lift upstairs.'

'And that room number would have been quoted at some time on the faxes from Kyoto,' Z argued. 'So others in the company who had access to the files would have known as much.'

Yeadings sat back in his chair, grim-faced. 'You're both determined not to limit the possibilities. You're right, of course. The frame's vast on this one. Vast and empty. With a choice of scenarios for two alternative corpses. As we can't eliminate either man as the intended victim, we'll have to carry on with parallel assumptions.'

'So why not split the graft? I'll throw my hat in for Imura, with prime suspects the Matsukawa women in collusion,' Beaumont suggested.

'Which leaves you, Z, with Matsukawa as the intended victim, if you accept.'

'Why not, sir?'

'And who will you have in your sights?'

That wasn't so easy, but she wasn't stymied. 'A. N. Other, sir. It leaves the field wide open.'

'Um.' Yeadings tapped his lips with the end of his ballpoint pen. 'There's quite a bit to fill in with Imura's known movements. Less on Matsukawa's, since he's not long been here. To balance the workload, Z can take over the school end again.'

Beaumont hesitated. He didn't care for anything to slip out of his hands, particularly after his visit to the Coulter home. But he was sure he was on to a winner with the murder, so he'd let her have the minor case. The silly Jap kid wasn't abducted at all. She'd just slipped off for a further spot of nooky.

It seemed a good point to make his report on his visit to Petworth. The other two listened keenly as he summarized his conversation with Mrs Coulter.

'Did you meet Maddie's father?' Z asked.

151

'Yes, he came in from splitting logs, and complained the house was overheated. And I saw some of his recent sketches. Including Mayumi. One really excellent likeness of Maddie. Several of his wife; caricatures, almost. I wonder she hadn't had them burnt. In fact she seemed quite proud of one or two. No sense of humour, maybe. The finished paintings were of people who looked faintly familiar but I couldn't fix names to. He's a popular artist all right.'

'What did he have to say about Mayumi being there?'

'He admitted he'd agreed to Maddie inviting her, but she seems to have kept a low profile while he was in the house. He did, however, do a couple of pastel drawings of her on Christmas afternoon. The next day he and his wife flew out to Switzerland. For the lowdown on what happened after that, we'd have to question Maddie again and her brother; but according to Mrs C they did have other guests and got through a lot of provisions between them.'

'We'll certainly need a list of their names,' Yeadings agreed. 'So that'll be your chore, Z. Anything more to report, Beaumont?'

'No, sir. What's the full rundown we've got on Imura's movements?'

Yeadings turned back to the VDU and scrolled through the data.

On receiving the fax sent via Dr Walling, Imura had checked in at the Bellhouse at approximately 2.15 p.m. Sunday, 8 February. He ordered a light meal served in his room.

He then used the hotel facilities to send faxes to Frankfurt, Kyoto, and Kobe. Copies obtained showed these to be in Japanese, and the last one was also in code. Translations of the first two showed they were concerned with business matters. Matsukawa, as recipient of the last, had been questioned by phone and claimed that this message concerned the return of his daughter to school and confirmation of Imura's intended flight next day to Wrexham.

Mr Imura had spent the afternoon on a work-out in the hotel gym followed by a swim in the indoor pool. At approximately 5 p.m. he left the hotel on foot, handing in his key, and had returned by 7.30 p.m. when he ordered drinks in the bar. At 7.43 p.m. he had made a phone call to Denham airfield concerning a flight booking made for him by the Kobe office. He then went through to the dining room for dinner, leaving at about 8.15 p.m. and taking the lift up to his room.

'He liked to keep active,' Beaumont commented drily. 'But there's a significant blank when he was out, betweeen 5 and 7.30 p.m. Haven't we traced any taxi used by him? Or did someone arrive and pick him up? I mean, what would he do outdoors, on foot, for two hours and a half on a freezing Sunday evening, marooned in open country?'

'Walk into Gerrards Cross?' Z suggested. 'There's only one main street of shops and they'd all be closed.'

'Attend church,' Yeadings added with a touch of mischief. 'That should be interesting for you, Beaumont, doing the rounds of them all to find which one. But there is also a cinema.'

His last words had a sound of finality about them and the two sergeants rose to go, but the Boss had saved a little titbit for the last.

'It's not confirmed yet, but we've just had a phone call from Zermatt, Switzerland, from the lady whose silver wedding reception was at the Bellhouse. The London newspapers were late reaching her with mention of the murder, but she decided to call us. About something she'd spotted in the hotel's ground floor ladies' room between 8 p.m. and 8.30.'

'The *ladies'* room?' Beaumont echoed, suspicious.

'Yes, a young Japanese girl in a grey overcoat, and she was rinsing her face at the basins. The lady thought she'd been crying.'

Fourteen

No one in the team was to get a free trip to Switzerland in winter sports season, because the silver wedding lady was due back next day. That was also when half-term would send Maddie and Julia home for a week.

Z added the printouts of Beaumont's report on his Petworth visit to her already bulging file on Mayumi's second disappearance. It worried her that so much paperwork represented nil progress in tracing the girl's whereabouts. To date May hadn't contacted school or family, and there had been no genuine sightings since her photograph had been circulated in the media. The number of false ones had drained resources less than usual because the missing girl had some distinctive oriental features. Even then, claims that she had been seen in Edinburgh, Waterford, Sunderland and Bristol had still needed to be followed up, if only for elimination.

Most seriously, no ransom demand had been received from a kidnapper. Two grim possibilities increasingly haunted the woman DS: that Mayumi was already dead, or else being held by some dangerous nutter as a sex slave.

As she worked again through the accumulated data, Z was interrupted by a phone call from Oxford. It was the policewoman sitting in at the Radcliffe hospital, reporting that Elizabeth Matsukawa had briefly regained consciousness that morning and recognized her husband. After further sedation she was expected to make a good recovery, and might even be fit enough for questioning the next day. Z chalked on the duty board that she would be absent then at Oxford. Meanwhile she had a fancy to take a second look at Greg Coulter's studio in Rathbone Place, West London.

As she parked a few doors away a woman was speaking into the entry-phone. Z hurried to get through the door before it closed again behind her.

'Ullo,' the woman said cheerfully. 'Bitter, ain't i'?' She was a thin, hard-faced, artificial blonde.

'Not so hot,' Z agreed cautiously. 'I haven't met you here before, have I?'

'Likewise. Still, I'm not exackerly meant to be seen. I do the cleaning. Offstage, you might say. Edie Swann,' she introduced herself brashly.

Z produced her ID and instantly the cleaner curled her lip at sight of it. 'I thought you might be one of that lot,' she lied. She'd meant police, but would probably have used an alternative description: 'the Filth' or 'pigs'. With narrowed eyes, as if smoking from the corner of her mouth, she waited for what was to come.

'Do you clean for all the occupants of this building?'

'With me mates Linda and Maureen, yeah.'

'At what times of day would that be?'

'Depends.'

'On?'

'Whose place. Most offices they work mornings from nine, so we do them evenings, from six onwards. Others work evenings, so guess what.'

'You do them mornings. How about weekends?'

'I take free, like anyone else. Just 'op in to do Mr Coulter's studio for a coupla hours Sat'day mornings, on my own. Can't get in there workdays with all them tricky lights and cables.'

'No Linda and Maureen for that job? Why's that?'

The woman darted her a shrewd glance from between mascara-stiff lashes. 'They've got kids to look after. Me, I'm on me own since me feller pushed off. And with it being weekends, the pay's time and a half. No point in letting anyone else in on that.'

'So, apart from you, nobody ever uses the studio from Friday until Monday?'

'Just a young feller who sees to the dark-room. That's only once in a blue moon. And then, just a week or so back, there was that young model stayed over on the Friday night. Not working, though. Just scrounging a bed.'

'Had you seen her here before?'

'Nuh. Just another kid really. They get camera-struck, some of them, pestering Mr Coulter all the time. Want to put on the glam and be cover girls. Think they can pay with pussy power, but he's not slow to let on it's boys he goes for.'

'Edie, I'm going to show you a photograph. I want you to tell me if you've ever seen this person before.'

The cleaner took the glossy of Mayumi and nodded. 'Yeah. That's her. The one who kipped here. A Chink or Jap, isn't she? Spoke good English, though. But a bit hoity-toity.'

The lift arrived and she stepped in backwards, blocking the narrow entrance, and with one thumb pressing on the OPEN button.

'Thank you, Mrs Swann. Can I have your address? I'm afraid I'll have to ask for a written statement from you later.'

'Do I get paid for it?'

'No. But if you refuse I could make it awkward for you. For withholding information from the police.'

'And obstructing them in the performance of their dooty, or some such. I know, I know. All right, no harm in asking, I guess.' With impatience she dictated an address in Paddington.

'Had anyone else been in the studio that weekend when you saw her?'

'I wouldn't know, would I? Came in on Sat'day morning all bright and early, ready to vacuum and polish. Found her still asleep on the studio couch. Said she was a friend of the fam'ly. If you'll believe that, you'll believe anything. Still, one or other of them two must have let her in. Never saw her here again, so they'll have shooed her off afterwards, Mr Coulter or that Danny friend of his.'

Z let out her breath in a sigh of satisfaction. So at last she had a positive sighting of Mayumi to fill in the lost hours of her first disappearance. And, as half-suspected, Maddie's brother Greg had been involved up to his elegant neck.

'And have you seen this girl again anywhere else, since that one occasion?'

'Nuh. She been up to sumpthink naughty then?' Apparently Edie only skimmed her tabloid newspaper.

Z ignored the question. 'So, if it's not cleaning time now, what are you doing here, on your own?'

'Come back for somethink I lost, haven't I?'

'Really?'

'Yeah, reelly. Me gold bracelet. Musta fallen off when I was cleaning the doctor's brasses up on the second floor. Don't suppose I can report it missing to you, can I?'

'You just did,' Z said tersely. 'Not that it'll do you any good. You should drop in at your local nick and fill in a form, if you don't find it today.'

'There! Never any around when you want them. And then no bloody good to you when they are there,' Edie Swann said scathingly. 'Well, so nice to meet you, I don't think.'

With this final scorn for the forces of law and order she was swallowed up by the lift doors, leaving Z to go up by the stairs. She took them two at a time, grinning to herself at the outcome of the chance encounter.

Arriving opposite the frosted glass panels of the studio's office she could just make out someone moving about inside. There was the mercifully muffled sound of rap music. She had a moment to wait after knocking and then Greg Coulter opened up, clicking his fingers, his shoulders jigging to the rhythm. Now the music was overpowering.

His stare was fixed but with his back to the light she couldn't tell the state of his pupils.

It was only marijuana. She recognized the smell. And Greg wasn't bothered whether she knew, lazily smiling and challenging her to take up the puritan stance.

'Busy?' she asked. 'Shan't keep you long.'

Mockingly he placed his right hand on brow, then on heart, and bowed low, with a sweeping gesture to indicate she might enter. '*Mi casa, su casa.*'

Nice touch, but it should have been in Arabic, not Spanish. He wasn't playing with a full deck at present, she observed. Which perhaps made it a good time to tackle him.

'Lies have a way of bouncing back on one,' she murmured, walking past him and on into the studio. 'So I've come back with the same questions and one or two more.'

'Couldn't stay away,' he drawled, following. 'How very flattering.' He turned down the music but its pulse continued, and his torso kept swaying in time.

Z went across to the shawl-draped couch and sat squarely in the middle. 'Cosy,' she said, patting the cushions. 'For just one night, she must have been grateful. What I'm curious about is how she got so far as this at that time of night.'

'*She?* Which of the women in my life . . . ?'

'Come off it. You've already played the gay card. Or have you forgotten your earlier defence?'

He leaned against the opposite wall and closed his eyes. 'I haven't the least idea what you're talking about.'

'Do you remember who I am? What I came about before?'

'Lady Fuzz.' He opened his eyes and used them to stab at her. 'Lies, you just said. What lies?'

She took her time pulling the notebook from her shoulder bag, turning back the pages to find the right place.

'All right. No need for such a performance.' He was impatient now. 'You came asking questions about Maddie's friend May, the Japanese girl. You must know I wouldn't for the world do anything to upset my little sister. She's the only female I've ever met that was even half-decent. So it follows I wouldn't hurt her friend. I'd done some studies of her over Christmas. She posed for me. They both thought it a great joke. I told you about that. You've seen the prints, worn the T-shirt. So what's the problem?'

'You also stated that you hadn't seen her since that occasion.'

'That's so.' He waited for more, and suddenly she was unsure.

'You still maintain . . .'

'I stick with that.'

'She didn't come and pose again for you at this studio the first weekend she went missing?'

'She did not. I never work weekends.'

'And you spent all the time, from Friday noon to Monday noon, at your Kensington flat in the company of your friend Danny?'

'If I said so then, that's how it was.'

'Are you quite sure about that? There's nothing you'd like to change?'

'Been a lot of water under the bridge since then, but one weekend's much like another. Either we stayed in or we went out. Same difference. I was all the time with Danny. In any case I wasn't bloody here.'

She got the feeling he didn't want the issue any more complicated than it was already. Impatient with her persistence, was he really aiming somewhere near the truth?

'Let me ask you one more thing. How many sets of keys are there to this office and studio?'

He frowned. 'I have a set, Danny another. Then the cleaning woman, and the agent for the owner of the building. That makes four.'

'What about the lad who sees to the dark room?'

For an instant that shook him. There was a brief narrowing of the eyes as he registered that she'd already checked up on his arrangements. But his voice was, if anything, more casual when he replied.

'I lend him my set of keys when I need restocking in there. Which I haven't done in cat's ages. Prefer to do my own skivvying with the chemicals.'

'I see. Can you give me something more precise than "cat's ages"?'

He thought. 'A couple of months, say.'

So perhaps the dark-room lad was a little friend he'd tired of. 'Right. Thank you, Mr Coulter. I think that's all for the moment.'

'My pleasure.' Although obviously relieved, he was as scathing as Edie Swann had sounded. Z reflected she wasn't proving popular in Rathbone Place. Not that it bothered her. Policing wasn't about getting yourself loved.

It was clear what she had to do next, but first she must pick up DC Jeffreys or another Met officer to stand in as witness. She used her phone from the car and after being referred from number to number finally ran him down at a bookshop in Chelsea.

'Why not?' he answered her invitation. 'Just finished with a big haul of crack here. Give me the address again and I'll meet you outside.'

She was going to look silly if Danny wasn't at home, but even while she waited for the DC to appear, she recognized a jaunty figure loping along the pavement towards her with a bag of groceries in his arms. He jogged up the house steps while she watched in her mirror. Two lucky encounters in one day. After running into Edie Swann, perhaps this visit too could come up trumps. When Jeffreys arrived she explained to him the line she intended taking.

'OK, OK, I'll come clean.' Danny's grin was meant to be engaging. Prancing from one crêpe-soled foot to the other, he wagged his open palms like a batman guiding in an aircraft. There was a monkeyish vitality about all his movements, and despite herself Z had to admit she found him attractive. Or might have done, if he wasn't Coulter's catamite.

He flung himself into a chair and hugged one foot on his knee. 'I got a phone call from May, wanting me to pick her up at the school gates; borrowed Greg's car keys and did just that. He never knew I'd even seen her. Mebbe he exaggerated, saying we were together from noon that Friday to noon on Monday, but I was with him off and on. We don't live in each other's pockets any more than a married couple would. So he knew nothing about my private arrangement with May. I just kept stumm about it, like she asked. Which suited me just as well, because Greg doesn't care overmuch for me showing an interest in girls.'

'In under-age girls,' Z reminded him.

'I swear,' Danny said, holding his right hand high, 'there was no sex involved.'

'So what exactly was this "private arrangement" with her?'

'She simply wanted somewhere to kip overnight, and I lent her the studio.'

'And went to all the trouble of commandeering your friend's car, driving out to the school, waiting for her in the road near the driveway, and delivering her to Rathbone Place. Why go to so much bother to satisfy a young girl's whim when the obvious thing is to say, "No way, José"?'

'She's a nice kid. I'd met her over Christmas at Greg's folk's place in Sussex, and I liked her. And let's say I owed her a favour. Manalive, I wasn't doing anything criminal, just giving her a lift and letting her use the studio as somewhere to stop over.'

'Removing her from the lawful care of Dr Walling, the school's principal.'

'Hell, I grew up as an alley kid. I know nothing about

161

boarding-school rules. I just assumed all the kids went home weekends.'

His casualness was almost convincing. Except that, according to a witness, he'd parked the car beyond the school gates with its lights off, waiting over an hour until May could effect her escape.

But Z was prepared to let him off lightly for the moment. He might be more chastened when DI Mott sat in on a later interview.

'But that wasn't the end of the matter, was it?' Z guessed. 'Next day you took Mayumi to her mother's place in Wiltshire.'

'Ah.' He tilted his head to squint at the ceiling. 'So she hitched a lift with me down as far as Salisbury. You'll appreciate I was doing the noble thing there, setting her on the right route for home.'

'Why Salisbury? You could have taken her the whole way. And explained everything to her mother when you got there.'

'I would have,' he said disarmingly, 'but May has this independence thing about going the last lap on her own. She just dismissed me part way; insisted on catching the local train. It was nothing saucy I did to put her off, I swear. She'd simply planned it that way all along.'

And there Z was inclined to believe him, having seen Mayumi walk out alone to Imura's helicopter, head held high, claiming that that way it felt less like being arrested.

'So what did you see as May's reason for slipping out of school like that?'

If possible, Danny seemed to become more relaxed at that point. 'Which is exactly what intrigued me. But she wasn't confiding in me that far. I know she intended a meeting with her mother, but she was in no hurry to get to her; seemed to be putting it off as long as she reasonably could.'

'However anxious that delay would leave Mrs Matsukawa, and everyone else?'

'Others maybe, but not her mother. She phoned her from the studio as soon as she arrived. I was still there. I heard her.'

'Did you check the number she rang?'

'No. She dialled it herself, but I heard her chatting away. God knows what she said because it was all in Japanese.'

Z found this puzzling, because Elizabeth had claimed ignorance of May's disappearance until the local police informed her. 'Are you sure it was her mother she was speaking to?'

'Of course. She asked where the phone was because she must ring her mother, and it was certainly a woman's voice on the other end.'

'You listened in.'

Caught out, he looked boyishly sheepish. 'On the dark-room extension. I was as curious as you are. But was no wiser for my pains. Couldn't make out a single word either said. I don't speak Nip.'

'But you could grasp the tone of the conversation.'

He grimaced before replying. 'They sounded close, confidential, serious. Yes, it was her mum all right.'

Z considered him: an engaging rogue, no more honest than he had to be, but over this she was inclined to believe him. And it hadn't caused him any grief that he'd blown Greg Coulter's alibi delivered in his presence days before. But at that time she'd been probing for Greg's connection with Mayumi, and now Danny's admission, that he was the one involved, left Greg exonerated.

It was a strangely slack relationship between the two men, with one commandeering the other's car without permission and the other presumably on the loose in London while claiming they were together. Small wonder people's personal lives got into messes when honesty was so elusive.

'And since you left her at Salisbury have you had any communication with Mayumi – by letter, by phone or by meeting?'

'I have not, Sergeant,' he said, picking up her official tone and echoing it. He seemed to appreciate that that was the final question.

'We'll be needing a written statement, sir,' Jeffreys interrupted sternly. 'If you'll drop in at the station between four and five, I'll be there to help you with it.'

'I shan't need any help. My spelling's quite good, Constable. At least for the simple sort of words you'll be needing.'

'That's as may be, sir, but we have to be sure you cover all the ground. Saves time in the long run. Unless you want police visits on a regular basis.'

'Heaven forbid. Unless, of course, the Sergeant here was to take me on.' He let his eyes dance over her face, irrepressibly mischievous, his temporary unease dispelled. Z gazed evenly back, asking herself what Mayumi would have made of him, how far he could have charmed her. Greg Coulter's lover he might be, but that didn't exclude the rest of the world, whatever the gender.

'Happy?' DC Jeffreys asked her on the steps outside.

'Not really. This is just information on the first time May went missing. We've nothing yet on where she might be now, or even if she's gone willingly. There could be no connection between the two occasions.'

However, there was some progress to chalk up. 'We may get a lead from that phone call Mayumi made to her mother,' Z said hopefully. 'I could know more tomorrow when I visit the Radcliffe. We heard today that Elizabeth Matsukawa has come out of coma, and I'm expecting to question her myself. There are definite discrepancies she'll need to explain.'

164

Fifteen

Beaumont hadn't been idle. Next morning he met Z at the Incident Room with an item that set her further questioning Elizabeth Matsukawa's part in recent events. On the night of Imura's murder the car she had rented from Avis had been recognized in the Bellhouse car park.

A software rep had hired it the previous week, when his company car was off the road with a bent wheel rim. He'd memorized the licence plate and it just sprang out at him when he pulled into the parking precinct with a client. No, he hadn't seen anyone leave or approach it, nor noticed whether anyone was sitting inside. It was too far away, and the overhead lighting hadn't shown up the interior. But he was certain about the number and model, a red Vauxhall rented from Avis.

So now Elizabeth's name was coming up on both inquiries: for her daugher's first disappearance and Imura's death. Z realized, before Yeadings actually put it into words, that Beaumont had equal need with herself to question Mrs Matsukawa.

'You'd better go to the Radcliffe together,' the Boss said. 'But don't spend too much time there. I feel it in my bones that the pace is quickening. We could soon have developments elsewhere.'

'Where does he mean?' Z asked, as the two sergeants went out to Beaumont's car. 'What's likely to come up?'

Beaumont looked owlish. 'Dunno. There's no guessing what the Boss feels in his bones. It's certainly not arthritis.

But later today the silver-wedding woman gets back from Switzerland. Not that we can expect much that's new from her. By phone she's already identified Mayumi from a faxed sketch I had off old Coulter. She was definitely the Jap girl in the ladies' room at the Bellhouse.'

'Which means that both she and her mother were there that night. Elizabeth would have driven them over from Amersham. It would only take about twenty minutes. They must have intended seeing Imura.'

Beaumont nodded. 'And they would have been at the hotel during the period in which the pathologist says he was killed. A pity the mother wasn't sighted too. Do you think the girl could have driven across on her own? Fifteen years old; most kids of that age have had some experience behind the wheel.'

'Elizabeth wouldn't have let her take the car. Unless Mayumi escaped without her knowledge and that was when she went missing.'

'No. Her mother had the same car later for driving north. But it does seem that May had disappeared by the time she left. All witnesses say there was only one woman in the car when it crashed. The whole area was toothcombed in case a passenger had been flung out. Absolute zilch. It looks like she'd stashed her daughter away somewhere safe beforehand. And you might ask why she needed to. Had the girl gone berserk and attacked Imura, or was it simply to avoid the estranged husband getting access to her?'

Z shook her head. 'Mayumi couldn't have killed Imura. All that blood! According to this woman at the Bellhouse – what's her name anyway? – May was only rinsing her face. Because she'd been crying. There'd be more to show than a few tears after a carve-up like that.'

'So her mother did it, and was still out of her mind when she crashed the car. The girl either guessed what had happened or was a witness. Either way she panicked and fled to friends. Your best bet for finding her is to ride Coulter and his boyfriend into the ground until they come up with more info. If she was such close buddies with them she'd have let something slip. If they haven't got her stashed away somewhere themselves.'

'Not "they",' Z decided. 'Coulter's not involved, I'm almost sure. Danny's too anxious for his previous adventure with Mayumi to be kept in the dark. Especially from Greg.'

'Because Danny's a bisexual and he was having it off with her?'

'Because Greg knows he's bisexual and would *assume* he'd cause to be jealous. But I'm not sold on the idea of Danny making a play for Mayumi, even given the run-up from their meeting at Christmas.'

'Come off it, Z. Get real. Don't say you didn't find him dishy yourself.'

Z considered a moment. 'I did actually. There's an animal magnetism about him. I was attracted in an amused sort of way. But I doubt if it would work with May. Not for her to go all the way. She struck me as a pretty wary little person, and in charge of herself; more of an observer than a high-diver.'

'She's a kid, and kids go for sensation. It just takes a little arousal and the defences go down. Who knows what he used: drink, drugs, a smooth tongue? It's been happening since the world began. Always will. Remember those come-hither photos of her that Coulter took? Was she being an observer then? Watching from the sidelines? No, she was too damn good at putting herself across.'

'That was an act: aping the role of sex symbol. Fantasy; not for real. And maybe she knew she was safe with Greg Coulter. He doesn't let females come close. Except perhaps Maddie. From what he said, he does seem genuinely fond of his young sister.'

At the Radcliffe Elizabeth had been moved from the ITU to a private room. Yasuhiko Matsukawa came out to speak to them, and Z introduced her fellow sergeant.

167

The Japanese seemed to have aged by ten years since she saw him in North Wales. He was uncertain whether to address her, as someone he'd already met, or Beaumont because he was a man. Uncertainty wasn't his line, but he clenched his jaw and spoke to the space between the two detectives: his wife was still in an extremely delicate state, both physically and mentally. They were to exercise the greatest caution in whatever they said to her.

'How much does she know of what's happened?' Z demanded.

'Nothing,' the man said, blank-faced. 'And I don't want her told.'

'She must realize she was involved in an accident.' Beaumont's voice was flat and a touch disrespectful. There showed a momentary smouldering in Matsukawa's eyes.

'She knows she was driving a car which crashed. She remembers no more. Neither where she was going nor where she had come from.'

'Is she still sedated?' Z enquired. 'Will she understand what we are saying?'

Matsukawa hesitated. 'There is nothing wrong with her brain. It is just that she doesn't remember.'

Z nodded. 'Trauma shadow. Sometimes memory can get wiped from a period before the accident equal to the time of unconsciousness after it. I met her a day or two earlier. I'd like to start talking about what happened then.'

'So long as you do not upset her.'

'Mr Matsukawa, we share your anxiety. We have the same desperate need for information that can lead us to your daughter. Please trust me.'

Mention of Mayumi brought another flash of animation to his face. How could I ever have thought him inscrutable? Z wondered. His pain was quite naked, before the eyes slitted and the mouth again became a straight line. 'Then we will go in.'

Elizabeth lay almost flat, a dressing strapped near her right temple where the hair had been shaved off. The rest was spread loose over the pillow, a dull grey-gold. Beyond the livid bruises and the dark hollows round the eyes her face had barely more colour than the bed sheets.

'Elizabeth,' Z whispered, 'hello. It's DS Zyczynski,' and the eyes came open.

'There was no need to ask if she remembered their meeting. 'Sergeant,' she croaked. 'Help.'

Did she mean Z had helped before, or was this a desperate plea?

'That's what I'm here for,' Z promised. She reached for the hand on the coverlet, and saw that Matsukawa held the other between both of his. For a moment she felt distaste, as though some unpleasant current passed between the three of them. Which was stupid and superstitious. All the same she wished he wasn't there.

'Could I ask you a few questions, sir?' Beaumont asked woodenly.

'Not now, surely.'

'We've only a limited time for this visit, sir. I must remind you we are pursuing a murder inquiry elsewhere, which must be our most urgent concern.'

Z was aware of the man's reluctance, but he gently relinquished Elizabeth's hand and moved away, leaving the two women together. 'Where were you off to when the car crashed?' Z probed.

'I don't know. I don't remember being in a car. I don't remember anything about that night.'

She sounded so wretched that Z squeezed her fingers in sympathy. 'So we'll go further back. Now, tell me, Elizabeth. Where did we meet?'

'At my home. When May – was missing.'

'Right. And do you remember that the previous evening, Friday, she had phoned you?'

Elizabeth looked perplexed. 'No. May phone? She hadn't rung me for weeks.'

'Perhaps you've forgotten. It would be well after 9.30 p.m. Perhaps ten or later. She spoke to you in Japanese.'

169

'No. No, you're wrong. We never speak in Japanese – unless her father's there. He wasn't, was he?' Elizabeth sounded increasingly confused.

'Maybe I have got it wrong.' (Or Danny had!) 'Let's go on to the next day. Do you remember that May turned up that evening when I was with you? And how it was that she left next day?'

'Heli – copter.'

'With—?'

'Mr Imura. You drove me – to the school.'

'Yes. You went to see Dr Walling, didn't you? And she gave Mayumi an exeat to go with you to your hotel.'

'Yes.'

They were approaching the area where she needed the greatest caution. One cry of alarm from Elizabeth and they'd be denied further contact. She covered the flaccid hand with her own. 'Then what did you do?'

There was silence. Z watched the woman's panic as she thought back. Not troubled by encountering a blank. No; it was the memory itself that distressed her. It was as well that her husband couldn't see the fleeting expressions that distorted her face. Elizabeth shut her eyes again, deliberately cutting herself off.

'Elizabeth, after dinner together where did you and Mayumi go?'

There was no answer. The eyes stayed fast shut.

'We know it was to the Bellhouse Hotel. To see Mr Imura again. Why was that?'

'No. To school. I – took May back.' She sounded terrified. It could be a lie. Across the room Matsukawa's voice broke off abruptly as he turned to listen, so Z left the gap in events unexplored and went on unhurriedly.

'What time would that be?'

'We were early. Before nine.'

'So did you see Dr Walling again?'

'I – dropped May – at the front door. She insisted.'

This time Z believed her. It was another instance of

170

May needing to go the last few steps alone. It was something which happened before that moment that Elizabeth was concealing: their visit to the Bellhouse. And why should she be so distressed, unless she knew about Imura's murder?

Z lowered her voice. 'Elizabeth, it's important that you don't leave anything out. We know you were at the Bellhouse. The car was seen there, so was May. You'd better tell me. Why did you take her?'

Elizabeth's face screwed in pain. She was fighting against tears, and made several attempts to speak before she got the words out. 'To deliver – a letter. For her father. May's – apology.' Her voice sounded hollow.

'I see.' But she wasn't sure that she did see. 'So what did Mr Imura say?'

Elizabeth's head rolled on the pillow. 'I waited. In the car. May—'

'May went in alone?'

'He'd gone to bed. She – slid it – under the door.'

'Do you mean she never saw him?'

'Yes.' But again Elizabeth was keeping something back.

'I think that's enough.' Matsukawa came to the other side of the bed and faced Z with authority.

'Yes, I agree. We don't want to overtire her. Thank you, Elizabeth. I'll probably come and see you again. And bring May.'

'Give her my love.' Elizabeth's eyes closed wearily.

'She doesn't know Mayumi's missing,' Z whispered to Beaumont when they were outside.

'What about the murder?'

But she couldn't answer because Matsukawa was on their heels.

'Sergeant.' He addressed himself to Beaumont. 'My wife is due her medication. She will be asleep for some time now. I can spare an hour to visit your superintendent.'

'Right, sir. Can I offer you a lift?'

171

'I have my own car. It is just a question of finding my stand-in chauffeur. If he's not in the hospital . . .'

'Don't trouble, sir. I can drive you. It's not far. Sergeant Zyczynski will take my car.'

Slick, Z thought. The female put down, and the boys chummy together. God knows what Beaumont hopes to get out of the man when they're *tête-à-tête*, but he'll have a damn good try.

At least she would have her mind to herself on the journey back. But not even that until she'd grabbed some coffee in the hospital waiting area and written up a verbatim report on this latest interview.

By the time Z reached the Incident Room at Gerrards Cross, Mr Matsukawa had seen the Boss and was on his way back to Oxford. He'd refused a lift in a patrol car, on arrival summoning his regular chauffeur to fly down, recover the Daimler from the Radcliffe car park, and pick him up. Z was impressed by the affluent set-up.

Whatever Yeadings made of the man, he was keeping it to himself.

Beaumont reported verbally that out of consideration for Elizabeth's weakness, Matsukawa had kept from his wife news of May's second disappearance and Imura's murder.

'What do you think, Rosemary? Does she really not know?' Yeadings asked Z.

'Elizabeth can't have known about May. She sent her love to her through me. And she was quite clear that she'd returned May to the school after dinner at the Crown. She said she'd left her on the doorstep.'

'So where's the memory loss Matsukawa warned us about?'

'It may be genuine over her reason for driving north on the night she crashed. She wasn't able to tell me about that. As for what happened before that journey, I think it was a convenient pretence to keep her husband from

172

questioning her too closely. She's not prepared for him to know everything. Maybe she doesn't trust him, or else there's something she needs to keep under wraps.'

'Such as?'

Z paused for thought. 'She's panicky. I believe her claim that she delivered Mayumi back to school. But suppose, after that, she went back to reason with Imura at the hotel.'

'You think she did it?'

'Not the murder, no. But remember the seam mark from a glove? If she'd found number 14's door ajar, as the porter did later, she could have pushed it open and gone in.'

'And seen the body?'

'Which could have decided her to get right away, overnight. God knows what she thought had happened there. She knew Mayumi had spent some time in the hotel. Perhaps the girl too had seen the same and yet had said nothing to her. Panicking like that, Elizabeth would have been driving wildly and that's how the accident happened. She might even have imagined her daughter somehow involved in the killing—'

'Mayumi couldn't have done it, because in the ladies room she was seen still wearing her school clothes. And we know the killer would have been covered in blood,' Yeadings put in.

'Too complicated,' Beaumont said dogmatically. 'If Mrs Matsu went back to the Bellhouse after dropping the girl off, it was probably to have it out with Imura. And the argument got out of hand. While his back was turned she reached for a knife in her handbag—' He shrugged, turning his palms up.

'Did you actually mention the Imura killing to her?' Yeadings asked Z.

'I couldn't outright: that was too risky. At first she wouldn't admit she'd driven to the Bellhouse with May. But once I'd got it out of her she claimed she'd waited

173

in the car while her daughter went in. And she'd only had it on May's say-so that the girl didn't see Imura. It seems May had written a letter for her father which she pushed under Imura's door. The trouble is that SOCO never found anything of the sort in the room. So either it didn't exist, was pushed under the wrong door, or Imura managed to destroy it before he was attacked.'

'No ashes or waste paper found in the room,' Beaumont reminded them.

'Or this could be one other object the killer took away with him,' Yeadings suggested. 'And why would he do that?'

'What language was it in?' Beaumont asked.

'If it was written with an ordinary pen, not a brush, I'd assume she wrote it in English, but I didn't get so far as to ask. We weren't given much time, and Matsukawa was hovering.'

'You'll need to go back when the woman's stronger. Let me have a list of the questions you intend following up with.'

'Yessir.'

'You certainly upset her when you mentioned the Bellhouse,' Beaumont recalled. He regarded her with his perky puppet expression and she knew what was coming. 'My bet is that Imura's murder would have been no news to her.'

Z hesitated before answering. 'We have to accept that possibility.'

The silver wedding bride was a Mrs Patricia Willoughby. She made her statement in a mixed air of gossipy excitement and pretended horror. 'Just fancy, that ghastly murder taking place upstairs while nobody had the faintest suspicion! What a thing to happen on my anniversary! And that girl I saw – she was involved, wasn't she? It was in the same newspaper, her running away from school a second time. Both Japanese. The murdered man, I mean, and the girl I saw in the ladies' room. Well, there has to be a connection. Do you think she did it?'

Z took care of her, sorted her observations from her assumptions and got an orderly presentation on paper. 'If you'll wait while I have it typed, you can sign it and we needn't bother you again,' she offered.

'Oh, I don't mind,' Mrs Willoughby assured her, seeming to find near-fame in a murder case a suitable relief from post-holiday anticlimax.

Yeadings scanned the completed statement after Mrs Willoughby had left. 'Mmm. Nothing new here. No oceans of blood in the handbasin.'

'She would have included that if she'd half a hope I'd accept it.'

'Not really a ghoul,' Yeadings said sadly. 'It's those safely on the outside who have a relish for gory detail. Now, Z, what next?'

'Dr Walling again, I think. If Elizabeth left May on the doorstep – and I believe her over that – why didn't anyone say they'd seen or heard her? We haven't searched the school grounds since that first time. Suppose she's hidden there somewhere, suffering from hypothermia and hunger.'

Yeadings sat sombrely slumped in the revolving chair. He knew she hadn't really meant 'suffering'. Given the time lapse and the grim weather, the more likely word was 'dead'.

'I'll arrange a search for first light tomorrow. We'll just let the girls get away for half-term this afternoon. Then we'll take the place apart. Should have done this before. Meanwhile get to Dr Walling and question the staff.'

There were limousines, Range Rovers and hatchbacks parked in the approach to School House, with a huddle of parents chatting around them. A few girls escorted by adults were issuing from the front door with hand luggage. Glancing up Z saw Dr Walling at her observation window.

She waited in the hall just clear of the scrum by the school office where pupils were being signed out. She guessed that since Mayumi went missing all security precautions were being increased.

The uniformed maid appeared at her elbow. 'Sergeant Zyczynski? Dr Walling would like to see you. Will you follow me please?'

Dr Walling turned from her window to welcome Z. 'I'm afraid you find us in some chaos, Sergeant, but fortunately most of the girls are awaÿ by now. Things will quieten down shortly.'

'You've a huge responsibility ensuring that they all leave with the right person.'

'We use a well-proved system. In these days of common divorce only a parent with legal access can sign for a daughter. We get to know their faces.'

'What happens if illness or some other crisis prevents them coming?'

'They inform me in writing and name a substitute. Then I'm afraid we ask for identification when that person arrives.'

'I see.'

'I'm trying not to be intrusive, Sergeant, but I must ask if there is any news of Mayumi.' There was no mistaking her anxiety.

'Only a small detail. Mrs Matsukawa was well enough this morning for me to question her. She told me that she returned Mayumi here before nine on the Sunday night, dropping her at the front door and then driving off.'

'Here? Or at Cavell House?'

'Here, at the main building. She left when she saw May ring the bell.'

Dr Walling was almost speechless. 'I don't understand. I wasn't available myself, but there were staff on duty. They weren't expecting her because she would normally have reported back to her own housemistress. But the bell must have been heard. It isn't out of order.'

'Perhaps I could speak to whoever was on duty then?'

But there was little to be learned from the sports instructor who acted as janitor over the maid's free weekend. She hadn't heard the doorbell herself, being at the rear of the building, but one of the younger girls told her it had rung. When she unlocked and opened up there was no one there.

She hadn't doubted the child, but assumed the village boys were having a bit of fun again. They'd been a nuisance the previous summer, ringing and running off. In November they'd even set off two thunder flashes under the Head's window just before midnight, and everyone in the building had been shocked awake.

'Did you go outside and look around?'

'Just to the end of the terrace, but there was no one there. No car or bicycles as far down the drive as I could see.'

'No sound of a car or voices?'

'Nothing.'

So there had been a considerable delay if she'd missed hearing Elizabeth drive off. 'Were there marks in the snow where someone had arrived and then walked away?'

The woman thought a moment. 'Nothing distinct. There was barely any snow at all then. It was more as if they'd tramped around a bit.'

'More than one person?'

'I couldn't say, I'm afraid. But there was no trail worth following.'

'And anyway you'd assumed it was boys larking about?'

'I wasn't expecting one of the girls to be returning. There had been no note left for me to let anyone in.'

'And, of course, May had misunderstood that she should report direct to Cavell House.'

'Apparently. It was the first time she'd been granted an exeat for an evening.'

'So if eventually she'd realized she wasn't expected here, she might have walked down to Cavell House?'

'I expect so. It wouldn't have been totally dark. There are globe lights all along the shrubbery path.'

The shrubbery. Yes, an ideal place for someone to lurk and jump out on an unsuspecting passer-by. 'Would you walk me that way now? I'll need another word with Miss Goss.'

At Cavell House, departures were more advanced. Only two cars remained in the courtyard, and while Z waited for Miss Goss to come free, the last girls came out with their mothers. This left only one still sitting in the guard room, her suitcase on the floor beside her. It was Julia and she looked thoroughly disgruntled.

'Everyone's gone but me,' she complained when she recognized the policewoman. 'I've got to wait for Ma to finish in court, because Pa's gone to sit with Grandad.'

'Is he ill? I'm sorry. I didn't know.'

'He's had a stroke, and they've sent him to hospital.'

'You must be worried.'

She looked less worried than annoyed. 'Even Maddie got away on time,' she grumbled. 'Her brother's taxi was the first to turn up. Lucky thing! She's gone to stay with him in London.'

'Really?' Z wondered if Greg would turn out his boy-friend to make room for her at the flat. Surely she'd not be lodged on the couch at the Rathbone Place studio? 'Why isn't she going home?'

'I suppose Stephanie's too busy, or away. Greg offered to come instead, and Stephanie gave him a note for Miss Goss.'

'I see. Does that mean it's the first time Greg's been to visit Maddie?'

'Yes. If I had a smashing brother like that I'd make sure he took me out every weekend. I know *I* wouldn't have looked so miserable.'

'Miserable – Maddie?'

'Sick as a pig. With a chance like that!'

Z smiled at the admiration in the girl's voice. Greg had

obviously gone over big with her. Julia even managed a look of dewy femininity. She wasn't to know it would have been wasted on him.

'I could see he was Maddie's brother the second he came in,' Julia said proudly. 'There's a look of her about him.'

Well, love's blind, Z thought. And Julia's hardly got a reputation for shrewdness.

Sixteen

Whoever had welcomed the computer age as a means of saving trees should be pulped himself, Yeadings decided, involved in the intricacies of fanfold stationery. In the days when it arrived flat, information had been easier to handle. Now, because he'd told the office staff not to bother tearing off the edges, they hadn't separated the sheets either.

After an hour spent coping with paperwork equivalent to a fifty-year old oak, he'd extracted only a few new facts. One item covered details of the two phone calls made by Elizabeth Matsukawa from the Crown Hotel at Amersham on the evening of her crash: the first was to a Jed Barrow at her home village in Wiltshire; the second to an ex-directory number in Wrexham which proved to be the home of Mr Ichikawa.

And Jed Barrow, it ensued, had once been the village Plod, later transferred to Salisbury and promoted to sergeant. Maybe he kept an eye on the house when Elizabeth was away. Yeadings looked forward to a one-to-one chat with the man as soon as his phoned request caught up with him.

As for Ichikawa, he was ignoring all faxes and e-mail to the Frankfurt convention. How long did these junketings go on? There couldn't be all that much to discuss about the marketing of toys.

It still wasn't known why Mrs Matsukawa had been in such a hurry to reach Wrexham. (A repeat of that question was on Z's list for her visit tomorrow.) Her connection with Ichikawa could be quite innocent, but Yeadings felt it must be significant, whether purely personal or concerning some business deal.

Had she intended consulting the man over her strained relations with her husband? Or was she flying to him for protection, out of her mind after killing the hated Imura? Could he even be her lover? Perhaps she thought he would provide her with an alibi. If so, she must have assumed Ichikawa would be equally glad that the man was dead.

But when push came to shove, could one really believe she had slit a man's throat the way Imura's had been? That hadn't been tentative or the result of sudden overwhelming rage. It was cold-blooded, demanding considerable skill. What did anyone know about Mrs M's physical training? Had she ever followed a course in self-defence – which included the use of weapons?

His ponderings were interrupted by a WPC who produced a new single sheet from the printer. A detail from Traffic, not normally Yeadings' line of country, but it did show that the trawl for Matsukawa items was being thoroughly carried out.

He read it with a dry smile, recalling the man's refusal of a lift back to Oxford. Instead he had ordered his own car to collect him and had his chauffeur flown down.

He might be regretting that now, because in a tail-back on the M40 an articulated lorry had run into the rear of his Daimler. In the ensuing argy-bargy between the two drivers a motorway patrolman had almost to tear the chauffeur and the other man apart. As normal routine both had been required to take a breath test. Both had consumed just over the limit of alcohol and both had been detained.

Yeadings wondered whether the Japanese had continued his journey by taxi or patrol car. He wouldn't have the highest opinion of road conditions in the UK, with two incidents in the family within a matter of days.

He was lucky that an over-zealous PC hadn't charged him with aiding and abetting a drunk driver.

Perhaps as a precaution the truck driver should be vetted for a connection with the man. If Matsukawa had been sitting in the rear as expected, instead of up front with the chauffeur, he could have been seriously injured.

Julia had lost precious hours of her half-term break, and she intended her mother should know how annoyed she was. But on arrival at school Mrs Olney-Pritchard's mouth was set in courtroom-battle grimness. It warned the girl to sit back silently in her corner of the car and watch oncoming headlights stabbing at them through the dark.

'You haven't asked after your grandfather,' her mother accused when they had been half an hour on the road.

'How is he?'

'Not good. But stable, they say. Daddy's staying over with him tonight.'

'What good will that do?'

'All the time that Grandfather's unconscious, he'll keep talking to him, playing music tapes. Anything to get his mind back on track. Maybe tomorrow you can relieve him for a while.'

'What, go to the hospital?'

'Well, I can't. I'm in the middle of a hearing. And we don't want Daddy crocking up as well. He's got enough on his plate at present.'

Julia had the sense not to utter aloud what she felt: that this was going to be one bloody awful half-term. But at least she'd have Granny to herself. They'd plan some trips out together, hiring old Barling's taxi, go to a theatre and have some really decent meals.

'I'll look after Gran,' she offered.

'You'll need to. I'm quite worried about her. It's been a shock, having your grandfather whipped away like that. I don't really like leaving her on her own. They haven't spent

182

a day apart for the last fifteen years or so. She's sedated for the moment, but tomorrow—' She was frowning at the road ahead.

'Tomorrow what?'

'We'll see.'

It didn't sound promising.

Apart from security lights the house was in darkness when they arrived. Her mother heated some canned soup for Julia and left her to make the toast while she rang through for a progress report on her father-in-law.

'No change,' she said as she came back. 'I'd hoped for better news by now. You can start on your supper. I'm going across to the bungalow to make sure Granny's still asleep.'

Julia took a tray into the lounge and turned on the television. She caught the end of the 9 p.m. news, with a repeat of the headlines. Two boys of nine and eleven were being held in connection with yesterday's train derailment in which a fifth person had now died; the Queen and Prince Philip were attending a reception at the American embassy after the first night of the Bosnian war film; the richest haul to date of drugs, including crack and amphetamines, had been made in a combined raid by Customs and the police in Chelsea; in Buckinghamshire the Thames Valley police had been dragging parts of the River Colne for the body of the missing Japanese schoolgirl.

Julia almost choked as toast lodged in her throat. She hadn't imagined anything so shitty could happen. May *dead?* Not just gone absent, but *murdered*; and her body dumped in a river? The police must have some reason to suspect that. But surely they were wrong. She couldn't believe it could happen to someone she actually knew.

She felt too shaken to mention it when her mother came back fussing. Granny was still knocked out by the pills the doctor had left; for herself she'd got another long day tomorrow in court and was going to bed now.

183

Julia might as well make it an early night too. She'd see her at breakfast.

Yasuhiko Matsukawa had accepted a lift with the police in a mood of cold fury not improved by severe pain in the neck caused in the crash. The rear of the Daimler had been stove in, and he was lucky to have chosen to sit up front with Gryff Lloyd.

The accident was none of the chauffeur's fault, but his failing the breath test was. When police took him away Matsukawa had washed his hands of the man, disgusted at the risks he had unknowingly run if the chauffeur was concealing an alcohol problem.

At the Radcliffe he had an orthopaedic collar fitted in Accident and Emergency before going to check on Elizabeth. Her alarm on seeing it seemed quite out of proportion to the injury, but it didn't displease him. It gave hope that his wife still felt some affection for him, and offered a safe topic when his mind was full of Imura's death and his missing daughter: both subjects to be kept from her at present.

The hospital staff were discreet, and she wasn't ready for newspapers or television. However, tomorrow the police would be questioning her again, and it might not be possible to hold them off. He kissed her forehead as she was settled down for the night, shrugged on his overcoat and went out to pick up a taxi.

The DC tasked to protect him trailed fifty yards behind his cab and kept him in sight until the lift light showed he had reached the Randolph Hotel's second floor. No one had taken any undue interest in the Japanese, but it was the obvious place he'd choose to spend the night, so his guard couldn't stand down.

He contacted the security officer and ensured that the hotel register was beyond the reach of passers-by in the foyer. Then he arranged to sit up overnight in a vacant room two doors from Matsukawa's. Superintendent

Yeadings had stressed that Imura might have been killed in mistake for his chief, so Matsukawa could be the next victim. You didn't cut corners when the Boss laid facts like that on the line.

Rosemary Zyczynski stayed on late at the Incident Room checking through the case analysis. The last entries, identifying the two phone numbers Elizabeth had contacted from Amersham, reminded her that she still needed information on Mayumi's call from Greg Coulter's studio on the night of her first disappearance. She riffled through the paperwork on her desk in the CID room, and a scribbled note of the number was there, phoned in to her personally, so it had not yet been passed to the computer.

The figures struck her as familiar. The code was Wrexham's. She went back to the analysis room and there it was up on the chart: the same number that the girl's mother had phoned from Amersham. When Danny had been eavesdroppping, Mayumi was speaking in Japanese to a woman at Ichikawa's home address.

But perhaps not so much a woman as a girl, one of almost her own age, because Ichikawa was a widower and his fourteen-year-old daughter's Japanese chaperon didn't live in.

Again Z felt the stirrings of a certainty that the clues to Mayumi's disappearance lay in North Wales. Tomorrow she was due to see Elizabeth again in Oxford. She remembered with unease her own last words to her: that she would come again *with May*. Perhaps Elizabeth had been too dopey at the time to remember that promise, but she just might. It seemed better, in that case, to see the Ichikawa girl the first next day, in the hope she might provide some lead to where Mayumi was now.

She reached Wrexham shortly after eleven the next morning. The weather was less severe than the last time Z had taken that route, but the overnight thaw made some parts of the road treacherous with flowing water. Z phoned

Ichikawa's home address and was told by the housekeeper that Eiko was at lessons and could not be seen before 5 p.m.

There was no point in fuming over the delay. Either private tuition took no account of half-term breaks, or else it kept to different dates. In the interim Z decided to drop in on Gareth Quilliam at the nick off Chester Street.

There she received a warm welcome. 'Where's the DI?' she enquired, and thankfully found that Frank Henderson was absent.

'Gone to sort out a spot of family trouble,' the canteen gossip informed her.

'A domestic, or his own family?'

'His sister Gillian. She rang up all of a flap about something: Frankie had to come out there on the dot.'

'Said she was his sister anyway, but you know Frank,' a constable chipped in.

'It was her,' Quilliam said shortly. 'I took the call and I know her voice.' He set a lemon tea in front of Z, boasting, 'See, I remember your preference. So how's the case coming on?'

There was little new to report, not that she would have given much away at this stage. They had been lapping up the media coverage, since the murder had connections with their area.

'Did you ever see the Ichikawa daughter with any of the Matsukawas?' she asked. I've come up this time to have a word with her about Mayumi.'

'You won't get very far. They may make talking dolls at the factory, but this one has the audio works left out.'

'You mean she's deaf and dumb?'

There was a chorus of disagreement. 'No,' Quilliam said. 'She's hog-tied, that's what. Isn't allowed a normal child's freedom at all. Doesn't even go to a local school like some. Has a local tutor and studies at home. Only goes out with her Japanese chaperon.'

'What does she do for exercise?'

'Visits the firm's gym. They're quite hot on their own kind of aerobics or whatever.'

'Would she do martial arts?' Z asked hopefully, and there was a roar of derision.

'If only you knew the little mouse,' Quilliam said. 'I guess the nearest to weight-lifting she's allowed is stuffing cherry blossom into vases. And bowing and scraping over the tea ceremony.'

It wasn't encouraging. After a he-man's helping of hot-pot, Z decided to fill in with a second visit to the Matsukawas' house. Maybe this time she would get a look inside, and with luck a little gossip with Mrs Lloyd on the state of her employers' marriage.

Just before the turning down towards the river she recognized the red face and sandy hair of DI Henderson at the wheel of a Datsun just opposite, waiting to come out. Watching for oncoming traffic, he hadn't noticed her and she sighed with relief. From his heavy scowl she guessed he might have welcomed the opportunity to let off steam.

This time the electronic gates of the house were shut so she pressed the bell and announced herself through the entry-phone. A woman answered, to the effect that her husband was away in Chester and she should come back another day.

Chester? So either she lied or was misinformed. Lloyd covering himself because of the drink-driving charge?

'Mrs Lloyd? It's you I want to see, not your husband. And it has to be now, because I return south tonight.'

Reluctantly the woman agreed, pleading the start of a bout of flu to keep the interview short. But the black, iron gate slid slowly sideways to allow Z to drive in, and closed again after her.

She'd been away when Z called before, a tall, stiffly gaunt woman with deepset eyes the colour of Welsh slate, and carroty, frizzed hair which she wore tied in a bunch. She was no Welshwoman; from her slight accent Z would have guessed she was an expatriate Scot.

187

She wasn't much help. She continued rigidly standing when she'd seen Z to a seat in the elegant glass-walled lounge. She said she hadn't seen a lot of her employer's wife. Elizabeth Matsukawa came along quite often when the house was being decorated, but she hadn't moved in herself at that point. Since then the Matsukawas had been mostly travelling in Europe. As for the daughter, she'd been introduced to her during the girl's summer holiday but beyond that they had barely spoken together. Gryff could say more because he'd driven her about, but he wasn't expected back until late that night.

By which time Z would be on her way home.

Questioned about the Matsukawas' relationship, Mrs Lloyd was uneasy, finally saying that nobody ever knew about a marriage except the two involved, and even then one of them was often in the dark. An odd remark, but evidently all Z was going to get out of her.

As she left the house the sun, sinking behind black trees and throwing dramatic rippled reflections over the river, reminded her of the other time she had come, in snow. The landscape here had moods, and a rare rich beauty that appealed directly to the emotions. There was a vibrancy and a rough splendour that got through the build-up of city values and moved her.

If I lived here, she thought, I'd be a different person, uninhibited, a bit wild. Not a policewoman, that's for sure.

Her next visit was to the girl who might have been Mayumi's friend. Eiko Ichikawa was all they'd said she was. Even forewarned, Z wasn't prepared for the tears that welled in her eyes and rolled down her cheeks when she mentioned Mayumi. Like everyone now, she had heard that her friend was missing. She had no idea where she could have gone or whether anyone might have wished to harm her.

'To harm her family perhaps? Her father, because he's powerful and wealthy?'

188

Eiko kept her eyes lowered and shook her head. Z tried another tack.

'When she rang you a week or so back, what did you talk about?'

'School.' She didn't attempt to deny the call.

'Just that?'

'She – took a holiday. From school. To visit her mother.'

'Is that really all you discussed?' Z was sceptical. It didn't sound urgent enough to make Mayumi ring as soon as she reached the studio.

'Are you sure she didn't give you any message? Did she tell you anything you didn't know before?'

The girl thought a moment. 'Only . . .'

'Yes?'

'That perhaps her father comes soon. From Japan.'

A sigh escaped Z. That had to be it. May's disappearance was planned to cause a panic that would bring Matsukawa back to Britain. For some reason Eiko had to be told. Perhaps so that she would pass the news on.

'Did you tell anyone this?'

'Just Papa.'

'And what did he say?'

Eiko stood silent a moment. 'Nothing. He had to go out to the factory. So I went back to bed.'

When he knew the boss was coming Ichikawa went out: that was significant. 'Do you know when he came back?'

'No.'

'When did you see him next?'

'We had sushi together at one o'clock, like always.'

'This was next day?'

The girl nodded.

'He's away at the moment, isn't he? When do you expect him back?'

And then the flood-gates opened. The child gave a moan of despair and covered her face with both hands. From her chair where she had sat listening, the Welsh

189

governess rushed to gather her into her arms, crooning comfort and at the same time directing savage grimaces at the policewoman.

'Really, I don't know how you can go on so! Harassing the poor child. You should be ashamed. I shall complain to Inspector Henderson. It's not right at all.'

What did I do? Z asked herself as she was hustled out. Why shouldn't I ask when Ichikawa's coming back?

Unless Eiko's afraid he isn't going to.

She drove through hanging mist, the tyres slathering on flooded roads, and the windscreen wipers' swish was a metronome governing the tempo of her thoughts. She saw again DI Henderson's red face and ruffled sandy hair as he sat waiting for the traffic to clear. Then she was recapping on her visit to Mrs Lloyd; the woman's defensive, taut face; her reluctance to give information; the bunched frizz of carroty hair. Gryff Lloyd being away to Chester this time instead of his wife as on the previous occasion. She remembered him telling her then that she'd gone to buy a hat to wear at someone's wedding. What had he called her? Gillian?

No, that was the name she'd heard a PC in the canteen using, for DI Henderson's sister. Then, snap! She'd connected. Henderson had been absent, answering an urgent call from his sister. And he'd been coming back from the direction Z was bound for. She had avoided running into him by a matter of minutes.

It wasn't a great leap of logic to assume what would be obvious to anyone with local knowledge. Gryff Lloyd had married Henderson's sister.

And other things were fitting together now: Mayumi phoning Eiko with a message that her father was on his way from Japan; Ichikawa then leaving to make certain preparations. And next day Elizabeth phoning him, perhaps to explain that it was Imura who'd come instead, so there must be a change of plan?

So what was that plan? One in which there was possibly

some collusion between Elizabeth and her daughter. And it seemed that, even warning Ichikawa, Elizabeth hadn't been in time to countermand any previous orders.

More and more it looked as if one of Yeadings' surmises might be correct, that Elizabeth had put out a contract on her husband's life. Imura had just been unlucky: the wrong man, but in the right place at the right time. Murdered by mistake for his boss.

Which meant that Matsukawa was still in the killer's sights.

Seventeen

Near Shrewsbury Z pulled in at a service station and filled the tank. Last time she returned this way she had called on the Olney-Pritchards. As she passed the entrance with its board advertising the garden centre, Z saw that the heavy rain had almost cleared the grounds of snow. Some celebration must be on, because it looked as if every light in the big house and the grandparents' bungalow was on full power. Of course, they would have Julia home now for a week. No doubt the girl was revelling in the fuss her family would make of her.

'Julia! Julia, she's gone!'

Her mother stormed in, a plastic raincoat over her head streaming water on to the Chinese rugs. 'You'll have to help me look for her.'

'Who?' Julia sat open-mouthed. The last she'd seen of her mother she was bound for bed. Now it seemed she'd been outdoors again.

'*Gran*, of course. I told you how worried I was about her.'

'You said she was asleep. She'd taken some pills.'

'That was half an hour ago. I got upstairs and I remembered her mail was still here on the hall table, so I slipped down so she'd have it for the morning. There isn't time when I'm rushing off to court.'

'But how can she be missing?'

'She isn't anywhere in the bungalow. Oh, don't waste

192

time asking questions. Help me find her. She must be somewhere in this house. I left our back door unlocked. Maybe she came in that way. I could have missed her in the dark.'

Julia stood up, still confused.

'Oh, come on, girl! Don't just stand there. Take the top floor and work down. I'll try the cellar and work up towards you. If we don't find her—'

'What then?'

'Well, she must be wandering about outside. And it's absolutely *pelting*! She could catch her death.'

They had searched the whole house, and there was no trace of the old lady. 'Maybe,' Julia suggested, 'she got up and went off to see Poppa in hospital.'

'How could she get there?' her mother snapped. 'The last bus has gone and Gran doesn't drive. Anyway she's not in my car. I looked. Another thing—'

'What?'

'She never dressed. Just pushed the bedclothes back and put on her slippers. She must be running about in the dark and the rain in her nightie.'

'She wouldn't do that!'

'You don't know. Since they took your grandfather away in the ambulance she's gone quite dotty. Not that she was ever one hundred per cent before.'

Julia stared at her mother. 'That's not true. You never liked Gran. You've upset her and she's run away.'

'Sane people don't run away. Come on, get your raincoat and wellies on; we've a lot of ground to cover.'

They tried the hothouses first but they were still locked. Shouting for the old lady they swept their torches round the shrubberies, stumbled over the ridged soil of the trial areas, and searched every foot of the driveway right down to the road.

'Maybe some driver will catch her in the headlights,' Julia said hopefully, scraping mud off her boots with a piece of broken branch.

'More likely run her down. She could cause an accident. I'll have to alert the police.'

'This happened at school. There were police all over the place looking for Mayumi when she ran away. *She wasn't mad.*'

'What has that to do with anything? Don't be such a fool, Julia. Your grandmother is an old woman, and she has delusions.'

Disconsolately they trudged back towards the house. 'Listen,' Julia said. 'I can hear a cat. It's round by the rubbish bins. Come on, it'll be soaked.'

The mewing grew louder as they rounded the protective hedge, and as their torches swept the ground it changed to a shrill keening.

She was there, hunched in a sodden mass, clutching to her breast a newspaper spilling vegetable peelings. Her wispy hair hung in wet, grey streaks over her contorted face and the end of a rotted carrot hung from one corner of her mouth.

Sharp screams punctuated the gibberings as they closed in, anonymous dark shapes against the night sky terrifying her.

'No! No, don't beat me! Where is he? What have you done with him? No, no! Cut him down!'

'Gran!' Julia called and ran to take her in her arms but the old woman's nails reached out and scored her face. Her boots slipping on the wet flagstones, the girl fell forward into the mass of stenchy rubbish spread about the bins.

Much later, after the ambulance had left, Julia was still shaking, unable to get warm. Her father had been recalled to comfort her. Now she was the one everybody was concerned for, but it was no consolation. She knew now: Gran *was* mad; and for the same reason that Poppa was so silent and had those old scars on his wrists and back.

It all went back to the war, getting caught by the Japs in

194

Malaya, their being torn apart and held in prison camps, starved and tortured. By the Japanese.

'It's something we've tried to forget,' her father said. 'But it's not always possible for the people who went through it. Sometimes – very rarely, though – when Gran's upset or unwell it comes back on her. She fears she'll be herded up and sent away, and there'll be nothing to eat. So she tries to find any food there is, whatever it's like, to hoard.'

'Scavenging in dustbins. That's horrible!'

'We hoped you wouldn't ever know. It isn't your generation's problem. We need to be forward-looking. When there were those VJ celebrations for fifty years of peace in the Pacific we put the last of it behind us.'

Julia glared at him. It wasn't behind. She knew now. She hadn't considered it before, except as dead history. But now it was different. She really knew because she'd seen what it had done. To Gran and Poppa, who were sweet and had never hurt anyone.

Hateful Japanese! And Mayumi was one of them. Hateful Mayumi, because she was callous too; she'd come between her and Maddie; she'd taken her best friend away.

Julia balled her fists, pacing up and down the length of her bedroom, all thought of sleep impossible. She had to fight back. Because of Gran and Poppa.

Since Mayumi was one of those monsters who'd done all those unspeakable things, why should she keep shut about what that beastly girl had been up to? She owed her nothing. Tomorrow, as soon as it was light, she'd ring the police and talk to that woman detective. It was time they knew the truth about Mayumi.

By the time she reached Oxford it would be too late to disturb Elizabeth, but Z called in at the Radcliffe for a report on her progress. In the corridor she ran into Matsukawa hurrying from his wife's room. He looked frantic, his normally pale face blotched with red, his hedgehog hair on end and half the collar of his black, executive overcoat tucked under as if he had dragged it on without noticing.

'Sergeant,' he called, almost running towards her. 'I was just going to phone. It has come. From the kidnapper.'

She made him sit down and asked a nursing auxiliary to get them both tea. 'Now, tell me what happened,' she said quietly. 'Was it a phone call?'

'No. A note.'

'Have you brought it with you?'

It had only just arrived, among a bundle of mail brought by messenger from the Wrexham office and addressed to him personally there. 'I tried to get the courier back, but he'd left by the time I got to this.'

'Who dispatched the mail?'

'Someone from Robinson's office. But read it.' He thrust a package at her, addressed to him in block capitals. It had gone through the post but the franking on the stamps was too blurred for the office of origin to be distinguishable. From the opened jiffy bag poked the end of a white envelope.

'I don't want to finger it,' Z cautioned. 'Have you shown it to anyone else?'

He hadn't. But, as he had read and re-read it, his prints must be all over the paper. Carefully Z drew the envelope out by its edges, and ignoring the unsealed flap, slit one of its sides with a nail file and used it to extricate and open the single page of writing.

It was a handwritten letter signed 'Mayumi'. There was nothing hurried about the evenly spaced, tidy writing. Which made it unlikely she'd written it under duress.

And it was an elegant but abject apology from the girl to her father for any distress she had caused by her foolish behaviour.

Z kept her eyes down, refusing to meet the despairing man's. 'This is the letter we told you of, which she wrote

196

you from your wife's hotel, and later pushed under the door of Mr Imura's room.'

Z thought back. Mayumi had done that because the DO NOT DISTURB notice was already hanging from the doorknob. And the letter hadn't been found by the scenes-of-crime officers during their search. Which meant that someone else had found it first and removed it. And that person must be the killer.

Mayumi, receiving no answer to her knock, assumed that Imura had retired for the night, so surely she'd heard no sounds of a struggle from inside the room. If Imura was already dead, the killer could have been in there, just the other side of the panels, listening, waiting until the coast was clear for his escape.

'You said you'd heard from the kidnapper. There's nothing here that says whoever sent this is holding your daughter, Mr Matsukawa.'

'It came from Imura's killer. It had to. There is also this.' He had picked off the floor a small scrap of paper which had fallen out when the envelope was withdrawn. Z read the five words stuck on in printed letters cut from some newspaper. 'Your daughter first. You next.'

A bald threat. No ransom demand to give any hope that the girl was still alive. Clever devil, Z thought. Maximum fear from minimum information. If there was to be any let-out it could come in a later note or phone call. There was a certain refinement of torment in it.

'I must get this to our scientific department at once, Mr Matsukawa. Superintendent Yeadings will want to see you tomorrow himself.'

The team met early and they heard Z through in silence. Mott had come over from Slough to join them, having seen his rape case through the committal stage on the previous day.

'So now we can at least proceed on the basis that Matsukawa was definitely the intended victim,' he said with

197

relief. 'The threat note makes that certain. First the girl, then there'll be another attempt on the man himself. So, if it is the killer who's holding the girl, how did he get to her?' he demanded.

'He could have heard her knock on Imura's door, might have peered out as she walked away, pocketed the letter on the off-chance of some profit, then followed her out to the car park. Elizabeth said she was gone about twenty minutes, which is why she left the car and went in to look for her. But we know Mayumi was rinsing her face in the ladies' room, maybe waiting there until she felt able to face her mother and the idea of school again.'

'So there was time for the killer to go down, maybe mingle with the silver-wedding guests, and follow either the girl or her mother back to their car.'

'And his own must have been left in the same car park. When they drove out he seized his chance and went after them as far as the school. But why? Did he even know who she was when he first sighted her?'

'He could have guessed. If he was sent to kill Matsukawa, and this young Japanese-looking girl came to the man's room, he'd know there was a connection, perhaps a relationship. He may even have known the man was to come from Japan because of the missing Matsukawa daughter.'

'Yes, we'll accept he could have known who she was. So he follows her mother's car to the school. Then what?'

Z frowned. Normally, if he'd driven in after them, Elizabeth would have seen his car as she drove out again. Except for one thing. 'There's a track off the drive near its top, a loop with an oval clump of evergreens in it. He could have parked up there, but that would mean he knew the school drive - had been there in daylight.'

'I like that,' Yeadings said almost dreamily. 'It brings us a connection between the school and the killing. Are we looking for one of the staff now? Or a parent of one of the girls?' It wasn't clear to the others whether he was being serious or sarcastic.

'It moves Mayumi's mother out of the frame,' Mott considered, 'if she's in the car being tailed.'

'Unless,' Beaumont said, 'she's in cahoots with the killer, had put out the contract on her husband and they had to get together to see what kind of mess it had got them into.'

'Right,' Yeadings invited, 'let's have scenarios from you all on that.'

'Neither of them could be best pleased that the wrong man had got himself killed,' Beaumont offered promptly. 'If Elizabeth then refused payment because he'd not killed the right victim, the hit man could have retaliated by snatching the girl. He'd have a hold over the mother then and every chance of a high ransom from the father once he'd finished pretending he'd done the girl in.'

'It needn't be pretence,' Z murmured.

'True, and he's still got Elizabeth's contract to top her husband. All considered, he could end a rich man.'

'Not if we nick him,' Yeadings said grimly. 'Angus, you come fresh to this. How does that smell to you?'

Mott grunted, running a hand through his blond hair. 'We've a time discrepancy. Elizabeth and the killer would have quite a bit to discuss, and Mayumi wouldn't have waited that long at the front door after she'd rung. Then the girl couldn't be snatched while Elizabeth was still there. It's hardly likely she'd permit her daughter to go off in the company of a hired assassin. I think she told the truth: that she dropped the girl and drove off immediately.

'I'd rather believe that even if she'd ordered the killing, Elizabeth didn't know the person who was to carry it out. There's more safety in that for both of them. Z has offered us Ichikawa as the middle man, and I'd go for that. Probably not Matsukawa's favourite person anyway, because at Wrexham he's been quick to clear him from the scene.'

'Ah, further to that,' Yeadings recalled, 'I've been in touch with a UK rep of the toy trade who's in Frankfurt at the conference. He can vouch that Ichikawa is alive and present there. He's met the man twice before. So we don't have to suspect the worst in his case. The total body count we have to date is still one knife-killing and one missing schoolgirl.'

And a young accountant who got shipped back to Japan in a hurry, Z remembered, but she kept that to herself because it was old news and probably irrelevant.

'Let's take another look at Ichikawa all the same,' Yeadings suggested. 'Z, you're saying that he could have been the middle man, passing the instructions to the killer, but not doing the job himself?' he recapped.

She nodded. 'After Mayumi phoned his daughter, he left the house as soon as she told him that Matsukawa was expected across from Japan. That was after ten on the Friday night that Mayumi skipped school. But he was at home next day for sushi at 1 p.m. On the Sunday of the murder he took his daughter to see Caernarfon castle. They were there all afternoon and evening.'

'A pretty public alibi. All right, so he didn't do the carve up himself.'

'In any case he wouldn't have confused Imura with Matsukawa.'

'When exactly did Mrs Matsu ring Ichikawa?'

'On Sunday afternoon from her hotel. This was after Imura had returned Mayumi to the school, and several hours before he was murdered. And we know she got through, but not who it was she spoke to. If Ichikawa was out, she would have left some kind of message on his answerphone.'

'In short she could have been trying to call the hit off, and the chain of command broke down.'

Yeadings sighed. 'Let's look at the innocents' defence. First for Mayumi: there's nothing to prove she expected her information to be acted on. She may simply have been confiding to her friend that she was trying to bring her parents together. Then when Eiko passed this to her father he remembered something at work that needed attention in case his chief should come to Wrexham. Then later, if Mrs Matsukawa got in touch with Ichikawa, it could be as a friend, purely to bring him up to date on family events. Any other implication remains hypothetical.'

'Which takes us full circle,' Mott gave as his opinion. 'We've accumulated quite a bit of information and a helluva lot more speculation, but as the Boss said, it all boils down to two facts. A murdered man and a missing schoolgirl. If we've any theories about who was responsible for either or both, we haven't a shred of evidence to back it up. Let's hope something solid comes from the lab's examination of the note Matsukawa received today.'

A WPC had been hovering outside Yeadings' office, and as their meeting broke up she signalled to Z. 'There have been two phone calls for you. I didn't like to interrupt the Superintendent.' She read from a message sheet. 'A Julia Olney-Pritchard. Isn't she one of the girls at that school the Japanese girl's missing from?'

'She is. Was she phoning from Shrewsbury?'

'She didn't say. But that's her number. Wouldn't trust me with a message, sounded very hush-hush. It had to be you. Maybe she has a schoolgirl crush.'

'Anything but, I think! Right; I'll ring her back.'

Twice, Z reflected, dialling the figures she'd been given: that made it sound urgent. But with Julia you couldn't put your money on anything.

The girl must have been waiting for the phone to ring. She answered it instantly and her voice was tense. 'Sergeant Z? There's something I think you ought to know. About Mayumi. I don't know where she is, but I do know why.'

She waited for an excited reaction, and when Z murmured something to show she was still there, the girl's voice grew waspish.

'She's pregnant, you see.'

Then exultantly, 'She's gone to London to have an abortion.'

Eighteen

Matsukawa had himself rigidly under control. Yeadings faced him across the table at headquarters and tried not to identify with his suffering.

A father himself, of a far more vulnerable daughter, since Sally was a Down's Syndrome child, he could imagine what turmoil the man was in. On top of this, with heavy commercial and financial responsibilities, perhaps sensitive to being regarded by some here as an alien, this man also had a severely injured wife. He had barely left her bedside since he arrived in the UK, and Z believed he was still in love with Elizabeth, however much she wanted her freedom.

'Our investigations have been held up,' Yeadings explained, 'by having to follow two lines of inquiry. Now at least we can assume that the intended victim was not Mr Imura at all, but yourself. You may be certain that all our resources will now be centred on that fact, and I must ask for your full cooperation in following the security lines we are laying down.'

'I understand,' Matsukawa said impatiently, 'but the main consideration is not myself. Right, so you have taken certain steps to ensure that I do not run unnecessary risks, but the first threat is not to me. You have read the note, you see what it says. First, Mayumi.'

Sudden emotion welled up inside him. Matsukawa beat on the desk with his fist. 'Now find my daughter! God knows what devil is holding her, or what he may be capable of doing! Surely you must have some idea where she could be?'

The light came on and she was instantly awake. She felt herself stumbling shoeless across cold flags, towards the bottom of the stairs. Her fingers were stiff as she gripped the railing, pulling herself to the top where the tray would be. Then her raised foot found only empty space and she froze, knowing she must already be there on the last step.

And there was no tray. No food. Nothing to drink.

The dull ache inside came in waves like the sea. Either she was famished or she had eaten too much. She would like to be sick, but nothing came.

And then she realized that she was still asleep. The light hadn't come on at all. It was still total darkness and she hadn't been called to her meal. The floor was hard under her body. She had to sleep on.

The dream was cruel, happening so often, over and over, and she was helpless to change it, although she knew it was just a dream. But the pain inside was real. It was the only thing that went on whether she dreamt the light was on or was off. Pain and a sense of desperation.

I wish, she thought. She didn't know what she wished, but she wanted it so badly, so hard.

In the repetitive dream there were incidents, like islands suddenly visible in fog above a river. A voice asking her over and over, 'Who are you?' 'Dolly,' she'd answer in her dream, because he had told her she was. 'Little Dolly Daydream.' And she'd hear him laughing. Then he asked, every time, 'So who am I?' And she heard her own voice saying, every time, 'I don't know. I've never seen you before.'

Then, 'Where are you, Dolly?'

'I don't know. I've never been here before.'

Again his barking laugh. 'And you will never remember any of this.'

She could hear his voice but she couldn't see his face. She couldn't see anything, not even the tray when it was left there for her. She just knew that it was, and that she had to eat and drink from it. Perhaps she was blind. No one had told her that she was; it was simply that she just couldn't see any more.

'Dolly,' she said aloud, and it sounded somehow familiar. But not quite right. 'Dolly?'

Then the dream started again. The light came on and she was instantly awake. (But how could she know it came on, if she was blind and couldn't see it? Someone had told her, then.)

. . . the light came on and she was instantly awake. Dreamt she was awake, dreamt she felt herself stumbling shoeless across cold flags towards the bottom of the stairs . . .

'I know how you all feel,' the Boss was saying. 'And I don't have to warn you how sympathy can paralyze action. So let's not hang about looking stunned. Let's go for the man behind all this.

'The warning and Mayumi's letter had been sent to Wrexham. Perhaps our killer doesn't know that Matsukawa's spending all his time in Oxford with his wife. That could narrow the field. Then the postmark: the lab is having it enhanced to identify the town of origin. That's something I have reservations about: we all know that enhancement brings out something that's not obviously there, possibly something the technician wishes to see.

'But the county shows up clear enough. The jiffy bag, one of millions on sale throughout the country, was posted here in Bucks. The address, which was written in block capitals with a ballpoint pen, is useless until we have a suspect's copy for comparison. By now there are no clear fingerprints except Matsukawa's own on the contents. The newspaper used to provide the five cut-out words was the *Daily Mail,* which anyone can get hold of.' He nodded to DI Mott who took over.

'Little enough to get our teeth into. Beaumont, I want you to go through the guest lists for both hotels again. Look for any connections with the Matsukawa family or firm; list new staff; sudden departures; anything out of the normal order of things. I'm going to see Dr Walling. Maybe a new face will help her remember something previously overlooked. Z, in view of this phone call from Mayumi's study-mate, I'll leave you to look into the claim she's made.'

'What's that, then?' Beaumont perked up suddenly, aware that some detail had escaped him.

'Just a touch of venom from the girl Julia, about Mayumi. Far-fetched, but it has to be followed up. Z can deal with it.'

Beaumont shrugged. Mott's words had a throwaway sound to them. Women's work, he assumed. Just the same, he noted that when they were dismissed, the Boss called Zyczynski back.

'Sir?' She tried to hide her impatience, eager to get this unexpected intrusion from Julia cleared from the inquiry.

'Who will you contact?'

'Maddie Coulter. If Julia knew anything about Mayumi, Maddie would know more.'

'Right. Get to it. Phone in what you find. And don't let Mayumi's father get wind of your inquiries. It could be a complete fantasy.'

Z looked up the Coulter address in her notes and phoned through, getting Maddie's stepmother on the line. 'Maddie?' Stephanie said. 'She's not here. She's spending a few days in London with her brother; back Tuesday. Try the studio, but you'll probably find they've gone off somewhere.'

The second call produced the studio receptionist. Mr Coulter was in the middle of a fashion session. It was impossible to disturb him. Zyczynski fumed, considered getting the Met to send someone round there, then decided the mere threat might produce the required result. She was promised that Mr Coulter would ring back at the first break in the takes. Z offered her number.

'Mr Coulter's *sister*?' The receptionist seemed surprised.

No, there was nobody there like that. Maddie had visited once during a session, but that was a year or two back. She'd not been very interested in camera work and complained about standing around with nothing to do.

Z thanked the girl and rang off.

So if Maddie wasn't with Greg, where was she? He'd certainly picked her up from the school. Julia had mentioned seeing him there.

What else had she said? Something that had seemed a bit odd at the time, but Z hadn't questioned it then.

She closed her eyes to think back. The girl's voice sounded in her head, treacly with admiration. It was the first time she'd seen Greg Coulter, but she'd have known him as Maddie's brother anywhere.

But why? They weren't alike. Zyczynski herself had been caught out by their dissimilarity, discounting the tall blond Viking because Maddie was dark, compact and elfin. Even Julia, notorious for missing the mark, couldn't seriously think they looked alike.

So maybe Julia had made the same blunder, mistaking Greg's boyfriend Danny for him. Could it have been Danny who came to the school claiming to be Greg? And using a taxi.

Dr Walling had explained that for security reasons unfamiliar people collecting the girls had to show an ID. Danny had admitted calmly borrowing Greg's car earlier on. What was to prevent him taking his friend's driving licence this time for ID?

She rang the studio a second time and asked for Danny. He wasn't there. She riffled through her papers for the phone number of the flat he shared with Coulter. There was no answer when she rang it, not even a machine.

Too many people were going missing in this case, but she was sure now that it was vital to track the man down. His name had been coming up too often. For an accepted homosexual, he was getting surprisingly involved with schoolgirls.

She recalled the dark-eyed, mischievous face, his quirky charm. She'd found him attractive herself. How much more so he'd seem to inexperienced girls.

The Boss had asked her to come back to him on this, so she followed him into the Incident Room where he was discussing allocations with the office manager. He looked up quickly. 'Z, what news?'

She had barely finished explaining the impasse when a call was put through. Greg Coulter sounded impatient. 'I hear you wanted to speak to me.'

'Mr Coulter, I'm sorry to interrupt your session, but I need to contact Maddie and thought she might be with you.'

'Maddie? Good God, no. Why should she be? It's half-term, isn't it? She'll be at home. Have you got their number?'

'I have, thanks. I've obviously been misinformed. I assumed from what Mrs Coulter said that you were picking her up from school.'

'Stephanie thought that? She'd know better than to ask me! No, that's her chore, however much she'd like to wriggle out of it.' He sounded bored and dismissive.

'One other thing, Mr Coulter. I'd like to have a word with Danny.'

'Can't help you. He's gone off for a couple of days; didn't leave a number. You could try here, or the flat, late on Tuesday.'

'Thank you, goodbye.'

Tuesday again. Stephanie had thought Maddie was with her brother until then. Danny and Maddie had to be together. What were they up to? Some kind of private mischief that relied on Greg's not being in contact with his stepmother. They wouldn't have reckoned on an outsider checking the two stories against each other. It could be Maddie who'd told Stephanie that her brother would pick her up from school.

Yeadings was waiting tense-faced for Z's comments. He

would have gathered enough from her side of the conversation to know where things stood.

'How serious is this?' he asked.

'I'd like to think it's irrelevant to the case.'

'This Danny had a connection with Mayumi, who later disappeared. Now it seems he and Maddie have gone off somewhere together.'

'But he's left a clear trail behind him. Although he used a taxi this time at the school, someone there – like Miss Goss – would be able to identify Danny from a photograph. He can't be risking an abduction.'

'Unless he's a nutter.'

Z didn't reply.

'Well, is he?'

That wasn't fair: she was no trained psychologist. 'I wouldn't have thought so. A bit of a sexual pirate probably, and seeing Maddie as ripe for adventure.'

'Which isn't enough to justify our chasing them up. On the other hand, if there's something more sinister going on . . . Could they be involved together in hiding Mayumi? The warning to Matsukawa was posted from down here. Either of them could have done that.'

'At school Maddie wouldn't have had an opportunity. And why should Danny drive out from London to post it here?'

Yeadings hummed with pursed lips. Finally he said, 'The three of them could be in collusion. It wouldn't be the first time an apparent victim had arranged a false abduction to raise cash. Leave it with me. You'd better stick with checking the story that Mayumi is pregnant. It is an alternative we have to cover. Since Maddie's not available, have another chat with Mayumi's friend at Wrexham, the Ichikawa girl while Mott tackles the school.'

'Right, sir.'

So it was back to Wrexham; again distanced from the murder inquiry. Beaumont would be stealing a march on her with the main case while she was diverted to tittle-tattle.

*   *   *

Back at the Radcliffe Matsukawa found that Lloyd had delivered the replacement Daimler. There was no time to find an alternative driver; he would deal with the man's excess alcohol charge later. He had enough to concern him with the delivery of another small padded bag redirected by special messenger from Wrexham. It too had a smudged date stamp showing only the county of Bucks. But inside was something that gave him both hope and a terrible new fear. With trembling hands he placed the tape in the car's cassette player.

The deep, distorted voice which came through demanded half a million pounds in ransom with a time limit of twenty-four hours. Where could he raise that much in used notes of small denomination, even given three times that notice? There was also the expected warning that informing the police would mean instant death for his daughter. Matsukawa felt crushed between two impossibilities at a moment when his mind refused to function with calm logic.

'I cannot risk it,' he said aloud.

'Sir?' Lloyd still stood by the car door, watching him with a worried frown, flat cap held tight under his uniformed arm.

'That is all. You may go.'

The man started away then turned back. 'Is it a ransom demand? Shall I get the police?'

'No, that's the last thing I want.' Matsukawa hesitated, glared, then admitted, 'It is about ransom, yes. But you must say nothing to anyone, you understand? I have to consider her safety . . .'

'Is your daughter all right, sir?'

'I have no means of knowing. They will ring back at nine tonight to tell me where to leave the money. I can raise a part, but nothing like the whole sum.'

'You could explain that. They must give you more time. And you should demand to speak to your daughter, to make sure . . .' His voice tailed off at the enormity of the suggestion.

To make sure she was still alive. Yes, the man was right. He at least seemed to have his head on straight. A man to rely on when no one else could be trusted.

'I need half a million pounds sterling,' Matsukawa said desperately. 'I can spare that. I will pay anything if only she comes back safe. But I need time. I shall have to borrow, to get cash. If I demand so much cash the police are sure to be informed. No bank will supply that much in old notes without becoming suspicious.'

'You have until nine then, to get as much as you can. Perhaps the kidnapper will take less, to get it settled quickly. It's your only chance.'

'And then I must deliver it to them.' Matsukawa's voice was sombre, as he remembered the Superintendent's words: that without any doubt he had been the intended victim when Imura was murdered. Perhaps the full amount was not so important. What the kidnapper really wanted could be that he should follow instructions and walk, unwary, into an ambush.

That was a risk he must take. And even then, with his own death, could he be sure the killer would keep his word and let Mayumi go?

'We have to make sure,' he said, 'that my daughter is in safe hands before I expose myself. After that, we shall have to see what happens. There is no guarantee of anything.'

'Wait until he rings. See what he wants you to do. Maybe we can set something up. He will be expecting the police to follow you. When he finds you are alone he may relax his guard. I could be hidden in the car, armed, in the boot.'

'I cannot ask this of you. There is too much risk. It could all go tragically wrong.'

'I'm a crack shot. I was in stickier spots than this in the Falklands.'

Matsukawa looked at the chauffeur and saw him in a new light. He stood erect, disciplined, grimly in earnest. It was a lot to ask of him, but at least there would be a

210

witness present; and if things went badly wrong, someone remaining to bring Mayumi back to her mother.

At Wrexham Z eased out of the driving seat, stretched her stiff limbs and surveyed the police parking area. It was so full that she'd been obliged to take the reserved space of a superintendent. Which reinforced her intention to cut her visit to the minimum.

In the CID office DI Henderson was slumped at his desk, his eyes red-rimmed, his tie askew and shirt unbuttoned. 'Miss bloody Zebra-kinky,' he greeted her.

Across the room Gareth Quilliam's hands rested on his keyboard. 'Hullo, Z. What's it this time?'

'The Ichikawas again. Is he back yet from Frankfurt?'

'Expected tomorrow. You're a bit early.'

'It's the daughter I most want a word with.'

'As prime suspect for the Imura murder?' Henderson demanded with heavy sarcasm. 'No, I forgot, it's your colleagues dealing with the *crime passionnel.* You're on the kiddy stuff.'

She knew she should rise above the man's jibes, but that did hit too near the mark for comfort. Not that he seemed to understand fully what the French expression meant. Vicious the killing had been, but not *passionnel.* There'd been no love interest.

'Need me along?' Quilliam asked her.

'Thanks, but I don't want her intimidated by numbers. She's a minor, so either her governess or the Ichikawa housekeeper can sit in. I just dropped by to say I was on your patch again.'

'See you later for a tot then?'

'Miss Zebra-kinky isn't choosy about company,' Henderson assured him harshly, 'so long as you pick up the tab.'

Glad it still rankles, Z told herself, grinning, and left with a wave to Quilliam.

This time she wasn't kept waiting for the end of Eiko's lessons. The girl must have seen her getting out of the car, because she came to the door herself. 'Is there news of Mayumi?'

'Not exactly. More of a rumour.' She was watching Eiko's face and the hopefulness didn't falter.

Z declined the offer of tea, wanting to get the interview over and return to base. But the subject was a delicate one needing careful handling. She began by asking how well the two girls knew each other, whether Mayumi had written from school.

Three times since New Year, Eiko said. The first time when Mayumi had been staying with an English friend in Sussex. It was interesting to read about the strange family.

'Do you think I might see that letter? Perhaps the other ones too?'

'You think you will find a clue?' The girl's almond eyes momentarily went almost round.

'There is just a chance.' But it didn't seem likely that Mayumi would have confided in such a naïve youngster if she'd been in the kind of trouble Julia suggested.

The first letter was by far the most interesting. The sketches of Maddie's parents and their casual departure abroad, abandoning their guests, were written with fresh humour. Among others Maddie's brother and his friend were described in almost clinical detail. There was no trace of special feeling for either of them. They had struck her as quite foreign to her experience of men, but without any consequent glamour. More interest was shown in the house itself, and the surrounding countryside. At the end Mayumi mentioned she had let Maddie's brother take some photographs which were quite clever, but they weren't suitable to keep.

'Is it possible,' Z asked, 'that Mayumi felt specially attracted to this man or his friend?'

Eiko giggled, putting a hand in front of her mouth. 'Oh no. She is not like that. She does not even care for Toru, the man she is to marry. She thought I was a little goose because I . . .'

The child's voice quivered and suddenly she burst into violent sobbing. The governess swept her into her arms and rocked her, glowering at Z over Eiko's hidden face.

'Because you love someone,' Z said sympathetically. At fourteen a girl can so easily imagine herself heart-broken.

'So much,' sobbed Eiko. 'And I shall never see him again.' She was peering round the woman's bulk, eager now to share her distress.

Z shook her head sadly. 'Did your father disapprove?'

'Father? Oh no!'

'Mr Ichikawa arranged the betrothal,' the Welsh governess said reprovingly. 'The two young people were engaged by their families when she was ten.' Her stiffness implied that the doings of foreigners, particularly rich ones who employed her, were odd but not to be questioned.

'And you loved him, Eiko. So what happened?'

'No! No, you cannot ask me! You cannot!'

Of course. Z remembered now the item of gossip learnt from Mrs Benyon. There was a young man suddenly sent back to Japan. Although there was a rumour about his fiddling the accounts, she'd thought it was for being over-familiar with two girls, one of them the local bank manager's daughter, the other Eiko.

'I'm sorry to have upset you,' she said softly. 'Of course I won't ask if it makes you unhappy.'

It took a little while to talk Eiko round to less painful subjects, and pregnancy was certainly not to be one of them. But as soon as she was smiling, however wanly, Z thanked her, said goodbye and left.

If there were two girls in this missing young man's romantic history, the sure source for the Eiko story would have to be her rival. So, if Mrs Benyon could supply her name and address, that was where Z would be heading next.

213

Nineteen

Libby Davies, the bank manager's daughter, was not a child like Eiko. From her appearance and self-confidence, Z guessed she would be twenty or even a little more. She explained she had met Yoshio when her father, interested in Japanese investment, invited him home for a meal.

She was aware of his engagement to the fourteen-year-old Eiko and seemed not to find it unusual. 'Different countries, different customs,' she said airily. 'At least they were genuinely attracted to each other, and Japanese females are expected to make a good marriage, whatever else they miss out on. Of course, a man in those circumstances doesn't have to be a monk while he's waiting, but Yoshio was different; a bit prudish actually, and worshipped the ground Eiko walked on.'

'So there was nothing between the two of you?'

'There was a helluva lot, but we didn't sleep together, for all I gave him the opportunity. No, it was a meeting of minds, I suppose. He was great to go around with, to watch his reactions to us as foreigners. He was quite different from the other Nips here; open-minded. A really nice man.'

'You must have missed him when he was recalled.'

Libby's face darkened. 'What's all this about – these questions? It's over, finished. That bugger Imura! Don't tell me you're after the one who did him in. He should be given a medal.'

She rose from her chair to stalk up and down the room,

frowning, her arms tightly clasped across her chest. 'I saw Yoshio just before they shipped him out. What a mess! He could barely walk, and to hear him breathe – he must have had a punctured lung, but they never let him see a doctor.'

'Are you saying Imura had him beaten up?'

'Did it himself. Crazy boy, he knew the man was a black belt. But he had to go and challenge him. Not that Imura kept to the rules of combat. There wasn't any part of Yoshio's body he didn't damage, except his face. There wasn't a mark on it; it had just gone white as a corpse.'

'You said Yoshio challenged him. But why?'

'A point of honour. He was terribly upset, furious, because Imura had insulted Eiko – been familiar with her in some way, when he was staying with her father. Yoshio didn't tell me the whole story, and he made me swear I'd never let on what I did know, for Eiko's sake. It's part of this *giri* thing they go on about: what's expected and proper. So I stayed shut, until you came asking questions.'

'What about Eiko's father? Did he know what had happened?'

'He must have, because from then on Imura went to stay in the Matsukawas' new house, which they hadn't yet moved into. But Ichikawa couldn't do anything to the man, being lower down the hierarchy. Imura's next to God in that firm, the old lecher.'

'And, the way Ichikawa saw it, he couldn't complain to Mr Matsukawa without shaming Eiko.'

'Exactly.' Libby spun on her heel. 'But you needn't think his only alternative was to await his moment and kill Imura, because I know he didn't. He was away at Caernarfon on the day of the murder. I was there myself that Sunday and I saw him, as late as eight in the evening.'

Today Elizabeth Matsukawa was sitting out beside her bed, surrounded by flowers. There were huge mixed bunches stuffed willy-nilly into urn-like metal vases belonging to the hospital, more tasteful baskets with soaked oasis, and the traditional minimalist display of three perfect stems from Japanese staff members at Wrexham.

Elizabeth, still drowsy from painkillers, smiled at the diversity on offer. It summed up so well her own position; her hotch-potch nationality.

She had persuaded her husband to go for lunch, otherwise he would have prevented the tall fair-haired detective from getting to her. DI Mott, unconcerned whether her missing daughter was, or was not, pregnant, had agreed not to raise the subject with her. His main object now was to discover how closely Elizabeth and Ichikawa were in league over any attempt on Matsukawa's life.

Elizabeth, smiling at the handsome detective, had trouble concentrating on his words. 'When exactly I knew my husband was on his way to England? Well, I assumed it. Dr Walling had reported Mayumi missing. I knew he would be alarmed.'

'But he didn't contact you about what he intended?'

'No. Perhaps he thought I was at Wrexham. There may have been a message waiting for me there.'

'So you warned Mr Ichikawa that he was on his way.'

'Did I? Yes, I think you're right. It's such a muddle.'

'And then, after Mr Imura took your daughter back to school, you rang Mr Ichikawa again, from the hotel at Amersham.'

'Yes. I remember that. I wanted him to warn my housekeeper to change the arrangements. To prepare a room for Mr Imura, instead of for my husband. But he wasn't at home. I left a message on his machine.'

'Did Mr Imura normally stay at your house?'

'He had done so once before. He was given a guest room.'

'Did you discuss anything else? Any other plans for your husband which would need to be changed?'

'No. Should I have?'

She looked so confused, so willing to help but uncertain

216

how she might do so. Damn it, Mott thought, the woman's worth an Oscar, or else she has nothing to do with any skulduggery.

If Ichikawa had set up the hit for Matsukawa, he could have done it without any help. And when she phoned with an innocent request for a guest room to be prepared for her husband's replacement, whoever Ichikawa had hired for the job was out of touch, so the hit couldn't be cancelled.

'I thought,' Elizabeth said uncertainly, 'that that nice lady detective was going to come and see me, bringing my daughter.'

'I'm sorry. She's very busy at present, working on the Wrexham end.'

'Why Wrexham? Mr Imura was killed in Buckinghamshire.'

'We need to fill in some background on him,' Mott said gently. No need to alarm her by suggesting they now saw her husband as the intended victim.

'If you haven't any more questions,' Elizabeth said, stifling a yawn, 'I think I'll have a little snooze.'

As Mott looked back from the doorway, she appeared asleep already.

His phone call caught Z at Wrexham nick. 'What progress?' he demanded.

'In short, Ichikawa had motive, but no opportunity.'

'We never thought he did it himself. Any lead to who he might have used?'

'Not so far. How did you get on with Dr Walling?'

'Frozen out. The very idea, that one of her young ladies had been having a spot of nooky on the sly! But she treated it seriously enough to call Matron in from her holiday and they checked the books. Mayumi had reported all her periods on time and requested the usual sanitary protection.

'It seems your Julia has a reputation for getting things in a twist, but Dr Walling was surprised at the sudden outburst of spite against Mayumi. Up till then she'd shown no open hostility. Jealous, I guess, that the other girl's hogging all the limelight.'

'Maybe.' Z sounded doubtful.

'Look, I want to see Ichikawa myself. You can come back and I'll take over at Wrexham.'

'He's still away; returns tomorrow.'

'Right. That gives me a little more time. You could drop in on Mrs Matsu. She was asking after you. And think up some reason why you haven't brought her daughter along.'

That, Mott thought grimly as he rang off, should put you in your box, girl. Never make rash promises in a missing person case.

At least the drive back would afford a chance to sort things in her mind, Zyczynski decided; but the incidents she'd covered danced elusively apart without forming any conclusive pattern. They were all there, like the tumblers in a complicated lock, but the one key fact was missing which would make the whole mechanism turn. Or else I already have the key, she told herself, and I'm fitting it in wrongly.

Mott's phone call lingered with her: Dr Walling's surprise at Julia's sudden hostility. It was true she'd not shown real malice before. Not the sort that would invent the scandal of a teenage abortion. Well, Julia was at home now, and available. Z could do worse than try to clear up that small point.

It was Julia's father who answered the door to her, a well-built man of fifty, red-faced and beginning to run to fat. 'Look, it's a bad time,' he pleaded. 'My father's just died and everyone's upset.'

'It is important,' Z insisted.

He let her in and went to find Julia.

She came in, sullen and apprehensive. 'Dr Walling's been on the phone. You told her,' she accused.

218

'Wasn't that what you intended? Anyway we had to check up. Don't worry; if you thought it was true, you did right to tell us. Let us do the checking. We often get reports that lead nowhere.'

'It *was* true! I know because I saw the package in their secret box.'

'What package? What secret box?'

'A pregnancy kit. It said so on the label. She'd used it. The result was positive. That wouldn't be wrong, would it? They have this box, see? It's supposed to be magic, to make things disappear. Last term Maddie put in—' She stopped abruptly.

'Go on.'

'You have to swear you won't let on, because Maddie would get into awful trouble.'

'I can't give any promise, if it could help us find Mayumi or solve the murder.'

'No, it's got nothing to do with that. Well, I'll risk it. Maddie's no good at maths, and she must have seen the end-of-term exam papers on Goss's desk after they'd been photocopied. And she sneaked one. So she knew what sort of questions we would get, and did a bit of swotting up. Then Mayumi found it and wanted to hide the paper. She didn't know I saw her bury their box under our window with the paper inside. I dug it up for a lark, because she wanted to believe in the box. And I flushed the bits down the loo, so she'd think the magic had actually worked. Japs are terribly superstitious.'

'Yes, but what has this to do with . . .'

'That was last term. Well, this term I thought I'd dig it up again and see if she'd hidden anything else. And she had. It was this kit stuff, in the chemist's bag she'd bought it in the week before. She'd had a dentist's appointment and two sixth-formers took her. I bet they'd gone into the chemist's to try out a lipstick or something, and they never saw what she was picking up.'

It sounded possible, even if you subtracted the fact that

219

it was Julia telling the story. 'Are you sure the pregnancy result was positive? Because Matron's quite sure her book's right and Mayumi was issued with all the . . .'

'She might have issued them, but she can't prove they were used, can she? Or that Maddie didn't use twice what she actually needed.'

An almost manic brightness shone in the girl's eyes. There was certainly malice at work here.

'Julia, what is it about Mayumi that you hate so?'

'She's Japanese! Isn't that enough? What they did to Poppa, my grandad. And now he's dead! It's inhuman. And Gran. She's gone right round the bend. I found her.' Julia was anguished, fists balled, writhing with the memory of that rainy night.

'She was eating putrid stuff out of the rubbish bins! She thought they'd taken Poppa away to prison camp and she'd be caught again herself. And they'd beat and starve her!'

'As ever, Julia got it wrong,' Z told Mott when they met up. 'But there could be truth in the story all the same. If Mayumi had gone for an abortion she might have called on Danny for transport, as she'd used him once before. But it was *Maddie* he picked up from school at half-term, not Mayumi. So if the kit showed positive for someone, why not her?'

'So Julia gets the storyline right, but the characters wrong.'

'Maddie's the rash one, the one who's sure she knows where she's going. Only, lately she's fallen a bit apart. We thought it was because of Mayumi's disappearance, but there could be a second reason. I think that this Danny's been a whole lot more than a chauffeur to the girls. At Christmas he fancied his boyfriend's little sister. Under-age sex is statutory rape, and anyway neither of them dared let Greg Coulter know the outcome. So while Maddie lay low at school, Mayumi got in touch with Danny, and forced him into setting up an abortion for Maddie at half-term.

'Now we know the reason for May's first disappearance. She was putting pressure on him to get her friend out of trouble. He'd need to act to save himself from a stretch of prison. When she'd got his promise of cooperation, she continued her journey to her mother's home and let it appear she was working to get her parents together again.'

Mott grunted and sat back stunned. 'Devious little baggages. And all this has got mixed up in our murder case. They should both be charged with wasting police time and resources.'

'Write it off, Angus. Poor kids – just imagine. Cooped up in that respectable school for young ladies, trying to handle a dilemma like that on their own. And now that all that is offloaded we should be able to see more clearly what's still relevant to Imura's murder.'

'A failure to murder Matsukawa; and don't forget that the killer's still out there somewhere waiting for a chance to earn his money with the right victim. I'm off to Wrexham to put pressure on Ichikawa the minute he gets back in this country.'

'I wouldn't be so sure.'

'About Ichikawa?'

'About the intended victim being Matsukawa. If Ichikawa had it in for anyone it would have been Imura. Let me tell you about his daughter, Eiko Ichikawa, her fiancé Yoshio, an attempted rape and its violent consequences. Believe me, this is going to set us right back at square one.'

Twenty

Yasuhiko Matsukawa finished his letter, read it slowly through twice and sealed it in an envelope. Then he removed his neckbrace and went to help Elizabeth back into bed. He had to steel himself to sit with her while she pecked at her lunch tray and complained in an exasperated way about Z's failure to pick up their daughter from school and bring her to visit.

'Surely Dr Walling would permit it under the circumstances? It must be getting near half-term anyway.'

'Perhaps that is what she is waiting for. Too long a break would interfere with Mayumi's academic work.'

They were interrupted by a nurse with Elizabeth's medication and a glass of water.

Soon, Matsukawa told himself, she will be asleep. I must contain myself until then.

He scoured his mind to find an acceptable subject to talk about with his wife, but could only think of Mayumi's situation, the uncertain outcome of what he was about to do, and the risks he and Lloyd would be running. He was impatient for action and at the same time almost paralyzed with apprehension. Perhaps it was wrong not to consult with Superintendent Yeadings, but if the detective insisted on sending police back-up, then the kidnapper – already a killer – might be alarmed and . . .

Not Mayumi, not his little flower! Such a beautiful child and in her own way so daunting. She was her mother again, a person apart, open, and with that trusting lack of wariness that can make life precarious. They thought, these Western women, that they could blandly decide what would happen, and were capable of taking care of themselves. So he admired their courage, and suffered for their recklessness.

Tormented and constantly undermined by their contrary independence, yet he had to acknowledge his need to keep this hold they had over him. No woman ever had been for him what Elizabeth was. And he knew that if Mayumi were lost – through his own wrong action now, or inaction – he could never hold on to his wife.

Yet he could not simply do what the kidnapper asked, pay up and let him walk away, because he would always be there to strike again. There would be no safety for any of them, because for some reason he was the man's chosen victim.

He had to take the chance Lloyd offered. Lloyd, the ex-para who had been trained to kill. Despite that one instance of a weakness for alcohol, he was unquestionably loyal because his future lay in Matsukawa's hands.

Elizabeth sighed and he leaned forward to stroke her hair. It clung to her gaunt cheekbones and spread thinly over her pillow. For the first time he caught the glint of silver in it. The thought that they might not grow old together was like a pain.

'I'll sleep now,' she said dreamily.

'I will stay till then.'

It didn't take long. As her breathing settled deeper he touched each of her hands in turn, kissed her forehead and murmured, 'Sleep safe, my life.' And he slid the envelope under her pillow.

My life, he thought, as he walked away. I have said goodbye to it. Lloyd may get the killer, but that devil will take me first: he must put right his mistake in killing poor Imura. It is his *giri*. As it is mine to go and meet him.

He waited in the dark for the phone to ring. Lloyd had

wanted to be there too, but Matsukawa was afraid his presence might somehow be sensed by the man on the other end of the line. Instead, in black sweater, jeans and trainers, the caretaker-chauffeur waited in the hotel garage, a knife slid down inside his right sock, a service revolver weighing solid on his thigh. Already in the Daimler's boot, cushioned on rubber, was his pump-action shotgun and the tape-recorder. He rehearsed in advance all the ways the action could go. He felt taut and capable. It was like it had been with the Argies. This waiting phase was the thing you got high on. It sorted the men from the boys.

Matsukawa had refused to allow an intercept on the hotel's line to his room. He insisted that all police action must be held back until after the kidnapper's final instructions.

The alternative was to intercept at switchboard level, and then secrecy would be impossible. So, instead, the man shadowing Matsukawa had to rely on his own ability to pick up significant movements and report them in. It was possible that the Japanese would comply with the kidnapper's demands without informing the police.

Mott, on his way to Wrexham, wasn't happy about it, but he counted on nothing happening until Ichikawa was back in North Wales and had set himself up a strong alibi. When and how he would contact his hit man was anybody's guess. Yet it might be that the killer had already received his instructions, or had *carte blanche* to choose his own time for setting up the trap.

Rosemary Zyczynski allowed herself time off to go home and snatch some sleep. Of late her work hours had been irregular rather than long, but she admitted to brain fatigue from the sheer frustration of circling the same old data without any sense of achievement. She knew, simply knew, that she had all the information needed to crack the case, and yet . . .

She hung fresh clothes over a chair, stripped off, and crept gratefully under her duvet.

A little short of two hours later she came awake, only half free of her dream, hearing herself murmur '*crime passionnel*'. Surrounded by faces silently mouthing, she saw them fade even as she struggled to identify them.

One, cozily familiar, had been nothing to do with work: Beattie, her landlady, dumpy, plump and defiantly red-headed, fresh from the beauty parlour; but clinging to her arm was little Eiko weeping for her banished fiancé, and behind them a distracted Lady Macbeth figure wringing her hands. She was faintly recognizable as the Matsukawas' housekeeper, her tawny hair loose and tangled on her shoulders. Without hearing any words Z had known she was calling for her brother. He was to drop his work and rush to comfort her.

Which had actually happened, Z remembered, stumbling to the shower. As the streaming water struck her fully conscious the connection came through. Henderson's sister – Gillian – had red hair. That explained Beattie's intrusion. Her redness came from a bottle, but without it she'd be a more faded tawny than Mrs Lloyd.

A devious thing, the subconscious, sorting and filing the junk taken in by the waking senses. And then nudging the data to produce hunches. So what was this enigmatic little memory worth? Was it gem or grit?

Z considered: Gillian Lloyd, upset, needing her brother's shoulder to cry on. Why? What else had been happening at that time? Matsukawa was in the offing himself, replacing the dead Imura; Elizabeth was injured in hospital; Gillian's husband, involved in a minor traffic accident, was being held by Thames Valley police after breathalysing positive.

Yes, that last would worry her. She'd want to know what the police were going to do about it. A criminal record could affect his driving job. Then Matsukawa might think again about keeping the couple on at the house.

Maybe DI Henderson had phoned through to find

how seriously Thames Valley police were taking it. He would possibly be told that Lloyd could get off with a caution.

She'd talked with Mrs Lloyd almost immediately after Henderson's visit, and by then the housekeeper had been slightly *distraite* but nothing more. All of that figured. But how did it affect the crimes under investigation?

And *crime passionnel* – the mixed sex, jealousy and revenge motive? That quote of Henderson's could have some connection with Eiko's fiancé. Yoshio had attacked Imura on a matter of honour, because the man had forced himself on Eiko. The black-belt Imura had made short work of the young man, and had him crated for return to Japan, where he presumably still was. If Imura's killing was really a *crime passionnel,* then it was to avenge the parted lovers. Which pointed to Mr Ichikawa again.

But hadn't the team now decided that Imura's death was a mistake, and the intended victim was his boss?

God, I've gone another full circle, Z groaned. Let me get this straight: Matsukawa has everything going wrong for him, which implies there's an enemy; but to date we've no motive for his murder, unless it's to ensure that Elizabeth inherits. For Imura as victim, there was motive enough, but as his arrival was unannounced, had there been time to plan and carry out his murder? The common prime suspect for both was Ichikawa, with the missing link of a hit man.

'Dammit,' Z said aloud, pulling on a sweater and leggings, 'I can't do this alone.' She left the house and drove to the Incident Room, stopping only to pick something up from a shop on the way. If she had the luck to find Beaumont there, she was confident he'd grasp the message in what she'd bought him.

He was scowling over the analyst's wall charts and humming through tightly closed lips. He barely turned his head to see who had come in behind.

'Prezzie,' she said, handing him a carrier bag.

He looked at the Body Shop logo with suspicion. 'I *smell*, or something?'

'Look and see.'

He took the bag cautiously, mistrusting her grin, and peered in. 'A loofah on a handle. Ah, a back scratcher.'

'I scratch yours,' offered Z, 'and you . . .'

'I should be so lucky!'

'Figuratively speaking.'

'Believe me, it's your figure I was thinking of right then.' He grinned back. 'OK, we trade ideas. Let's go scrounge some coffee in the Boss's shack.'

And there, exchanging theories, with Yeadings listening, they were interrupted by the phone call from Oxford.

'Woodman reporting in,' the Superintendent said tersely over his shoulder. 'Matsukawa's just left the Randolph Hotel, driving himself. Our man's on his tail. They're taking the A44 towards Chipping Norton.'

'Where's the chauffeur?' Beaumont demanded.

'No mention. I think you should both go over and find out. If it's not his normal day off, it could be significant. Matsukawa doesn't normally get behind the wheel.'

They bundled into Beaumont's Toyota and Z set the radio to the Boss's channel. The next call came almost instantly.

'He's bypassed Chipping Norton, taken the A34 towards Shipston on Stour.'

'That's out of our area,' Z told Beaumont. 'It's Warwickshire. The Boss will be notifying the local police.'

'Not if he wants it kept quiet. And we don't know for certain that it's the set-up for the rendezvous.'

'It has to be. Matsukawa was waiting for news, on a short string between his phone and Elizabeth's bedside. He wouldn't get a sudden urge for a scenic drive.'

They were just short of Oxford when the next news came. Woodman had lost the Daimler at traffic lights when an articulated lorry came in between. Then he'd put on speed again on leaving the town. So far there was no sign of Matsukawa's car ahead. He could have turned off earlier on to a minor road.

'We'll have bugged the Daimler in the Randolph garage,' Beaumont said confidently. 'The trouble comes if he has to leave it and pick up another.'

Z checked back to Kidlington control. 'There was a bug,' she was told, 'but for some reason it's not operating.'

'He's an electronics wizard,' Beaumont groaned. 'Betcha that's the first thing he'd look for. But it does prove he's on a special mission.'

'So what do we do?'

'Our nuts. What's your fancy?'

'Give it some wellie to Shipston on Stour, then toss a coin.'

'That's a slim chance, but the only one. Here goes then.'

Matsukawa smiled grimly. In his driving mirror he'd been keeping a close watch on following cars. The first suspect had turned into a petrol station, where a white-haired woman had got out to handle the pump herself. The second had hung on further but he'd lost it in the centre of Shipston on Stour, taking his left turn on to the B4035 in the lee of a bulky transporter. For the next five miles there was no traffic behind until a tractor pulled out of a farmyard and comfortably crawled along in centre-road. If the police had been taking an interest in his movements they were well thrown off the track by now.

His phoned instructions had been to proceed to Chipping Campden and pull into the car park of the Cotswold House, enter the hotel and wait in the lounge for ten minutes. He followed the directions precisely. There was a further minute and a half to wait and then a call came for a Mr Fuji to answer the phone at reception.

His hands trembled as he waited for the detested voice to make its demands. They were simple enough. He should return to his car and play the cassette tape which was now in the Daimler's audio system.

Certain that his every move was being observed from close by, he sat again in the driving seat and pressed the play button.

The same voice, grimly sardonic through its muffled distortion, gave him his final orders. He was now to turn off into a narrow country lane and proceed for five miles to Draycott, park for five minutes, then turn in the direction of Blockley. Once through the village he should leave the car and walk on as far as the next field gate, climb over and make for the clump of trees at the field's far end. In there, when he reached a small pile of stones, he should prostrate himself on the ground with his arms widespread. If he valued his daughter's life he should keep his eyes firmly shut.

'And Mayumi?' he asked the tape. 'Where is she?' But the tape whirred on emptily without speech. He drove his fist painfully into the dashboard.

It all rested with Lloyd now. The ex-para must threaten the man but not kill him outright. Not until he'd confessed where the girl was being kept and the truth of it had been checked.

Matsukawa tasted bile in his throat as he wrapped his coat tighter about him and stepped out into blustering wind. But what did the cold matter? He had only a short while to live. The man hadn't said how many minutes he was to wait this time. He just hoped it would be enough for Lloyd to get out of the carefully modified car boot and creep up on the assassin.

If only he could be sure that Mayumi would be finally released, he could endure anything, even abjectly pleading with this monster. This anonymous enemy. There was no reason he could think of that anyone should hate him so much, but in climbing high one could step unknowingly on others' faces.

That would be happening now to himself, ground into

the earth, his mouth and nose filled with the mud of dank English woodland. That was to be his last sensation, his degradation.

But surely to some purpose? The killer had to show compassion for an innocent child.

'So where now?' Beaumont asked.

Z shook the folded map. 'I'm not familiar with this neck of the woods, but it seems he took a direct route out of our area. If the kidnapper's on the ball he'd have expected that tail we put on earlier, and he'd assume we'd contact the next county as soon as Matsukawa entered it. If I were setting this up I'd halve the risk by making him cross the next border too. So let's go left at Shipston and we'll get into Gloucestershire. It's only a B road but it's deep country, and out here a Daimler could be uncommon enough. Let's hope for news of a sighting.'

She ran a finger down the map. 'Oh no! If he turns back on himself and drives due south, he'll come to Upper and Lower Slaughter. Do you think that's where Matsukawa's being led? What kind of twisted black humour is that?'

Twenty-One

Because Tuesday was his morning for drawing his pension, old Tom Wetherby had afterwards loaded his string bag with an eight of Heineken and, true to long-established custom, stopped half-way home to rip the lid off the first can.

Squatting on the gate to a field of kale, he gulped noisily, lifting his face between mouthfuls to feel the watery sun on his weathered cheeks and reaching feebly into the thin fabric of his jumble-sale jacket.

Idly he considered the flash car parked half a mile back. Belonged, like as not, to one of them hunt lot. Nobuddy round here ran a crate like that, not even the farmers fattened on them Europayan subsidies. Wasn't like it in his day, when all he got for his eight acres was barely enough to raise a family on, plus a back that felt like it was broken.

Funny about that car, though. The boot left unlatched and half an inch open, like it wouldn't shut proper. So he'd had a peer in. And there'd been cushions inside. Then under the cushions (because natcherly he'd had a poke around) some odds and ends includun a pump-action shotgun.

Never had one of them neither. Just a good old over-and-under double-barrelled that he'd sold for only half what it was worth, only he'd been a bit strapped for cash at the time. Well, all the time really.

Why cushions anyway? Most people carried their dogs

231

in the rear with a bitta cage in between. Took a man with a fancy car like that to cram the poor bloody beasts in the boot. There was an air vent, though. Had it drilled special like. Ve-ry co-sy. Haveta be careful, that bloke, he don't get squatters movun in!

Tom brayed with laughter at his own wit and made a mental note to save that comic gem for next time he met Harry. Harry had—

He lifted his head as a distant cry was repeated, and this time he took notice. Wasn't no fox. Nor no rook neither.

And then he saw the far-off figure stumbling in a zigzag run, like he was blind. Or drunk. Or blind drunk. Only it didn't seem funny, somehow. Tom screwed his eyes to watch as the man collapsed and disappeared in the greenery below the skyline.

A queer'un. Or just ornery sick? Not his business any-way. Mebbe somethun to do with that flashy car back there. If the bloke that parked it had gone off pottun rabbits and put an arseful of shot into some tramp instead, it was best not messed with.

Only it might be somebuddy he knew, from the village like. Couldn't have furriners comun in and shootun up folk who belonged. So, takun due care like, no harm in havun a look-see. Could get home that way anyroad. Just a bit further round.

The man lying on his face in the kale was no local. When Tom turned him to see his face he proved even more of a foreigner than expected. After the city suit, the Asian features. 'A bloody Chink,' Tom marvelled.

There was a whole lot of mud over the front of him, and a gory splat on the back of his head which had trickled dark blood forward over his face. He couldn't get his hands up to clean it off because they were lashed together behind with a leather strap. Which hadn't made it any easier to run. The man's eyes were open, pleading.

Best find out a bit about him before lettun him go,

Tom decided. Didn't want to risk a maniac attackun him.

'Who dun this then?' he demanded of the winded man.

'Kid—'

'Kids, eh?' Nothun surprisun these days, the way they were brung up. Not even dragged up, some of 'em. Just left to get on with it themselves.

'Napper,' the man said breathily.

'Yeah. Took a right wallop there, diddun you?'

He looked so under the weather that there seemed no harm in lettun him loose. Tom reached for his old horn-handled pruning knife and cut into the leather strap. 'There, how's that then?'

The pain as he moved his arm forward was excruciating. Matsukawa saw red flash over the backs of his eyelids. The muscle was torn in his right shoulder and he had to take the weight off, nursing the elbow in his other hand. Still he couldn't get to his feet. 'Lloyd,' he blurted. 'He ran after him, the man who attacked me.'

It took a few minutes for Tom Wetherby to get the story straight and to realize that this was one of the very few times when the police might be of some use. But the foreigner wasn't having any. 'Lloyd,' he insisted. 'Find Lloyd first. I heard a gun go off.'

Tom found the second man about ten minutes later, a few yards into Gayters Wood. He looked in a worse state than the first, his hands bloody and one arm peppered with shot. 'Got away,' was all he could say before losing consciousness again.

Z had left the car at Cotswold House to make inquiries in the bar. Two of the men in there had seen the Daimler about an hour before and had remarked on it in the hotel. It was assumed it belonged to the Japanese businessman who had lost his way and was resting with a mineral water in the lounge.

'And then?' Z asked, but nobody had noticed when the stranger left because of some dispute in the bar over a damaged dart.

'For such minutiae are mighty empires lost,' declared Beaumont ponderously. 'Still, we're obviously on the right route.'

About to rejoin the car he heard the *hooh-hah* of an ambulance fast approaching from the direction they'd come by. 'Let's not get held up,' he snapped, putting the car in gear and shooting out to get ahead. The lane became narrow and twisting. It took some skill to keep clear of the vehicle bucketing along behind.

'Maybe . . .' Z began, and then spotted the Daimler parked up on the verge. 'Oh God, we could be too late!'

A dumpy old man was waving both arms frantically from a hundred yards down the lane. Beaumont drove past and left the car in a passing point. As they ran back the old man was beckoning paramedics to follow as he scuttled over the fields.

Matsukawa was sitting up now, head in hands. His briefcase with the money was gone: fifty thousand pounds that was all he'd been able to raise in the short time allowed. And the kidnapper had taken it uncounted, being under pressure to get away.

'What about Mayumi?' Z asked anxiously. 'Did you see the man?'

Matsukawa groaned. 'Before Lloyd got to us he said she was already free, making her way back. I had my face down in the mud, with a gun in my ribs. There wasn't a chance . . .'

But could anyone believe the kidnapper? Balked of killing the victim he'd sought all along, would he let Mayumi reach safety?

'Let's get on our way,' one paramedic ordered. 'They'll both do for now, but they need to see a doctor promptly. You can have their stories later.'

'I'm travelling with them,' Z said firmly. 'Beaumont will

stay and see the SOCO's team goes over the ground. Not that they're likely to find much after we've churned it all up.'

Lloyd was the hero of the moment, although furious at letting the kidnapper get away. Z took his statement as they rode to hospital. The injuries to his hands came from beating off a knife attack. He'd been about two minutes behind Matsukawa as he entered the wood. That was the closest he dared approach because the first part was in open country and the kidnapper could be keeping watch. As he came upon them, Mr Matsukawa was on his face, hands secured behind him. The man's shotgun was pressing into his spine.

Lloyd had leapt on to the man, fighting to wrest the gun away. It had discharged once into the trees as they struggled in close combat. Then the man had thrown down the shotgun and was lunging at him with a knife, aiming for the throat. Lloyd had managed to twist free, his hands cut to ribbons, and as he dodged behind a tree he heard the gun go off again.

'I thought he'd finished Mr Matsukawa off,' he said hoarsely. 'Then I realized it was me he'd winged. I ran at him and he turned tail, grabbed the briefcase and made off. I had a revolver. I could have shot him, but my hands were useless for aiming and we needed to take him alive. I kept following, but I guess that's when I blacked out. I'm sorry. Can't describe the man. He was wearing a balaclava, but he ran like the wind. Must have been a good bit younger than me.'

He paused for breath. 'When I came round someone was swearing and breathing beer all over me. Said his name was Tom Wetherby, a local. He phoned for help from the Daimler. The rest you know. Look, can you get this typed up straight away and I'll sign it. I need to get home and see if my wife's all right. She's had enough scares this past week to last her a lifetime.'

Matsukawa's bedside statement was more lengthy and delivered haltingly. Yeadings had come in person and the Japanese was aware of the Superintendent's grim expression when he admitted to keeping the police in the dark about the kidnapper's instructions.

'I could not risk it,' he pleaded. 'My daughter's life was on the line.'

And still was. No one put it into words, but the knowledge hung over them all.

'He told me,' the distressed man insisted, 'that Mayumi was already free. She was making her way home.'

'Which home?' Yeadings asked gently.

'To the house at Wrexham, surely? Or perhaps to my wife's place in Wiltshire. I didn't ask.' He was appalled at his own failure to get it straight, wanting so much to believe the man that he'd accepted such vagueness.

'We'll have people on the lookout for her at both ends,' Yeadings assured him.

Z, signing her report and looking for the date, stared at the calendar. Tuesday: she remembered then, that on Tuesday Danny was expected back from his break. And Tuesday was when Stephanie Coulter expected Maddie back from a supposed stay in town with her brother. They seemed to belong to another world.

At least there were some loose ends she could tie up now if she questioned them separately. Accepting that there was a perverse kind of honesty in Maddie's lying, she tried her first. Her stepmother answered the phone and agreed to call the girl.

'Mind, she seems hardly awake. I guess they've been having some late nights.'

'Miss Zyczynski?' said a subdued, little-girl voice she had difficulty in recognizing.

'Maddie, how are you?'

A short pause, then suspiciously, 'Fine. Why do you ask?'

236

'Because I guessed.'

A longer pause, but at least she didn't argue or act the innocent. 'Did Doll tell you?'

'No. Mayumi's still missing.'

'God, how awful!'

'It was Julia actually, but she'd got it rather wrong. She'd thought it was Mayumi pregnant, not you; and that that was the reason she'd gone missing.'

'Oh, Julia's such a fool!'

'A fool with troubles of her own. When you feel you can forgive her, get in touch. I think her world has started falling apart. You could help her.'

'You – you won't have to spread all this about me, will you?'

'I don't see any immediate need. You must decide for yourself who you confide in. It's risky not letting on what's happened to you.'

'I could tell Dad, I suppose. He just might understand. Oh, it's so squalid!' Her voice rose in protest. 'Having my inside sucked out, like being vacuum-cleaned. You wouldn't want anyone to know. And Dad would blurt it out to Stephanie. Then Greg would get to hear and he'd simply kill Danny.'

'Not actually kill, I'm sure. It might not harm Danny in the long run to get himself sorted.'

There was a small, gasp-like chuckle from the other end of the line. 'He is a bit of a shit, isn't he? I've only started to see it *since*...'

'A liberal education,' Z told her. 'Put it down to that, and know better next time. You'll be fine, Maddie. Go back to saying you know who you are and where you're going.'

'I guess. But I'm such a liar too!' The brief laughter died in her voice. 'About May; can't you do anything?'

'Just go on searching. I think we shall know soon, one way or the other.'

*   *   *

Like an automaton the girl continued walking, almost unfeeling now in her weariness. It had started to rain again quite heavily, and passing cars threw up sheets of water so that one side of her school coat was spattered with mud and her legs were drenched.

She wasn't quite sure of the way, and she seemed to have been walking for days, but she managed to follow what the signposts showed, knew she should be on the Ruthin road, in which case there'd be a roundabout at the end and she'd be able to ask someone how to get through the town.

Anything was better than having to make decisions for herself. She seemed to have forgotten how; couldn't get that part of her mind to work. If she could, she was sure she'd find something easier than this. She hadn't always walked everywhere, but couldn't remember what else she'd done.

On the left now there was a turning she had to cross. She stepped down without looking either way and a wavering siren which she'd been barely aware of was blaring suddenly right on top of her, then there was a squealing of tyres. A huge white shape loomed above. She was stunned by a voice shouting. Someone came up from behind and held her by the armpits while ahead a man was jumping down from the van, an ambulance. They were all round her, moving in. Men in white coats, going to stick needles in her and shut her away in the dark. She threw back her head and screamed.

Mayumi had been taken to the Maelor General Hospital.

'Sedated?' Yeadings asked the doctor in Accident and Emergency who had phoned in the news.

'Anything but. She's had enough rubbish pumped into her of late. We put her to bed in a private room while we analyzed some blood, and she fell instantly asleep. No food first, no bath, just sleep. She'll probably stay that way for the best part of twenty-four hours. You'll have to wait to question her, Superintendent.'

'I'll be sending one of my team across. Let her have access as soon as you possibly can, doctor. The kidnapper is a killer and still at large. He wants to get at the girl's father. It's vital she tells us about the man who was holding her.'

Yeadings replaced the receiver. 'This one's for you, Z, until DI Mott can get back. You know how vital it is to get her story quickly. Meanwhile our emphasis here is on protecting Matsukawa.'

'Sir?' Z stood her ground. 'Are we really sure he's in danger? Everything I've discovered of late points to a deliberate killing of Imura.'

'Not that old line again,' Beaumont objected. 'I thought we'd cleared that. How about "The girl first. Then you"? That was for Matsukawa all right.'

'But he's let Mayumi go. And her father.'

'On motive Z makes a good case for Imura as intended vicim,' Yeadings agreed slowly. 'But not every lecher gets topped as his deserts. We still have to guard Matsukawa. This was an interrupted murder attempt. But for Lloyd, the man would be dead now with half his body blown away.'

'Is there anything yet on strangers in the area, cars driving through before or after Matsukawa's Daimler?' Beaumont pursued.

'Nothing so far. We may raise some sightings from house-to-house inquiries. The locals are shocked, and eager to give what help they can. Someone will come up with information.'

Twenty-Two

Tom Wetherby had edited the account he gave to the police. He didn't see it made any difference to their inquiries. Since he'd given up his small-holding he'd had one or two brushes with the law over poaching and he knew it was important to watch what you told the buggers. God only knew what they'd make of him having opened the parked Daimler's boot after using the car phone. Probably accuse him of putting the pump-action in there, charge him with illegal possession or somethun. Might even make out he'd been the one dumped it after all that shootun.

Funny, though, that the gun had been left behind there. On first seeing the posh car abandoned in the lane he'd assumed it was some rich townee's who had hired the shoot, picking off the birds Tom had once considered his own right. Come to think, he'd heard a coupla shots let off as he left the store a quarter mile back.

Now he was enjoying his brief moment of fame. One of the benefits was the free nosh in the police canteen as guest of the girlie they'd brought along with them. She was a good listener. As he ploughed through his steak and kidney pie with double chips, he shared with her the hardships of his recent life. She seemed enough of a country girl to understand what it meant selling up in a recession and living off others' handouts.

'Useda bag the odd bunny or bird for me pot,' he reminisced rashly, 'until I had to flog me old over-and-under. A-course, I can still get me snares filled on the quiet, but

240

it's not like having a bang at 'em. Don't even taste the same somehow.'

Z got up and went to fetch his rice pudding with a dollop of strawberry jam. 'Ta, love,' he said, then a bright idea struck him. 'That Chinese bloke – Japanese, whatever – he's supposed to be rich, ain't he?'

'Seriously rich, I believe.'

'Well; don't suppose he'd be offerun a reward, like?'

Z kept her face straight. 'He could well be feeling grateful to you for finding him.'

'Yeah, that's what I thought. So s'pose he was. If he gave me enough, guess what I'd spend it on.' He looked wistful, despite the bulging hamster cheeks.

'What, Tom?'

'I'd buy meself a gun like what that Jap had. Pump-action. Cor, I'd really fancy one of them.'

Z kept quiet a moment, afraid of stemming the man's flow. But he was concentrating on scraping the last milky smear from his bowl.

'Pity he didn't use it then,' she suggested.

'Couldn't, could he? A-cause he'd left it in his car.'

She supposed he meant the Daimler, which Beaumont had driven back to Oxford, since it wasn't required for examination. It was probably now in the Randolph Hotel garage. A search was still being made in the wooded fields for tracks of any other vehicle.

'Do you mean,' she asked, sounding almost casual, 'that there was a pump-action shotgun in the Daimler?'

Tom hesitated. 'Sure; why not?' He began to look uneasy.

'I never saw one.'

'That's because you never looked prop'ly.'

'Tom, before we turned up you looked in the boot, didn't you? That's where it was?'

'Coulda been. No harm in that.'

But Lloyd, who'd hidden in there, was carrying a revolver, which in the event he'd been unable to use.

Why take along a bulky shotgun too? She wondered if Beaumont had checked over the car and found it.

'Tom,' she said, 'get yourself a tea or coffee. I have to make a phone call.'

Beaumont was still at the Randolph. He took Z's message in the bar. 'Sure, I'll take a look. Then what d'you want me to do about it?'

'Check if it's been recently fired, and if so bag it, and seal the car for forensics to go over.'

'Z, I don't get what you're after. If Matsukawa's got a licence for the gun, or this Lloyd feller, there's no offence.'

'Unless it's the one the killer's supposed to have used to pepper Lloyd's arm.'

'*Supposed?*'

'Lloyd could have fixed it himself, just as he could have slashed his own hands. We've been assuming that when he turned up the kidnapper escaped with the gun he'd been going to use on Matsukawa. But he didn't need to escape if he was never there. Yet the gun still has to be disposed of. Who's likely to look for it in the boot of the intended victim's car?'

'Are you trying to tell me Lloyd was playing his boss along, to get the ransom money? A hoax kidnap?'

'Just think. Matsukawa was on his face in the mud. He'd never see who came up behind, stuck a gun in his back, then trussed him. Before he was knocked unconscious he heard voices in the distance, sounds of a struggle and the gun twice going off. Some of that could have been recorded. So search the car for a miniature tape-player too. I'm going to insist on Lloyd's injuries being photographed. He'll think that's for victim compensation, but maybe the path lab will find they're self-inflicted.'

'How does that fit in with Matsukawa's version of what happened? What about the phone messages directing him to that spot?'

'Lloyd was never with him when the calls came. He was supposedly still in the car boot. But Matsukawa had to wait for the kidnapper to contact him each time. Which gave Lloyd an opportunity to get out of the boot unnoticed and use his mobile. I think we'll find that those areas haven't yet got the automatic trace facility on their exchanges, even if Matsuakawa had tried to use it.'

'Let me recap. You're saying that Lloyd followed his boss into the wood, threatened him with a gun, tied him up; then broke off when supposedly attacked himself; knocked out Matsukawa; pretended to fight off the kidnapper; shot his own arm; returned the shotgun to the car; went back to the wood; slashed his hands, and feigned unconsciousness.'

'Until Matsukawa could get himself free and come to find him. Luckily Tom Wetherby was in the area when Matsukawa staggered out of the wood. He'd heard two shots some time before, and was brave enough to investigate after everything had gone quiet. So there wasn't all that time to wait. And we happened along just after.'

'So it was all a hoax to get money out of Matsukawa? And telling him that the girl was already released was so much codswallop?'

Z took a deeper breath and plunged into her theory. 'Not if Lloyd really was the kidnapper all along.'

'Out to to get Matsukawa any way he could? And killed Imura in mistake for him? Possible, I suppose, if the room was in darkness when he got in.'

Z didn't argue that point. She was happy to let it go at that until she had enough substantive evidence to try her wilder ideas out on the Boss.

'So how about checking on that gun right now before Lloyd gets free of hospital and arrives to remove it?'

Superintendent Yeadings learned of Z's quest at secondhand when Beaumont proudly produced the shotgun.

Clearly it had recently been fired. Efforts were being redoubled to find any ejected cartridge cases in the woodland, with no success as yet. If Z's theory was true Lloyd could have retrieved them, having fixed up the gun to shoot his own forearm before hiding it again under cushions in the car boot.

Then, staunching the bloodflow, he had returned to the wood, slashed his own hands to give the effect of defence injuries received in warding off a knife attack, and perhaps stamped the knife, blade first, into the damp soil to conceal it. A metal detector should bring it to light.

The briefcase containing the ransom money could also be somewhere in the vicinity, since Beaumont had not come across it when searching the car.

While there was good cause for suspicion but still no hard evidence against Lloyd, Yeadings preferred him to be detained on medical grounds at the hospital. Since DI Mott had returned immediately on being told of the new developments, Z was off again to liaise with the North Wales police.

In the Maelor General Hospital, on the outskirts of Wrexham, the exhausted girl who had called herself Dolly slept on. She was also suffering from hypothermia and recent malnutrition. Blood analysis had shown the presence of apomorphine, an opium derivative with hypnotic and emetic qualities. Puncture marks on her right arm indicated repeated injections. In her present inert state there was nothing to show whether she was left-handed or not.

It had been the houseman's belief that the girl was foreign. No missing person answering to her description had been reported locally. How she came to be stumbling along the A525 from Ruthin was anybody's guess, but from the state of her shoes and torn tights she had been walking for some hours.

Evening brought the specific police inquiry concerning

244

a missing Japanese girl, and identification from a photograph was made before she woke up.

It was dark when Z arrived at the Matsukawa house, and she was refused entry when she used the phone at the outer gates. The housekeeper sounded hysterical.

'Mrs Lloyd, I have your brother with me. Will you speak to him?'

'Frank? What is it? Where's Gryff?'

Henderson, abashed, shrugged at Z. 'Let us in, Gill, there's a good girl, and we'll explain.'

'I've been so worried,' she babbled when they reached her at the front door. 'He came back at two in the morning and barely said a word. He was so strange. He wasn't here more than half an hour and barely spoke to me. Then he drove off again. I knew something was wrong. He's been quite frightening these last weeks.'

Z guided her to a chair. The woman was dishevelled, distracted.

'He's all right, Mrs Lloyd. Just having a check-up for some cuts to his hands and so on. He'll be fine in no time. Your brother's going to stay with you while I have a little look around.'

'Frank—?'

'It's OK, Gill. How about making us a pot of tea? This young lady's just had a three-hour drive.'

Z nodded encouragement. Slob as he was, Henderson had a soft spot for his sister. He couldn't relish his present double role of comforter and policeman.

It had taken ruthless persistence on Z's part to persuade him of her suspicions, but once she'd challenged him that Eiko wasn't the only one to suffer at Imura's hands, he had given in and admitted his sister's rape.

After unforgivable advances to the fourteen-year-old during his previous visit, the Japanese had needed fresh lodgings. Mr Ichikawa had arranged for him to use the still unoccupied house built for the head of the firm and

245

where the Lloyds were caretakers. There he'd had more success, forcing himself on Gillian when Lloyd was away, and scaring her into silence. She shared her secret only with her brother, imploring him to hide it from her jealous husband. And in view of her precarious state he'd done as she asked until a fresh hysterical outburst when Ichikawa ordered her to prepare for this second visit from Imura as house guest.

Gryff Lloyd was a hot-blooded Welshman on a short fuse, but now it was all over he was almost happy to confess to Imura's murder.

White with anger he had stormed out, to drive overnight to the hotel where Imura would be staying on the firm's regular booking. Familiar with the layout there from when he'd chauffeured Matsukawa, he knocked at Imura's door as the Japanese prepared for an early night.

He had been allowed in to deliver a message from the firm's chief. With the advantage of surprise, he'd slashed Imura's throat open from behind, but had to withstand a ferocious counter-attack while the man's strength ebbed with his life-blood. Then there followed the mutilation and the hideous amputated mess discarded in the bedclothes.

'Finally,' Z told Yeadings on her return, 'as we'd assumed, he showered and dressed in Imura's day clothes, taking his own bloodstained ones away in the dead man's luggage. When Mayumi's letter was pushed under the door he read it, and decided to keep it. Only later did he think of using it as a bait for the girl's father. And that letter was the clue that proved him the killer, because once we'd accepted him as the kidnapper, its reappearance also proved he was in Imura's room that night.

'As he left the hotel he caught sight of Elizabeth with Mayumi in the car park and followed them out to the school. There he waited while Elizabeth drove off, and persuaded Mayumi that her father had sent him to take her to the Wrexham house. Gillian never saw him smuggle the girl in, by now gagged and terrified.

'Every move he made after that was an impromptu effort to build the illusion of a campaign to kill Matsukawa, in which he'd be clear of motive, and to disguise that Imura's murder was intentional.'

'And we fell for it,' Beaumont muttered, 'till Z sorted out the Wrexham connection.'

Yeadings grunted and nodded to Z. 'So you left DI Henderson with his sister, went down and found the evidence in the cellar, where Lloyd had been holding Mayumi in the dark. What a bastard, going off and leaving the girl there, drugged, and without food for the past three days.'

'Why didn't his wife feed her?' Beaumont demanded. 'Is she that crazy?'

'She didn't know Mayumi was there. Gryff Lloyd's a pretty fearsome person when roused and Gillian was just about keeping her head together as it was. She even tried to conceal from her brother that Gryff had driven south on the evening of Imura's death, afraid that his duty as a policeman would force him to pass the knowledge on. She must have guessed by then that Lloyd was the killer, and she feared for her own life. *Crime passionnel*, as Henderson once let slip when he did get to hear of it. But he still did nothing to help us with the case.'

'Apparently the drugs Lloyd used on Mayumi were left over from a previous mental breakdown of his wife's,' Yeadings told them.

'Lloyd had discovered that they induced a semi-hypnotic state, and he injected it the way he'd seen it done.' Yeadings looked grim. 'The psychiatrist called in to sort the girl out tells me she was an ideal subject, as are all strictly disciplined personalities, brainwashed to be receptive. He's now working on her to free a naturally strong but suppressed self-assertion.'

'Her father will love that,' Z suggested. 'He's already given in to Elizabeth's demands that they spend the main part of every year in England. Now he'll have to get used to an assertive daughter too.'

'Mr Matsukawa,' Yeadings mused, 'is a very remarkable man. I've been listening to some of his ideas. He doesn't let the grass grow under his feet. He's already been in touch with the parents of the two girls Mayumi shared a study with, and persuaded them to keep their daughters on at school together. His thesis is that their combined experiences are character-forming. It is essential that they face all that has happened, assimilate it, accept their share of responsibility and realize that they remain in charge of their lives. Formidably progressive, don't you think?'

'Formidable for the school,' Z gave as her opinion. 'Dr Walling may be grateful she's soon retiring.'

Yeadings' face creased into a broad grin. 'She's determined the three shan't pose as heroines, but apparently she's the most enthusiastic of all. Progressive indeed. It's a long way from the original Three Little Maids.'